"Hey, Summer?"

"Uh huh?"

TJ picked up his flashlight and turned it on. "Would it be okay if I come downstairs with you?"

The relief that swamped her battled with her stubborn urge to prove she was absolutely fine. But before she knew which one was going to win the war, he added, "If we're both working, we can get it done much faster. I solemnly promise to follow all your orders."

Summer cleared her throat, painfully aware that he'd tacked on the last part to humor her. Still, she was grateful enough to accept the effort. "Don't think I don't know what you're doing, Officer Shepard. Humoring me."

His low chuckle rippled through the darkness and settled low in her abdomen.

"Is it working?" he asked as he moved closer to her.

A sensible request combined with that voice? It was working entirely too well...

Dear Reader,

Welcome to Horizon, South Carolina, home of the Shepard family. For generations, the Shepards have served in law enforcement, and they're the backbone of this small Southern town on the coast. In *A Hero's Rescue*, you'll meet K9 officer TJ Shepard and the new veterinarian in town, Dr. Summer Patel. There's a storm on the way that will force the two of them to work together instead of squaring off.

I love exploring new places, absorbing bits of story and color from both professional tour guides and the local experts who might serve me a Diet Coke with lunch or give me directions when I'm lost. South Carolina's Lowcountry is filled with thousands of stories, hopeful and heartbreaking and funny and rich with history. I hope some of that flavor comes through in Horizon.

If you'd like to know more about my books and what's coming next, please visit me at cherylharperbooks.com.

Cheryl Harper

A HERO'S RESCUE

CHERYL HARPER

Recycling programs for this product may not exist in your area.

ISBN-13: 978-1-335-46037-0

A Hero's Rescue

For questions and comments about the quality of this book, please contact us at CustomerService@Harlequin.com.

Harlequin Enterprises ULC
22 Adelaide St. West, 41st Floor
Toronto, Ontario M5H 4E3, Canada
www.Harlequin.com

HarperCollins Publishers
Macken House, 39/40 Mayor Street Upper,
Dublin 1, D01 C9W8, Ireland
www.HarperCollins.com

Printed in U.S.A.

Cheryl Harper discovered her love for books and words as a little girl, thanks to a mother who made countless library trips and an introduction to Laura Ingalls Wilder's Little House books. Whether the stories she reads are set in the prairie, the American West, Regency England or Earth a hundred years in the future, Cheryl enjoys strong characters who make her laugh. Now Cheryl spends her days searching for the right words while she stares out the window and her dog, Jack, snoozes beside her. And she considers herself very lucky to do so.

For more information about Cheryl's books, visit her online at cherylharperbooks.com or follow her on X @cherylharperbks.

Books by Cheryl Harper

Harlequin Heartwarming

The Fortunes of Prospect

The Cowboy's Compromise
Courting the Cowgirl
The Right Cowboy
The Cowboy's Second Chance
Her Cowboy's Promise
The Cowboy Next Door

Veterans' Road

Winning the Veteran's Heart
Second Chance Love
Her Holiday Reunion
The Doctor and the Matchmaker
The Dalmatian Dilemma

Visit the Author Profile page
at Harlequin.com for more titles.

CHAPTER ONE

THE CHATTER THAT normally filled the Horizon Police Department's squad room right before the morning shift change was absent as TJ Shepard filled his coffee cup. His K9 partner, Lucy, registered the tension in the air as well. As the most popular officer on the squad, the yellow Labrador normally caused a wave of scratches, pats and general happiness when she entered at his side. Today, every officer had their head down, scanning reports, and Lucy's eyes were locked on TJ.

Outside, dark clouds were forming on the horizon of the Atlantic Ocean to the east, but the warm spring sunshine made it difficult to believe a storm was on the way. Inside, the large screen in the center of the back wall displayed the current forecasted path of the first hurricane of the season. Alerts issued by the state and federal agencies tracking the storm's movement scrolled along the bottom.

One quick glance showed that Horizon was near the center of the path. Unless the storm weakened or changed course before landfall, most of South Carolina would feel the effects in some way.

It was too early in the year for a storm of this size.

The silence made sense. Everyone was focused because the storm coming was out of the ordinary.

TJ didn't really operate well in tense silence, however. He considered it part of his calling to lighten the mood. Getting the job done right always mattered in Horizon's PD, but there was a point when grim concentration on the job ahead hindered instead of helped.

"Lucy, take another lap. You didn't get enough attention for my liking." He motioned for the yellow Lab to circle the room again. This time, she got the affection she deserved in a slow ripple that spread from one desk to the next.

Lucy was highly trained for scent detection, but her ability to clear the atmosphere came naturally.

"Good morning," TJ said in a general address to the room crowded with desks. "Anybody heard from the chief yet?" He slurped obnoxiously as he drank the first delicious, scalding sip of hot black coffee. Noise here was standard operating procedure, storm or no storm. He would weather a few annoyed glares to get the morning back on track. "What's the current ETA on the storm's arrival?"

"Glad you asked, Shepard," Horizon's chief of police, Tom Shepard, said as he marched down the center aisle to stand in front of the screen. His office occupied the front corner of the first floor, allowing him to keep an eye on the squad room and the street that ran between Battery Park and Town Hall.

The chief bent to shake Lucy's paw because there was always time for the proper greeting for every officer. "All eyes up here."

His father never hesitated. The morning brief started on time, his goals were clear, and his rules for proper officer conduct did not waver. He always knew the right thing to say, the correct step to take and how to get any job done. TJ had always wanted to be exactly like him.

Gray at his father's temples and the bifocals that he was still adjusting to wearing were the only signs that the chief was slowing down.

That and his frequent remarks about retiring.

If that ever happened, it would mark the end of an era. No one who worked with Chief Shepard was ready to see him go.

Relieved to have some action in the room and the chief in control, TJ immediately moved to his desk near the doors that led to the town hall's public lobby but smiled when he met his sister's glance. Bee was leaning against the wall near his desk. Her usual spot allowed her to monitor what was happening in Dispatch while she attended the morning brief. The department's communications center filled a small square room between the chief's office and the egress point for the station's parking area, and Bee ran it as her own kingdom, ruled with an iron fist in a velvet glove.

Bee had learned that skill from their mother.

"Everyone's got the shift reports to review," the chief said. "Pretty quiet night overall. Patrol responded to one noise complaint and assisted the state police with two separate drug searches on the highway. Holding is currently empty. That's the good news." He hitched his duty belt higher as he motioned to the screen. "Storm's path remains largely the same, with a slight shift now to center on James Island."

He turned to show the approximate center of the storm path north and east of town on the map of Horizon that had hung on the back wall of this squad room for as long as TJ could remember. Even before he could read the words painted above it, his father would point them out.

We Serve.

The police department's motto was painted on the wall here and on both sides of all of Horizon's patrol cars. Wear and tear meant the map was occasionally replaced and the paint was refreshed, but that map, showing the city limits and surrounding areas, was as constant in TJ's mind as the Greek Revival building that had been converted to Horizon's town hall.

Chief Shepard, this building and that map had withstood time and many hurricanes already.

It was easy to trust that they'd withstand this storm, too.

"The hurricane watch was issued this morning. Tropical Storm Agnes is expected to make landfall in less than forty-eight hours. Current estimates put the storm at a Category Two hurricane. If this was September, we'd be more prepared. The size and early timing of the storm, falling outside of the 'normal' hurricane season—" the chief made air quotes around the word because there was really no "normal" anymore "—means that all the towns and cities in the impact area should already be making plans, getting ready." He sent a sweeping glance around the room over the top of his glasses. "Should, I said. We already know that many of our friends and neighbors are not taking this as seriously as I would like. Familiarity breeds complacency, and that is dangerous in times like this."

The chief paused to allow the gravity of the situation to settle in the room.

TJ raised one eyebrow at Bee, who smiled and tipped her head down to hide it. They were careful not to give their dad too much trouble while he was on the job, even if his delivery might remind them of how he settled them down at the dinner table with a stern glance and charged silence.

As a father, he had never raised his voice. He'd never had to. That expression would do the work.

"For the next two days, what is our job?" his father asked.

No one spoke. It was a rhetorical question. Everyone in the room had been there long enough to know the chief would answer it himself.

Unless he was driving home the point.

He tapped the motto painted in large blue letters over the map of Horizon.

"Shepard, what do we do?" his father asked again, peering over the top of his glasses to make sure TJ understood he should deliver the correct answer.

Law enforcement was the family business. For generations, Shepards had served Horizon, the state of South Carolina and the United States in law enforcement roles. Not all of the latest Shepard generation had stayed in Horizon, but only one of them had bucked the system and gone her own way to sell real estate of all things.

Tom Shepard's kids were expected to know the right response to this question above all.

"We serve." TJ watched his father nod. Then he took the scattered emotions that bubbled up and tied pride, anxiety and insecurity into a hard knot before shoving them way down. He knew this urge to always have the right answer for his father and the anxiety that came along with it was silly.

TJ was an adult, a trained law enforcement officer and good at his job.

His dad was a hero and *his* hero. Disappointing his father, even with something as small as an incorrect answer at the morning briefing, would stick with TJ.

Having him as a boss increased the pressure of the job. Daydreams about trying law enforcement somewhere else, in a place where he could be Officer Shepard without being one of The Shepards of Horizon, South Carolina, had been harder to shake lately.

They came almost as often as his father mentioned retiring.

The worry that he might not be quite as good at police work outside of his father's domain had to be squashed when it immediately followed.

"That's right. This is our community. We serve Horizon." His father waved a clipboard in the air. "I've got zones and assignments listed here. Dispatch also has this information. Today, in addition to the normal outstanding police work that I expect from everyone in this room—" his father paused dramatically to scan the room again "—we will check in on our neighbors and send the message that they should be securing their houses, gathering emergency supplies and making evacuation plans. At this time, we do not have mandatory evacuation orders, but moving inland is a strong recommendation." He ran his finger down the eastern edge of the Horizon map. "As always, these homes and businesses lining the Battery, the public beach and the coast are at the highest risk.

The mayor has called this morning to offer her support with any requests I need to make through the state for extra manpower or resources. I've already been in contact with the head of operations at the shipyard, the park rangers at Rocky Point Lighthouse and the school district superintendent. Television, radio stations… The top story is storm preparation."

TJ surveyed the other officers in the room. All eyes were glued to the chief.

His father tapped the clipboard. "Now is the time to make a difference. Preparation will save lives. Today, we focus on verifying that people are paying attention. Then we shift to safety during the storm, rescue and recovery. Emergency Management is already mobilizing crews for Charleston County. They are taking this storm seriously. It's our job to make sure our neighbors here do the same. Any questions on our orders for today?"

Bee stepped forward. "Chief, last night I had a conversation with Charlene over at the Sandlapper."

The seafood restaurant was a Horizon mainstay, situated on a dock jutting out into the bay. It had been there long before TJ arrived, and the crowds of day-trippers who continued to flock to the place were evidence that it would outlast them all.

"Are they making plans to close up?" the chief asked.

Bee nodded. "The restaurant's windows were

already boarded up, but Charlene was concerned about Shoreline Shelter and the animal hospital. She's on the list of emergency fosters for storms like this, but no one has contacted her. I told her to call today, but plans to evacuate the animals should already be in motion. This will be Dr. Patel's first storm with a direct hit, and Jewel is on vacation in Hawaii until next week."

Everyone in the room understood that it was the last piece that was truly worrisome. Jewel Edgecombe had run the Shoreline Shelter, which was connected to the Horizon Animal Hospital, for as long as Tom Shepard had been a police officer. When Dr. Patel had purchased the veterinary practice from Dr. Forsyth, she'd inherited the shelter along with it.

At the mention of Summer Patel, most of the eyes in the room swiveled his direction, but the officers tried to be stealthy about it. TJ picked up his coffee mug for another sip, determined to ignore the unwanted attention. He and the town's new veterinarian had encountered each other previously when she was in town to complete the sale of the veterinary practice.

It hadn't gone well.

She had parked in a no-parking zone. It was almost directly across the street from Town Hall, in one of Horizon's busiest tourist spots at the park.

Since every officer on the Horizon PD had spent too much time asking day-trippers to move, ticketing day-trippers who *didn't* move, and calling tow trucks for the ultimate resolution, TJ had had very little patience, and his tone and direct order to move her SUV had reflected that.

Her response had been to point out poor signage, poor curb markings and poor etiquette on his part.

And she'd made her argument firmly to him, the police chief, the mayor and probably anyone else she knew in Horizon.

Thanks to the mayor, there was now a new sign, new paint and new training on what was expected of city employees dealing with visitors to Horizon.

When the weather warmed and tourism picked up again, they'd see if the changes helped the parking issue.

TJ had a sneaking suspicion it would, but he'd kept one eye peeled for Dr. Patel ever since. He hadn't decided how their next encounter would go yet.

"I haven't had an opportunity to meet Dr. Patel yet, but I wonder if she has any experience with storms like this," Bee added. "She moved here from Atlanta. Hurricanes out there on the Island will be a whole new thing for her. Might be good to send someone by to see if she's ready."

"Thanks, Shepard." The chief scanned the list of assignments. "Looks like TJ is assigned out there to the Island."

This time, TJ froze with the coffee cup halfway to his mouth. The breeze stirred up by all the heads whipping around to stare at him rustled the paper on his desk. He set his cup carefully down on top of it.

The Island was a small piece of land that had once been attached near the town limits, but time and changing water flows had cut it off from the mainland. A sturdy bridge connected it to Horizon, but rising water was a threat during significant rainfall.

Bee's concern was valid.

His assignment to that zone, however, was a wrinkle in the plan. Dr. Patel might not be as receptive to his assistance.

His father turned to make sure he registered the assignment, so TJ nodded. Explaining that it was time to evacuate the animals should be simple enough to fit in his shift, and he and Summer Patel were adults.

They were neighbors, for that matter. His apartment was on the Horizon side of the bridge that connected the Island.

Whatever friction there was between them could be smoothed out. He would be extra professional to ensure success.

"Do we continue scheduled community outreach events today, Chief? Horizon Elementary is expecting TJ and Lucy in about—" Mark Rodriguez, the department's public relations officer, studied his watch "—four hours for Shep the

Safety Dog story time and to announce the winners of the Spring Safety art contest."

The chief frowned as he considered the question. "The superintendent has canceled classes for tomorrow. Verify that the teachers still want to have the story time first. Cancel all other extraneous events for this afternoon and the rest of the week. The situation is serious, but we don't need any panic."

"You got it, Chief," Rodriguez answered.

"Shepard, hurricane safety seems like a good topic for you to cover while you're there. Maybe those kids can take it back home and get some of their parents motivated. Everyone, disperse the message widely. Preparedness. Planning. Those are the words." Then he pointed at the words on the wall. "Remember the mission. Meeting dismissed."

"We serve," all the officers and staff said as they moved to carry out the chief's orders.

"Please follow me to the front desk, Shepard," Rodriguez said as he waved at TJ, "and Shepard." He pointed at Bee.

They followed Rodriguez to his cluttered desk in the lobby of the old antebellum hotel turned city hall. Horizon PD occupied the first floor with an auxiliary garage to one side and a sally port connecting to the courthouse on the other.

Before the Civil War, it had been one of the most expensive buildings in town, meant to host wealthy tourists visiting Horizon's beaches and seaside park. Afterward, it was repaired and took on a new life at the center of the town's administration. That meant they were always surrounded by history, even if it was a little cramped and some areas of the building were cold in the winter and hot in the summer. Modern additions had increased the space and function of the building, but the history added a special touch.

The mayor's offices took up most of the top floor, and the town's main fire station had grown out of the stables behind the building, fully modernized now but with a historic facade.

Every now and then, someone got the bright idea to build something modern for the police department. More than one developer had expressed interest in renovating this building into a boutique hotel or even a niche shopping center, but voters had successfully shut those outsiders down. History was important in Horizon.

"We need to choose the winners of the art contest. TJ can deliver the certificates and make the announcement, take photos, all of that, this morning." Rodriguez opened the file folder containing the drawings they were judging but waited for TJ to meet his stare. "The photos, TJ. You better get them this time. I want smiling kids. I want Lucy posing with the winners. I want community service, each with at least one thousand words in picture format."

TJ held his hands up in surrender. "I solemnly vow not to forget again."

Bee shook her head sadly. "You had one job at the Christmas parade, but there was not a single photo of Lucy doing her job, patrolling the crowds. How will we ever trust you again, TJ?" The wicked gleam in her eyes was evidence that she enjoyed watching her older brother squirm. Their sibling rivalry had softened, but it was obviously never going away.

He wanted to argue that his "one job" had actually been crowd safety. Lucy's had been as well, but it would be a waste of breath. Sometimes he got the impression that other officers viewed his partner as a mascot instead of an important member of the police force. Lucy was so good, she could find drugs and other contraband while also being the police department's version of a celebrity.

If he also got the feeling that they viewed him the same way, TJ tried not to let it get to him.

"That Christmas parade was a rough assignment for you." Bee patted his shoulder. "Isn't that also where you threatened to arrest Dr. Patel?"

"No," TJ said and shook his head forcefully. "I asked her to move her vehicle, and she hesitated, so I insisted. That's all that happened." Everyone had heard the story at this point. There was nothing to gain by defending his actions further, even if the repetition had turned into an annoying game of Telephone where every version that made it through the grapevine back to him was embellished.

Honestly, the more details he added, the worse he would look.

Bee pursed her lips. “Well, you’ll get a chance to solve two problems with one visit. Clear the air between you by helping her prepare for the storm. As long as you don’t cause another stir by forgetting the pictures, you’re going to come out way ahead today.”

Mark Rodriguez gave him a thumbs-up. “I believe in you, TJ.”

“Forget to take photos one time,” TJ muttered as he pulled the file over to flip through the drawings. They started strong and deteriorated in skill and clarity the farther down he went.

“I put the winners on top,” Rodriguez said breezily, “and I already made out the certificates.” He patted an envelope on his desk. “Just thought you needed to be familiar with them in case anyone asked any questions.”

“So what am I doing here?” Bee asked.

“Keeping him in line.” Rodriguez motioned his head at TJ.

TJ studied the last drawing of the bunch. It was a puzzle. “Why aren’t you going to do this yourself if you’ve already finished all the legwork?”

“Flip that one over. Mrs. Lamb put a hint on the back.” Rodriguez waited for him to follow directions. "We always say three officers review and choose the winner. All I need is your rubber stamp."

"Sea turtle," TJ read slowly and then flipped the paper back over to study the brown-and-green pile in the center of the page. There was a stick figure next to it, but every guess he could immediately form about the pile of roundish, misshapen blobs of brown and green…

Bee murmured, "Well, I see why the teacher added a note to help. Otherwise, it reads as mildly offensive."

Rodriguez tilted his head to the side before nodding.

"I can't go today because we're getting messages from Emergency Management about storm prep, and I want to make sure the website and all the social media accounts are updated as the situation develops." Rodriguez offered TJ the envelope with the certificates inside. "I left the *Shep Meets a Stranger* book and a bag of candy at your desk, too." He pointed. "Don't let me down."

TJ saluted. "You can count on me."

Bee grinned as she turned to go back to Dispatch. "Call me if you need a reminder, Tommy, and when you're talking with Dr. Patel, try some of that charm that normally has the ladies buzzing around you."

No one in Horizon called him Tommy.

Except for his sisters when they were trying to annoy him.

It was tempting to consider his life as a police officer in Charleston or Columbia. Everyone there would call him by the name he used to introduce himself.

Here he had to be glad Bee had gone with Tommy. She'd been pretty creative with nicknames growing up, and he didn't want a single one of them to stick.

"Shepard," his father said before TJ could motion Lucy out to the squad car.

TJ turned back. "Chief?"

His father tipped his head back. "After you check on the Island and visit the school, I'd like you to return to the station."

Since "station" meant desk work, reports and, even worse…phone calls, that dampened TJ's enthusiasm further. Smoothing things over with Summer Patel would have been a blip on an otherwise okay day.

Now there was paperwork looming.

"Okay, I had planned to patrol down the Battery and south of town, but…" TJ shrugged. "I can come back to the station before I do that."

His father shook his head. "You need to be here. As the storm gets closer, Command will center here in the station house. I want you observing closely how the department works with outside agencies."

TJ nodded, but he was confused. There had been other storms, but he'd always been on the ground, not locked up at the station.

"You missed a great deal of the planning while you were in Columbia yesterday. A man who will lead this department should have a solid grasp on how communications with outside agencies go during emergency situations. You'll be grateful for the exposure when the storm season is fully underway this fall and you're running the show." He tapped TJ's badge before turning on his heel and returning to his office. "We should still be able to get home for dinner on time tonight."

TJ was knocked off balance as he realized it was the first time he'd ever heard his father's timeline for the retirement he'd been threatening. There had been a hazy plan that TJ would follow in his father's footsteps *someday.*

He'd been picturing years in the future, while his father was thinking months.

And the chief had already determined how those months would go. He would train TJ here at the station house before handing him the keys to the corner office.

Then they would meet for dinner at home.

Just the image of being quizzed and critiqued by the man who was his old boss, the man whose job he'd stepped into, *and* his father over his mother's home-cooked meals elevated TJ's heart rate.

The line between father and boss shifted constantly, but the pressure TJ was under from each would rise with his promotion.

Pride at being judged worthy to step into the role battled with the unexpected timeline and the nagging question about how well he could fill the role.

His plan for the next family dinner had been to explain how well his visit to the annual meeting of the South Carolina Canine Officers Association had gone and his interest in running for a regional COA office so that he could serve on the association's Ethics Committee.

The state-wide meeting held in Columbia the day before had given him the chance to meet the leaders of the group responsible for training, certifying and advocating for K9 officers in South Carolina. The South Carolina COA was also part of a broader network of states cooperating to standardize K9 officer guidelines.

Walking into the group as a Shepard had been easy, as his father's reputation went far and wide. TJ had pursued the grant through COA to get the department its first police dog, even though his father had been certain Horizon operated well enough without a canine detection unit.

TJ and Lucy had breezed through the training required, and together they'd assisted with enough drug and explosive searches and seizures to prove TJ right.

Even Chief Shepard had been forced in time to admit Lucy's impact far exceeded her cost.

TJ had become a police officer because he felt the same commitment to Horizon as his father, but working with Lucy was the best part of his job. He wanted to make sure other officers like Lucy were valued and protected and that the handlers entrusted with them did the right thing.

He'd been energized by the meeting. It had felt like finding a purpose, his next goal to pursue.

This storm would only present a temporary pause, but his father's plans might change everything.

TJ glanced down to meet Lucy's stare. She stood, ready to go to work.

"Ten-four, Officer Lucy. We have our orders." TJ held the door open for his partner before trotting down the wide steps that led to the sidewalk where his car was parked.

Working with family was hard on his ego. It was a good thing he loved his job.

Meeting with a group of kids who treated police officers and firemen as superheroes would remind him of why.

And he was always ready to assist a neighbor, even one as prickly as Dr. Patel.

Figuring out what to do about how his father was sketching out TJ's future could wait a day or two.

CHAPTER TWO

DR. SUMMER PATEL had accomplished almost every goal she set her sights on because she had always been independent, confident and stubborn. If one trait failed her, one of the others usually kicked in. Right now, both stubbornness and confidence were failing, and she was fighting the urge to call her parents for help.

The only problem was that she'd made a pretty dramatic vow that she wouldn't do that, and not even facing a hurricane for the first time could convince her to back down.

Not yet, anyway.

For Summer's whole life, the key to doing what she wanted had been listening to her gut instead of her parents, even if she'd always done her best to make them proud.

She'd met all their academic requirements while stubbornly participating in extracurricular activities they could never understand: marching band, Shakespeare club and yearbook.

She'd chosen veterinary medicine instead of

orthopedics like her father, and when he had followed through on his threat to stop paying tuition until she reconsidered, Summer had scrambled to cover it on her own.

But walking away from the wedding her mother had been dreaming of since the sonogram showed "it's a girl," and the groom her father had chosen to take over his successful medical practice, had tested every bit of mettle Summer had developed.

The pressure to "come to her senses" had been unending.

Going her own way three hundred miles from home had been Summer's solution.

On a sunny, calm day, the distance from Atlanta to coastal South Carolina was perfect.

Today, she wondered if she should have pointed her SUV north to Tennessee instead.

It was hard to believe a hurricane was on the way. Clouds moved quickly, but the sun was out. The wind might be heavier than usual, but if the radio and TV were correct, the storm headed her direction was going to be a problem.

Right now, her focus was keeping the roof of the veterinary clinic in place.

"Anyone who can play the trombone while they march to 'Uptown Funk' can handle a loose—" Summer stared up at the roof and the piece of… something that was flapping in the winds stirred up by the approaching storm "—whatever that building-thingy is."

The urge to call her father for advice made her straighten her shoulders.

There was no guarantee Dr. Jay Patel would answer her call yet.

The devastation on his face when she'd announced the wedding was off had only been surpassed when she'd announced she was leaving Atlanta again.

Her mother would answer, but Lynn Carter Patel would tell her to pack up and hit the road, leave that dangling roof-thingy blowing in the breeze. They'd have the clinic listed for sale by Monday and be putting down a deposit for a new wedding venue.

"Daddy has never fixed a loose building-thingy in his life anyway," Summer muttered as she spun on one heel, caught the swaying tote bag she'd slung over her shoulder on the way out of her veterinary practice, and hurried across the expansive yard that lay between Horizon Animal Hospital and Shoreline Shelter. The animal clinic with the cozy attic apartment on the second floor framed one side. The long, narrow building that housed the rescues awaiting adoption was on the opposite side. Dense trees formed the third side, and the fourth was a tree line that grew sparse as it gave way to a marshy beach. The scenery had been the biggest selling point.

Proximity to the ocean was less attractive right now.

The tote held the hammer and screwdriver that

Summer had found in the junk drawer of the staff break room. Kima, the clinic's office manager, had waved heavy-duty silvery-gray tape at her as she'd headed out the door with the promise that "if all else fails, duct tape never will."

The shed situated in the short leg of the shelter's L-shaped building might have better tools.

Since Summer had no idea what would be required, she wasn't certain what she hoped to find, but a ladder would definitely make getting on the roof easier.

"Easier? You mean possible, Summer," she muttered and then glanced around to make sure no one was around. When she'd moved to Horizon, she'd planned to leave a whole moving truck full of things behind in Atlanta.

Like her history with the trombone, for one thing.

And the engagement ring for the wedding she'd walked away from.

And talking to herself.

Since she'd been in Horizon, she'd done her very best to keep her mouth shut and her ears open. That had always been the key to her success in new groups.

Keeping her mouth shut had always been important when she wanted to appear confident and was anything but. In this moment, her own thoughts delivered in her voice were the only pep talk available.

"Find a ladder. Get the job done. Desperate times, desperate measures and all that." Summer unlocked the door and stepped inside. When Dr. Forsyth had given her the tour around the place, obviously keen on making a deal to sell the practice he'd built so he could move up to Charlotte to be closer to his grandkids, she'd insisted on seeing every single nook and cranny.

Buying a practice of her own was a huge gamble. Not looking like a fool and avoiding catastrophic failure were tied for the top spot on Summer's list of career goals, so she'd been thorough in investigating both practices she'd considered buying.

Debate Club had been the one extracurricular that had pleased her father, but it had also given Summer experience in digging through statements for the truth.

Her elective business classes as an undergraduate had given her the vocabulary to ask questions about the practice's revenues and the interest rate on her loan, even if the answers had been over her head.

The sheer size of the business loan she had taken out meant Summer had been methodical at each step. Taking on that debt had her waking up in a cold sweat in the middle of the night.

Her compulsion to ask every question she could think of, to dot every *i* and cross the *t*'s, had lengthened Summer's inspections and shortened

Dr. Forsyth's patience and his transition timeline. As soon as they closed, he packed up what he could carry in his SUV and headed out of town, leaving her to find her own way.

But that thorough inspection meant she knew there was a ladder inside the shed.

The fact that she didn't know one tool from another? That meant everything else inside would be a mystery.

Summer didn't enjoy mysteries.

As she flipped the light switch next to the door, she thanked Dr. Forsyth for running electricity to the shed. The only thing worse than mysteries were *dark* mysteries. Rummaging through the cabinet along the wall turned up some big nails, some big screws, an electric screwdriver and some kind of powerful stapler that might be useful.

The ladder was leaning right where she remembered.

Large metal panels lined one wall, but no immediate answer as to their purpose came to mind.

"Not a priority, Summer." She slipped her arm under one of the ladder rungs and hefted it over her shoulder like she'd seen guys on home improvement shows do.

Summer immediately regretted it, but she clenched her jaw and hoped neither Kima nor Natalie, her vet tech, were watching out the window as she struggled to drag the ladder across the yard.

After the second cancelation of the morning,

Summer had tasked Natalie and Kima with contacting everyone who had an appointment scheduled for the rest of the week so that they could reschedule. There was no sense in staffing the office if the incoming storm meant few patients.

The relief on their faces had poked her concern about the storm like it was a bruise that popped up overnight. Neither of her employees had approached her about closing the clinic, so she'd assumed she was on the right track.

To be fair, she'd never really wondered if she was on the wrong track.

"Nothing less than a Category Three," she muttered to herself as she set the ladder up against the roofline. Evacuating was for Category Three storms and above. Part of the intense questioning she'd subjected Dr. Forsyth to had been about hurricanes, the land and buildings he was selling her as part of the veterinary practice, and how much she needed to worry about the two of them coming together.

She could still picture the way he held up two fingers in a victory sign.

That was how many times he'd evacuated in all the years he'd been there.

Twice.

"We're actually protected here in this little inlet," he had said as he'd pointed off into the distance. "Natural breakwater."

His tone had been very persuasive.

Maybe that was why Summer had failed to drill down deeper to ask about what he had done instead of evacuating, how he had prepared to stick it out on the Island.

Dr. Forsyth had been certain Summer would be safe here.

That confidence, added on top of the absolutely gorgeous view of the shoreline on beautiful days, had made it easy enough to convince herself that he knew what he was talking about.

But now there was a Category Two storm headed her way.

Life in Horizon had carried on as usual, so she'd followed suit. None of her neighbors had appeared to panic.

For days, she'd been listening to weather reports, watching and waiting to see if the tropical storm would strengthen or weaken, turn toward or away from her spot on the coast.

Today, all signs appeared to be pointing right at her.

The news reports had covered preparation basics, but in her head, she could remember Dr. Forsyth's sunny smile. She had a generator, but it suddenly seemed important to stockpile water bottles.

Just in case.

"Fix the roof first, Summer." The growing list of things to worry about would lead to paralysis if she didn't keep moving forward.

Just as she reached the roofline, an obnoxious rooster's *cock-a-doodle-doo* caused her to jump, which shook the ladder and froze her in place. "Russell Crow, when I find you..."

Summer had to leave the threat open-ended because she had no idea how to close the loop.

The rooster had shown up two or three days after Summer had, and the pen or coop or containment area that Jewel, the shelter's manager, had set up for Russell Crow was not doing the trick. He seemed to take it as a challenge to escape, and he was very good at avoiding detection until he was ready.

Everyone for miles around knew he was hungry for attention because of the crowing.

So much crowing.

She surveyed the yard in front of the clinic, the tree line at the edge and the flowerbeds directly under the ladder.

No chicken in sight.

"Maybe I can spot you from the roof," Summer muttered and scrambled over the top rung on her knees. Heights had never been particularly scary, but the wind, the fast-moving clouds, the not-quite rhythmic banging of the loose building-thingy and Russell Crow's disgruntled chortles below added too much atmosphere for comfort. "Find the loose thing. Reattach it and get back down, Summer."

As she scrambled up to the dormer window that looked out from her tiny living room, it was easy to see the loose metal piece banging against the roof. What was more difficult was figuring out what she might have in her bag of tools to address the problem. She tried and failed with the screwdriver and screws. The staples didn't go deep enough. One of the heavy nails worked to sort of wedge the piece against the roof, but it continued shifting in the wind. "That's probably coming loose again." She bit her lip. "Better try duct tape." The sinking feeling that she was failing gained speed and size as she ripped pieces of tape off and covered all the edges of the loose piece. The shifting stopped, but how much good would duct tape do in a hurricane?

Summer had no idea. That was just the most recent question she didn't know how to answer.

Before she could begin the slide back down to the ladder, her phone rang.

"Hello?" she answered after frowning at the unknown number.

"Dr. Patel," a timid voice said, "it's Hank. Hank Brown? I'm a volunteer over at the shelter?"

Summer exhaled slowly to contain her sigh. Hank and Hattie Brown were the nice couple who were, along with a couple of college-age helpers, running the shelter while Jewel Edgecombe was on her Hawaiian vacation.

Both of them spoke only in questions and gave Summer the impression that they would evaporate if she moved suddenly.

They were very good with the dogs and cats, and Jewel said they had a magic touch for finding human matches for the animals that came in needing homes. Keeping them from evaporating seemed important.

"Hi, Hank, what can I help you with?" Summer asked.

"This storm? Have you been watching the weather reports, Dr. Patel?" Hank cleared his throat.

"I have." Summer rubbed her forehead as she tried to guess what Hank's real question was. There was no way to miss the weather reports.

"Don't you think..." Hank cleared his throat again. "Seems like it's time to evacuate the animals?"

The weight of responsibility was crushing as Summer sat there.

On the roof.

Watching dark clouds building over the ocean in the distance.

With a nervous man and a big decision to make.

Russell Crow decided to remind her that he was there also. Somewhere.

She had no idea how to move all the animals out. The shelter was supposed to run itself, and she'd been working nonstop to serve all the patients left waiting until she reopened the clinic after Dr. Forsyth left. She didn't know much about the operations of the shelter, but finding one place to move the animals to seemed impossible. Summer and her two adult volunteers would have their hands full relocating the shelter animals.

"Should we call Jewel?" Hank asked.

Since Summer had no idea how to evacuate nine dogs and thirteen cats before the storm got there, his suggestion was tempting.

But this was a problem that should have a solution.

"Has the shelter evacuated before, Hank?" Summer realized how many things she still had to figure out in her new business. Taking care of her patients was always her first priority, but the rest—business plans, safety plans, evacuation plans—they had to exist somewhere, didn't they? If not, they needed to move much higher up the to-do list.

She'd treated the shelter as secondary because Dr. Forsyth had told her it was part of the package deal to get the clinic. He'd stated firmly that it was Jewel's domain. She ran it, took care of the minimal funding and staffing. He provided the space and the veterinary care.

That had seemed simple enough.

Evacuating in the face of a hurricane was not simple.

"We have evacuated, but it's been a minute? Jewel has a list of volunteers for emergencies?" Hank said. "We should call her?"

His readiness to give up already made no sense

to Summer. The answer was clear enough. There was a list and volunteers who knew what to do. All they had to do was find that list.

"Or we can check her files at the shelter. Could you and Hattie meet me there? We'll look for the list, and we can all make calls. It will be a rush, but you're right. We have to get the animals out." Summer rolled her head on her shoulders to eliminate some of the ache building there. "I can get some help at the clinic, too."

"Sure thing, Dr. Patel." Hank's tone had changed. Maybe he was just a man who needed a leader. His new certainty boosted Summer's confidence.

She had no trouble leading. Taking charge came naturally most of the time. In fact, it was the most common complaint she'd received romantically and from bosses, the fact that she didn't always work well with others. That actually made perfect sense. Summer wanted to do things for herself.

"Meet you there in twenty minutes," Hank said before he hung up.

Relieved to have come up with at least one answer, Summer started scooting down the sloped roof.

She slid to a stop when she realized the ladder was gone.

She rubbed her eyes and looked again.

"Still missing." Russell Crow agreed loudly with Summer's verdict.

Frustration bubbled up again as she tried to count the number of things she'd encountered that week that no one thought to warn her about. Neither of her parents, none of her professors and not a single one of the veterinarians she'd trained with had explained what to do if she happened to get stuck on a roof while a hurricane was moving in and a ladder disappeared and a rooster laughed from some super-secret hiding spot.

Summer learned quickly. If anyone had explained what to do in this situation, she would know the answer.

"Okay, options." She inhaled slowly, held her breath until her chest hurt and then exhaled. "Call Kima to get her out here to put the ladder back up." She extended one finger. "Wait for Hank and Hattie to show up." She extended the second one. "Sit here until the storm comes in and hope for a fresh start somewhere else with no roosters."

She'd reached for her cell phone when a car turned off the narrow road leading up to the animal hospital.

Summer watched the Horizon Police Department patrol car roll slowly down the gravel driveway and tried to guess whether this was a fourth option, an unexpected solution to being stuck on the roof, or more trouble headed her direction.

When the officer slid out of the driver's side, she realized he could definitely be both. She knew this officer. Their introduction had been rocky and ended up requiring mediation from the very nice chief of police.

If the police department needed a model for recruiting or maybe even a fund-raising calendar called "Hot Cops" or something similar, TJ Shepard would claim the front cover. His sunny blond hair made her think of the all-American boy next door.

Unfortunately, Summer had a type and this was it. Her fiancé, Dr. Dixon Brooks, would have given this officer some competition.

"Ex-fiancé," Summer muttered. Dixon had also taught her a valuable lesson.

Dixon's handsome face had been easy to fall in love with, but letting him and others tell her how to live her life had made her miserable. Keeping her guard up against making that same mistake twice would be smart.

The officer's arrival made perfect sense. On her trip to complete all the paperwork to buy the practice, she and TJ Shepard had turned a routine traffic stop into an event. Had she been partially responsible? Maybe. She regretted that her introduction to Horizon had been so combative, but every time she drove down the street where she'd signed all her loan paperwork and saw the new sign and painted curbs, she experienced a slight spark of vindication.

She'd been a little wrong at their first encounter, but she'd also been right.

Still, it would have been nice to meet Officer Shepard again somewhere more dignified than her perch atop the roof. Apparently, the universe was going to use him to humble her.

Again.

Somewhere in the near distance, Russell Crow was laughing at her, but hunting for the rooster would have to wait. Summer couldn't take her eyes off the man walking toward her.

CHAPTER THREE

EVERY POLICE OFFICER knew that the job was unpredictable. TJ had once been called to assist with a routine traffic stop, only to find a woman and her pet boa constrictor out for a road trip. He and Lucy both had been caught off guard by that one.

He'd expected his conversation with Summer Patel to be awkward, based on their history, but finding her seated at the edge of the roof of the animal clinic erased whatever rehearsed speech he'd had in mind. Her dark hair was blowing in the wind gusts, but he didn't detect any panic on her face.

That was a good sign.

He also wasn't seeing any signs of a warm welcome. Dr. Patel watched him, but the most favorable interpretation he could make of her serious expression was curiosity.

He wouldn't label it relieved or even particularly interested in why he was there.

Anyone in her situation should be glad to see him, shouldn't they?

As TJ walked across the grass, he noticed the ladder on the ground behind the bushes that lined the front of the Horizon Animal Hospital.

"Stay right there," he said as he reached down to pull up the ladder, "and I'll save you." Then he shook his head and muttered, "Exactly where is she going to go, TJ?"

The urge to smack his forehead with his hand was powerful. Wit and charm usually came more naturally to him, and he took a lot of pride in his ability to talk to anyone.

Something about this woman short-circuited his normal skills.

He decided to give it a minute for his words to float away in the breeze before meeting her stare. When the ladder was propped back up and steady, he braved a look at the doctor's face. He could read both intelligence and impatience in her eyes.

"Hold the ladder and I'll save myself, officer." She inched closer, and TJ decided she was used to having her orders followed. Her tone didn't allow for any argument.

That tracked with the way she'd argued with his request to move her car.

"Yes, ma'am. Go ahead. I've got the ladder." He nodded to encourage her down off the roof. "Careful."

For whatever reason, he didn't get the impression Dr. Summer Patel spent a lot of time with ladders or roofs, but she was steady as she returned to the ground, each step exploratory before transitioning to solid. Her grip was also tight enough to turn her knuckles white, so TJ took that as confirmation that she hadn't been as confident of being able to rescue herself as she'd sounded.

Not that he was going to mention that to her. She had already diagnosed him with foot-in-mouth disease. Sticking to business made sense.

Whatever she was going to say was lost as a rooster crowed loudly.

TJ laughed as the startled doctor placed a hand over her heart and then shifted the straps of the tote bag over her shoulder.

"That rooster," she muttered to herself. "He'll have me breaking my neck yet."

As TJ pulled the ladder down, he tried to find a clever icebreaker, but nothing came. When he couldn't fuss with the ladder any longer, he straightened to see that she was watching him with the same serious expression she'd had on the roof.

"'In my defense, I was left unsupervised,'" TJ read the words on her tote before smiling. "That explains a lot."

Flirting? Was he flirting now? Not well, obviously.

Did he have some undiagnosed issue with taking unnecessary chances? Flirting with Summer Patel was high-risk.

His joke thudded to land in the dirt between

them. The frown that flitted across her forehead was a warning. "Dr. Patel? May I call you Summer?" TJ asked as he held out his hand. "Let's make a fresh start."

She stared at his hand for a long pause before slipping her own in.

TJ only had a second to register the soft slide of her skin on his before she freed herself and returned both hands to the straps over her shoulder. "Officer Shepard." Her eyes were focused on his badge. "What brings the Horizon chief of police's son out today?" Her lips firmed into a tight line. "To save me."

Her emphasis on "son" was irritating.

She obviously hadn't forgotten that her complaint about his "abrasive manner" had crashed right at the feet of TJ's father. Something about her tone convinced him that she was reading "nepotism" between the lines.

Until he'd been forced to consider his readiness to step into the chief's office, that charge had never bothered him much, but today it poked a sore spot. TJ had to firmly remind himself the reason for his visit was to make sure Dr. Patel and the shelter animals were ready for the storm. Defending himself against an insult she hadn't even delivered would impede the success of his mission here.

The hard emphasis on "save" was a sign that he wasn't succeeding with his secondary goal, either.

So far, he hadn't managed to rehabilitate their relationship with this visit.

"Please call me TJ." He straightened his shoulders. "Law enforcement is the family business, so that clears up some of the confusion caused by so many Shepards in the station." Attaching his best charming smile didn't warm the doctor's expression. Not even a little bit.

When she didn't answer, just raised a single eyebrow, TJ nodded once. "Right. We are checking in on people in the highest risk zones today to make sure the storm preparations are underway." He scanned the front of the animal hospital and the shelter at the perimeter of the property. "Is that why you were on the roof, Dr. Patel?"

She hadn't made much progress if that had been the plan. At a minimum, the windows would need covering. Shattered glass would be dangerous and expensive to repair.

"Is it against the law to climb on the roof in Horizon?" she asked, but before he could figure out a way to answer that, the wind blew strands of dark hair across her face that she shoved behind one ear before shaking her head. "The wind had loosened—" she frowned before continuing "—something up there. It was banging, so I wanted to secure it before the winds got worse."

Then she crossed her arms over her chest. "Dr. Forsyth went to great lengths explaining how safe this place would be during storms. I asked every question I could think of about hurricanes before I bought it. He only evacuated twice in his time here." She waved a hand with two fingers raised. "And this is only a Category Two storm."

TJ nodded as he considered that. She was defensive before he said much at all, as if she believed she might be in trouble here and wanted to prove herself right. Cops saw a lot of that, too.

Her answer also explained her delay in response.

Dr. Summer Patel had trusted the wrong person.

He saw the effects of that often enough in his day-to-day work. Trusting the wrong person always led to danger.

"Dr. Forsyth was..." How could he say this politely? Trying to make a sale? Foolish? Or lying? TJ didn't believe the man had only evacuated twice in a decade or more, but it didn't seem prudent to cast doubt on the previous veterinarian like that. Summer Patel had memorized Dr. Forsyth's advice, and she was prepared to follow it. "Well, Charlotte's a good fit for him. Some people are meant to stay inland, you know?"

When she spluttered out a laugh, he hoped it meant he'd gone the right way. "People like me, you mean? I hope you won't be saying exactly that about my short tenure here to the next veterinarian anytime soon."

Her shoulders relaxed a fraction, so his did, too. Her reaction gave him hope they could still come to an understanding. Her eyes were beautiful when humor replaced suspicion.

"The decision to evacuate is yours, but the damage from this storm, especially with a nearly direct hit, will be extensive. Roof. Windows. Trees. All of that from the wind, but the water out here on the Island is the biggest danger. You will probably lose electricity for some time, and the bridge will definitely be impassable for a period." TJ watched her face as she absorbed all of this. "It's too bad Jewel's on vacation. She would have had you on track already, but it's not too late. The first thing you need to do is call Boogie Howard, get him over here to put up the hurricane panels. I know Dr. Forsyth stored them around here somewhere. Then get the emergency fosters out here to evacuate the shelter."

TJ propped his hands on his duty belt as she tipped her chin up. "Is a list of orders part of the rescue service provided by every Horizon police officer, or are you doing me a favor, Officer Shepard?"

The way she lingered again on "rescue" and "favor" was a reminder that Dr. Patel didn't let much slide. That would be a problem since he'd been making one misstep after another with her. Her laughter had been a brief bright spot.

"TJ, please, and this is intended as advice, best practices from someone who has been through these kinds of storms his whole life, to a new neighbor. I would do the same for anyone in your position." He tilted his head to the side. "It's also my job to keep you safe, so there's that."

"Fine." She loosened her tightly knotted hands. "If Boogie's real name is Brian, I tried to call him this morning to fix the loose—" she pointed at the roof "—thing, but I got no answer."

TJ forced his lips into a straight line, determined not to grin at the way she described whatever had come loose on the roof.

"That is Boogie. He was the Horizon High School Pirates' wide receiver who scored the touchdown to take the team to the state championships the year we graduated. That is a level of success you cling to around here." TJ shrugged. "He liked to dance in the end zone after scoring. Boogie will be on his obituary someday."

Her lips twitched before the smile broke through. "That seems unfair."

TJ nodded sadly. "Yeah, but his other choice is Brian, so…"

A gust of wind sent the hair across her face again as she chuckled.

Earning that real laugh felt amazing.

Watching her relax a fraction was even better.

"Thank you," she said. "I'm sure you have a lot to do to get ready for the storm. The Browns are on their way, so we can figure out how to evacuate the animals. I'll try Mr. Howard again."

TJ understood that to be his cue to leave.

Leaving without gaining her permission to call her by her first name felt like losing somehow, but he couldn't find a casual way to approach the issue until he saw Lucy's head in the back seat of his patrol car.

Then he wanted to smack his forehead again.

He had one foolproof lure to win new friends and influence even tough customers like Summer, and he'd left her sitting in the car.

"Before I go, I'd like to introduce you to my partner." TJ watched Summer shift impatiently from one foot to the other as he opened the door.

Lucy bounded out of the car.

"Meet Officer Lucy Shepard," TJ said and watched every bit of rigidity melt from the doctor's frame.

She immediately crouched before glancing up at him. "I know she's working. Is it okay to pet her?"

It didn't surprise him that the vet knew the correct protocol for addressing his K9 partner. "Yes, you two will be meeting again. You're Lucy's doctor, *Dr.* Patel." Hinting at his request to call her Summer by emphasizing the formality of her title was his best shot at bringing up the issue again.

And it worked.

As she settled onto the grass in front of Lucy, Summer said, "Please, call me Summer." She raised her eyebrows at him. "TJ." Her tone was clearly "Are you happy now?" but he was happy indeed, so TJ didn't feel it necessary to continue down that road.

Watching the way she talked with Lucy reassured him that his best friend wasn't included in the doctor's disdain. Whatever grudge Summer held, it didn't include Lucy.

"I thought police dogs all had to be named Bullet or Taser. I worked at Auburn's veterinary teaching hospital for a while. We examined a lot of military K9 officers there. I remember a Tank, for sure," Summer murmured as she ran her hand over Lucy's side, checking the fit of her vest as she went. "Symbolic of their roles as weapons, I guess."

Her tone was cool.

As if she didn't approve of the use of dogs on police forces.

TJ wasn't concerned that the doctor would find a physical problem. Lucy's safety and health were top of mind for TJ when they worked, so he never cut corners.

This wasn't the first time he'd met someone with a less-than-positive view of police dogs. That was why the COA and its officer standards were so important.

"Physically, Tank was in great shape." Summer smiled at the way Lucy wriggled closer to her lap. "But his socialization was an issue. I'm happy to see you don't have the same challenge, pretty girl."

TJ hesitated before speaking to gather his thoughts, but he had to say something here.

"Lucy is an officer, not a weapon or a tool that I pull out of a kennel when it's time to go to work and return when the job is over." TJ waited for Summer to meet his stare. The point was too important to slide past. He wanted the best care for Lucy, and it was important Summer understood what that looked like for TJ. "She's also a member of my family now. Forever. I will do anything to keep my family safe, Summer."

He held her gaze long enough to be sure she understood him perfectly.

Summer nodded. "Not a tool. Good. What's her training? Security?" She looked away to make silly faces at the dog, and Lucy grinned.

"Detection. Nose work. Her main skills are in drug and firearms detection, but she has helped with tracking missing persons a few times. She has a good nose." TJ crossed his arms as he watched Summer scratch under Lucy's neck, her weak spot. The dog leaned into her, and a beautiful smile lit up Summer's face.

If the doctor disapproved of dogs used in police work, she absolutely loved the dog herself.

And that was good enough for today. Educating Summer on COA's efforts to elevate police dogs from "weapon" to full officer status with all the protections and benefits they deserved was a discussion for another time.

"Lucy and I are due at the elementary school for story time, but if you need me, please reach out." Since his luck was changing, TJ pushed it. "Would you like my phone number?" He shrugged. "Or you could give me yours. Just in case of an emergency."

Summer blinked slowly as she ran her hands over Lucy's ears. "I have your number. It's 9-1-1, right?"

Outsmarted and a little confused by his own request, TJ nodded. "That will do it."

She made kissy faces at Lucy, and it was difficult to fight back the tiniest sting of jealousy.

"Load up, Lucy." After Lucy was back in her seat, TJ turned to slide behind the steering wheel.

Summer was watching them, the wind catching her dark hair again and sending it streaming out behind her. Maybe she hadn't known how to proceed before the storm, but there was something about her that convinced TJ she never made mistakes.

Or maybe that she never made the same mistake *twice*.

Here, she would make up any lost time and get her storm preparation on track.

That didn't completely relieve his concerns as he made the short drive to the school. Hurricanes were unpredictable, and it was hard to imagine how he'd face one if he hadn't lived through them his whole life.

Dr. Patel would need all the help he could give.

Summer.

Summer would need help.

"Safety. It's part of the job," he muttered as he pulled his cell phone out while he and Lucy walked up the sidewalk. When Boogie answered on the second ring, he said, "Boogie! What are you up to?"

"Busier'n a moth in a mitten. This storm's got me hoppin', TJ." The sound of a drill punctuated Boogie's words.

"Do you have time to head out to the animal hospital? The new doctor said she tried to call this morning," TJ said as he realized he might be digging his hole deeper with the pretty veterinarian. She hadn't appreciated his "rescue" earlier. Giving more help she didn't ask for could definitely backfire.

"Ohhhh, you know? I had a call, but I didn't recognize the number. Don't get too many of those that are anything but telemarketers." Boogie grunted as he banged something into place. "This storm doesn't seem too bad, but Doc was usually prepared out there on the Island. I'll call her soon as we hang up. I can make time. Doc's panels are quick to hang."

After TJ thanked him and ended the call, he opened the door for Lucy. Mrs. Lamb was waiting for him in the lobby. "TJ! I'm so glad we could work this in today. These kids have been talking about Lucy's visit and the contest for days." She hugged him as she had ever since she'd been his first-grade teacher. Horizon Elementary hadn't changed a bit, either. If they had refreshed the paint since he was a student, they'd stuck with a pale yellow that matched what he remembered from his time tearing through the narrow halls.

"Have you got your hurricane preparation done, Mrs. Lamb? We're out here making sure our neighbors are ready for the storm," TJ said as they walked past a few classrooms and a long stretch of bulletin boards covered in colorful spring artwork.

"You betcha. I've learned not to mess around with hurricanes. I have plans to stay with my daughter for the rest of the week. Riding these things out alone is not easy. Better to have some company, you know?" She patted his arm. "Would you like me to introduce you two again? Her divorce should be final any day."

It wasn't every day that TJ encountered a woman stuck on a roof, but offers like this one came with such frequency that he'd gotten good at saying no without saying N o. "Mrs. Lamb, how many times do I have to remind you that you have my heart?"

The way she rolled her eyes while she chuckled made TJ smile.

Entering the first-grade classroom reminded him why he loved his job.

The kids erupted in cheers.

Most of them were for Lucy, but his name was definitely mixed in.

After he finished here, he'd have to return to the station's command center. The dread he felt about being cooped up in the station was discouraging, but afterward, he'd check in on Summer Patel again. That small spark of anticipation felt good.

After the storm, when he had a spare minute, maybe he would figure out what that meant.

CHAPTER FOUR

SUMMER WAS STILL frozen in the yard, staring at the end of the driveway where TJ Shepard's patrol car had last been seen, when Hank and Hattie Brown rolled in, their tiny red Smart car bouncing along the gravel like a rubber ball. The idle question about how they managed to transport groceries home in the vehicle that appeared to be filled to capacity by two small people was wiped away in a sharp gust of wind.

"Afternoon, Dr. Patel?" Hattie said as she stood. When she spoke to Summer, she ended every statement as a question just like her husband.

Wind slammed the car door shut behind Hattie, and Summer was briefly concerned that their car would be lost, literally blown away. Clearly, the Browns needed to head back to higher ground ASAP.

"Thank you so much for coming out, Hattie, Hank." She motioned over her shoulder for them to follow her to the shelter's office. The motion was a habit left over from her life leading veterinary students who often trailed in her wake like ducklings.

Then she remembered that she wasn't teaching residents or working with her own vet techs and slowed her pace. "I should have been digging into safety plans for the shelter already. I know it's going to be a scramble to get this done, and I appreciate your help."

When both of the Browns blinked as if they were surprised by her thanks, Summer wondered if she was the reason they seemed permanently stuck on "flight" in the fight-or-flight response. Her job at Auburn's veterinary teaching hospital had required a brisk pace, managing students, residents, vet techs, patients and their owners. When she'd given that up to move home and accustom herself to life in one of the busiest full-service clinics in metro Atlanta, Summer had still moved quickly through her day.

Life in Horizon required a whole new outlook. Instead of a big team full of medical professionals and the critical support staff that kept the office running, the Horizon Animal Hospital had one full-time doctor, an office manager and two part-time vet techs. The shelter was fully staffed by volunteers.

That meant earning their good will was critical. Improving her working relationship with the volunteers at the shelter was an important goal.

Thinking about what she wanted for her clinic

and the shelter in the future had been bumped way down the priority list by everything required to keep her head above water. She had to find a solution for that.

After the storm.

Summer entered the code for the door to the shelter and then turned on the office light. Hank and Hattie had been handling the early-morning feeding and then coming in again around dinner time while Jewel was out of town. The shelter was lucky to have a small rotation of college-age students who traded off morning and afternoon exercise breaks.

As Summer entered the office, she immediately remembered another reason why she'd spent so little time digging into the shelter's operations. This office was small, dark and crammed with stuff.

During Dr. Forsyth's tour, she had tried to imagine what it must be like to walk into the office intending to adopt an animal. The picture wouldn't form, but she'd been relieved to discover that the rest of the shelter was spotless and organized. The animals were obviously the top priority, as they should be, but it was hard to see how anyone could work through the messy office.

The desk was mounded with…stuff. So much stuff.

It made her heart race to even consider the state of the shelter's records.

Jewel apparently used a flat filing system: she

piled everything on a flat surface and considered it filed.

The walls of the office were also lined with piles. So many piles. Large plastic bins were stacked high, a metal shelving unit held smaller plastic containers, and the door was framed by hooks with leashes dangling in tangled knots.

Nothing was labeled.

If there were any digital records for the Shoreline Shelter, the computer used to create them was absent. That made her think it didn't exist.

Any list of emergency fosters had to be in hard copy.

And it had to be on the desk or in the desk.

Since Hank and Hattie were hovering near the door, she assumed that meant the organization of the office was a mystery to them, too.

Hoping for the best—an organized set of permanent files—Summer pulled open a drawer on the right side of the desk. It was filled with three small bags of chips and a plastic tray of what must be very stale Girl Scout Cookies. The drawer on the left side had to be the shelter's version of the junk drawer. One quick glance showed scissors, a hammer, a handheld fan and an air horn.

No file folders.

Before she left for the evening, she was going to be brave enough to inspect the workroom's cabinets, too. If they were in the same condition as this office…

Being "hands off" with the shelter, as Dr. Forsyth had claimed in his sales pitch, wasn't working. That mistake fanned the self-doubt sparked by the storm. Until she'd made this move to South Carolina, Summer had been successful in eliminating the things that shook her confidence. Having it return here was discouraging.

She rubbed the ache in her chest building at the prospect of working in such chaos.

"Any idea where Jewel might keep this list we need?" Summer asked, determined not to let the simmering frustration escape. Disorganization had always turned up the heat under her anxiety, and there was almost no room left for it to grow without spilling out over everyone.

Hank cleared his throat. "We dug around through the paperwork on the desk this morning before we left, but…"

Hattie crossed her arms over her chest. "If we weren't going to evacuate, it seemed like a bad idea to go any deeper. Might mess up Jewel's system?"

"System" seemed very generous in this situation, but this was not the time to discuss that.

Summer bit her lip as she considered their options. The first three papers she picked up were bills. Were they paid? Important question. The tension in her neck and shoulders grew. "Okay… what else do we need to do to evacuate? Get food together." Summer ticked off the points as she paced. "Meds for any of the animals who'll need them for…a week or so?"

Hank and Hattie both nodded once.

"Which of you is better with sorting?" Summer asked.

Hank raised his hand.

"Okay, the two of us are going to work on big piles." A quick inhale and exhale of breath made it easier to think. "Bills." She pointed at the floor in a corner of the room. "Junk." Summer moved the trash can to the center of the room and made a quick wish that Hank was as good as he thought he was. If they didn't actually toss the trash out, there would be time for Jewel to ensure that they didn't get rid of something important.

Right now, nothing was as important as finding the list of volunteers. Quickly.

"And anything we aren't sure of, we'll stack here." She pointed at the floor in the corner closest to the desk. "Logically, I would guess what we need is underneath all of this." One wave of her hand was the best she could do to summarize the mess.

"Jewel will be mad," Hattie said slowly.

There was no question mark at the end of her statement.

As if this was the one thing certain in Hattie Brown's life: Jewel Edgecombe would not be pleased if they touched the nightmare of disorganization on her desk.

"Not as mad and heartbroken as the rest of us will be if anything happens to the animals," Summer said firmly. "Hattie, you go start preparing packages to send out with the fosters. Line up the meds, make sure they are clearly labeled for the dog or cat they belong to, and I'll check everything as the fosters arrive. We'll have to move fast to get this done."

Summer tried not to worry about what would happen if the list was as outdated as she feared from the state of Jewel's desk. What if the emergency fosters had moved away? What was she going to do if they couldn't find enough help?

Nine dogs. Thirteen cats. In the path of a hurricane because Summer had neglected to ask all the right questions.

They were depending on Summer to find the answers quickly.

The racing of her heart had her worried. If she had a heart attack on top of failing to make sure these animals were safe…

Maybe she should have one of the Browns ready to call 9-1-1 just in case.

The next thought, that she wished she'd taken TJ's phone number, stopped her in her tracks for a second.

"What could he do to help, Summer?" she muttered.

Hank paused in his rapid-fire tossing paper into the trash can to ask, "He who? Help how?"

The giggles that bubbled up surprised them both. Somehow she'd made Hank Brown speak like a Dr. Seuss character. The pressure of the storm had almost broken her brain so that nothing was funny but everything was hilarious.

Since Hank and Hattie both appeared to have their running shoes on in case Summer moved unexpectedly, she had to keep it under control. Getting the animals to safety was top priority, and she needed their help.

A quick cough cleared her mind. "TJ Shepard was here, checking to make sure the storm preparation is under control." That part of the equation was easy. Why she would want to call him now was less clear.

"Oh," Hank said with a nod. "Whatever it is you need help with, TJ can do it. You can trust him."

"And so handsome," Hattie chimed in from the workroom off the office where the food and medicines were stored.

Both of them were making firm statements now, all about how great TJ was.

And handsome. *Thanks for reminding me, Hattie.*

"Good looks don't equal good guy," Summer muttered under her breath. The sight of bare wood in the center of the desk lifted her spirits, but it took her a second to realize both Hank and Hattie had stopped to stare at her.

"TJ's a Shepard?" Hank returned to the breathy questions.

It sounded as if Hank was aghast at the suggestion that TJ or any Shepard might be anything less than hero material.

"Shepards have been leading Horizon ever since the town was founded," he added, his voice stronger. "The first Shepard in Horizon, Captain Emory Shepard, was a hero of the Revolutionary War. You've seen the statue in the park on the waterfront?" He punctuated his paragraph by dumping a small stack of paper in the trash.

Summer appreciated Hank's ability to talk and work at the same time.

That didn't mean she wanted to admit that she had seen the statue but had not cared in the least about who it was or their role in town or the Shepard family. She had a suspicion that would lead to more history, and no one had time for that right now. A noncommittal "Hmm" was her best choice.

Hattie leaned back around the door to shake her finger. "Every one of those Shepards is gold, Dr. Patel. Tom's kids are good people. TJ and Bee both followed in his footsteps here, but his daughter from his first marriage, Emery, and his stepson, Daniel… They don't live here in Horizon, but they're both some type of police officer, too."

Only-child Summer tried to imagine growing up with that many siblings. The fact that they'd followed their father's career did say a lot about the family, too.

Not that she'd ever really doubted that TJ was decent enough.

In their first encounter, his officious attitude had raised her hackles. She'd been a visitor in town who hadn't known all the parking rules, and she'd been following everything posted. Why had asking a question about his orders been an issue?

Had she been a little forceful herself? Possibly.

He'd had zero patience or interest in her side of the argument then.

Now, she just didn't appreciate his bossiness. Was that the right word? Know-it-all-ness?

Still, bossiness might have been part of the Shepard genetic makeup at this point, running in the family, bred through generations like the job.

Summer had fought for years to avoid being pressed into her father's mold. How much simpler would her career have been if she'd taken up orthopedics, joined her father's office and then taken over his practice when he decided to give it up for more time on the greens? There would have been no hard decisions to make, like whether or not she could meet her loan payment month to month. In Atlanta, hurricanes could have remained mysterious sources of occasional heavy rain and potential tornadoes.

All she had to do to make that happen was practice medicine that she hated every day and give up any ability to make her own career choices. At least that fight had prepared her to stand up and walk away from the marriage everyone in her life knew was perfect for her.

She had experience surviving big storms.

"We left out sweet Lila," Hank said. "She didn't get a badge, but you'll see her face all over town on houses for sale. Good as gold, the Shepards are. Don't see why you wouldn't call for help if any one of 'em offered it."

Hank's perplexed tone reminded her of the reaction she'd gotten from her maid of honor when she'd told her the wedding was off. Dr. Dixon Brooks was a catch, a successful surgeon and one of the most eligible bachelors in Georgia. How could Summer walk away from him?

The truth was that it hadn't been simple.

And it certainly hadn't been easy.

But it was the right thing for Summer.

Here, she knew that leaning too heavily on TJ Shepard would be a problem. Giving up her own independence had been a mistake before. Finding her own way, making her own decisions, had made her stronger. What she learned from this storm would make the next one easier.

TJ, who had followed in his father's footsteps and grown up in a town where everyone viewed them as legends, would never understand that.

In the middle of the storm, it was tempting to accept TJ's "rescue," but it wouldn't be right for her.

She'd moved to Horizon to solve her problems, not find new ones.

Besides, evacuating the shelter had a solution already. "I do need to get to know the Shepards better, but for now, we can take care of this problem by ourselves." Summer tapped the bare wood desktop. "More of this is all we need."

Hank nodded uncertainly. "When you change your mind, I have his number?"

"Dr. Patel, if we don't find that list, we can call and TJ will round up some troops, I bet." Hattie sniffed and disappeared back inside the workroom.

The Browns were persistent. That could explain their success at finding good homes for the rescues coming through the shelter. Persistence was a good thing.

Summer silently reminded herself of that while she weeded through the pile in front of her.

Determined to ignore their lack of faith in her and how it contrasted with boundless belief in TJ and the Shepards, she focused on a single task: methodically clearing the next section of the desk.

The clipboard she discovered filled her with hope, but it turned out to be a list of donors to the shelter.

"Very valuable information," Summer muttered as she put it in the corner nearest the desk.

Hank had cleared his own large section of the desk, so if the list of volunteers was in the clutter, they were closing in on it. If not, they'd need to reevaluate their options.

Before she could decide which area was most likely to yield results, another vehicle turned down the gravel drive.

It was a pickup truck with a sign that said Howard Construction on the side. The logo was a football, which had nothing to do with construction as far as Summer knew, but it totally fit a high school wide receiver named Boogie.

"Oh, good, Boogie's here. He'll get your windows all covered." Hank nodded as he scooted his next pile closer to the trash can. "I was wondering when you were going to get the hurricane panels up, Dr. Patel."

He'd wondered, but hadn't suggested she do it.

Helpful.

But when she considered the way they tiptoed around her, it made awful sense.

Instead of snapping, "Action is the natural antidote to worry," in the same tone her father might have used, Summer paused. That pause was filled with all the patience she'd managed to develop over a lifetime.

"Hattie, Hank, I'm hoping you'll call me Summer," she said as she stood. The way TJ had pressed the issue of using her first name and reminder that she needed to adjust her manner to fit Horizon's flow were fresh on her mind. If they knew her as Summer instead of Dr. Patel, the Browns could relax a little. They might use more periods instead of question marks and give her some friendly guidance when things like hurricanes popped up.

That was all Summer needed here, a little prodding. No “rescue” or orders. She was fully capable of making the right choices.

Hattie stuck her head back around the door frame to exchange a look with Hank before they both nodded.

She had no idea whether the request would smooth out things between them, but it had been easy enough. Before, demanding respect had been a big part of Summer’s daily battles at work and in her relationships. Success in Horizon appeared to rest on something different.

“Keep organizing. I’ll make sure Boogie has what he needs to get started.” Summer was halfway across the large grassy yard to the animal clinic when she muttered, “And determine how exactly Boogie Howard knew to show up here.”

Because she hadn’t had a chance to call again.

By process of elimination, that left TJ Shepard as the most likely person to have done it for her.

The confusion of emotions caused by that…

Summer blew out a breath as she approached the pickup.

Clearly, TJ had done her a huge favor by reaching out to the guy who could secure the windows that the Browns had been secretly worrying over.

She just as clearly hadn't asked for his interference.

Anyone else might be able to grasp the gratitude and brush the other away, but a lifetime of being surrounded on all sides by people who were convinced they knew what was best for her and determined to override Summer's opinions to the contrary had built a large, invisible bruise.

TJ Shepard had a way of poking at it.

The fact that gratitude and relief were swamping everything else would need some examination.

"Hey, Doc," Boogie Howard said as he slid out of his truck. He waved his cell phone. "Sorry I missed your call. Soon as TJ told me who was trying to reach out, I added your contact info. From now on, you won't have any trouble getting me."

Boogie offered her his hand. Summer shook it and immediately felt some of the fear and tension that had been building escape. Boogie's wide-open smile inspired confidence.

"I should have left a message." Summer hated that she'd made an error like that, especially in such an important moment. Admitting it wasn't easy. She wrapped one hand around the opposite wrist to squeeze it, a coping mechanism for when big emotions were too near the surface.

Eventually, she'd also have to come to terms with the certainty that she needed to thank TJ Shepard for taking over here.

Boogie waved his hand. "No problem. You did

’zactly the right thing, talking with TJ. That rascal is pretty good about connecting people like you and me.” He waved at the ladder. “See you got me started. Is the shed unlocked? I’ll get these panels up in a minute, put your ladder away and be on my way to the next stop before you know it.”

The urge to explain that she hadn’t involved TJ on purpose, in case anyone got the idea she needed his help, was washed away with a sting of tears that surprised Summer and alarmed Boogie.

Having Boogie take charge of hurricane-proofing the clinic was such a relief.

“Hear, now…it ain’t so serious, I promise.” He patted her shoulder awkwardly. “Any damage the buildings take from ol’ Hurricane Agnes, we can fix. Won’t be the first time, and I will bet money it won’t be the last.”

Summer nodded and managed not to lecture herself aloud about getting a grip.

Instead, she said, “There’s a loose…something up there.” Pointing at the roof was silly, but it felt right in that moment. “You will see some duct tape.”

Boogie laughed. “We call that ingenuity, Doc. I will see if I can do anything to shore up the mighty force that is duct tape for today, and when we’re on the other side of the storm, I will find a permanent fix.”

The urge to explain that she’d done the best she could with limited skills and resources reminded her so much of her old self, the one she'd left behind in Atlanta, that Summer had a surge of annoyance at herself. There was no need to apologize or explain, and Boogie wasn't asking for anything here.

It was refreshing.

Energizing.

The knot of problems that had almost frozen her in place on the roof was unraveling.

Before she could offer her brand of assistance, whatever that might be, Hank appeared in the doorway of the shelter. "Dr. Patel?" He cleared his throat. "Summer, I found the list."

When she turned to excuse herself, Boogie held up a hand. "I'll let you know when I'm finished." His tuneless whistle would have normally ruffled Summer's feathers, but today it was a sign that he wasn't worried about the job ahead.

What a relief.

Summer trotted back across the yard and met Hank's smile with her own.

"Good job, Hank." She took the wrinkled paper from him and counted fifteen names and phone numbers. Finding the single piece of paper wasn't easy, and she said a quick, silent thank-you to the universe that Hank had been right about his sorting skills.

They had to find places for nine dogs and thirteen cats. Did they have enough volunteers?

Obviously, more would be better, but there was no way to know until they took the next step.

The list wasn't a lot of information to go on, but it was what they needed to move ahead. "Come into the clinic's office with me. We'll get Kima and Natalie plugged in and start making calls."

CHAPTER FIVE

TJ SCRUBBED HIS hand down his face as he waited for the mayor to wind down. The storm's forecasted path had changed very little throughout the day, but the weather had finally shifted. The high winds and building clouds over town had pushed everyone's concern into high gear. The number of phone calls, emails and important messages handed to the chief had overloaded even his capacity, so TJ had stepped up to take Mayor Rainey Blackwell's call.

His father had immediately stepped outside. TJ really hoped he was coming back.

It had been a day that felt seventy-two hours long, and Rainey was still running strong.

As far as TJ could tell, the only job he'd hate more than being his father's second-in-command would be stepping up to first.

Adrenaline had gotten him this far. It might even carry them all through the coming storm, but if TJ didn't find a real meal soon, he might lose his patient demeanor.

Actually, there was no real doubt about it.

Rainey was a cousin three or four generations back in the family tree, but she was half a second from meeting a brand-new TJ.

When she paused in the list of emergency contacts she'd established for any communications overnight, TJ interrupted, "Hey, Rainey, email your list over and—"

"Already done," she immediately responded. "I copied the chief and Bee both, but I'm covering all my bases. If I need to reach out to the governor for assistance, I want to know ASAP."

Rainey had spent two terms in Columbia as a state senator with her sights set on Washington before returning home to take charge of Horizon's city offices. She was a big fish in a small pond at this point, but she never hesitated to throw her connections around when it could help the town.

Right now, TJ appreciated the sentiment, but if she hadn't already thought of how to get more resources ahead of the storm, he wasn't going to be much help. Her notes were all they needed. This phone call was Rainey making sure she hadn't forgotten anything.

Before he could say that, she'd launched into her plans for the next day.

His father walked into the cramped conference room they were calling "Command" for the storm and held out his hand. The chief didn't have to ask any questions to understand the situation.

Relieved to step back into second place, TJ handed him the phone.

His father said, "Rainey, we are on top of the situation." Whatever she said caused his father to close his eyes and inhale slowly. "Yes, the overnight shift has all this information as well. TJ and I'll be back on duty at seven in the morning, and we'll brief you on any new developments then."

His father nodded.

Then he nodded again.

"Of course, I understand. This is critical for all of us, but we need to get rest tonight. There won't be any tomorrow." His father waited patiently for her to agree and added, "Do not call me tonight unless something is underwater or on fire, Rainey." He held out a hand. "On second thought, if something is on fire, call the fire chief. We need food and sleep, and that includes you."

His words must have gotten through because his father said, "Tell your daddy I said hello," and ended the call. Their eyes met as the chief gave TJ the phone back.

"I swear, ninety percent of this job is telling people to settle down, one way or another." His father exhaled slowly.

The long day was easy to see on his face, even though TJ knew that his father was indestructible. The fine lines around his eyes were deeper, and his hair was rumpled as if he'd spent too much time running his hands through it. This man was miles away from the chief who'd led the morning shift briefing.

This Tom Shepard might actually be ready to retire.

"Did you mean what you said? Are you heading home?" TJ asked. It made sense, but he wondered if his father would rest or if he'd be up watching the weather reports and checking his phone for alerts.

"Absolutely. Your mother made me promise to come home as soon as I could. She doesn't agree there will be plenty of time to sleep after I retire. I didn't have any interest in hearing her talk about balance again, so I caved immediately. She's right. She always is. We—" his father motioned between them "—have had a long day, and there are a few more on the horizon. A thing every leader has to learn is when to take a break. Burnout is real, and it will end your career in law enforcement long before you are ready if you don't guard against it, TJ."

This wasn't the first time his father had warned him about burning out. He'd heard Chief Shepard tell more than one new hire the same thing.

The aspect of the job that TJ loved most was that it was unpredictable. His days were never the same.

Until he was forced to sit at a desk all day.

Or in a conference room with a constantly ringing phone and endless reports to read or write.

Too many days like today could definitely add up to burnout.

His father clapped a hand on TJ's shoulder. "You did good today. How do you feel?"

Drained.

Exhausted.

Like he'd been stuck in jail all day on the wrong side of the bars.

Imagining a lifetime of days like this? Depressing.

Really depressing.

Especially compared to how he'd ended the day before, energized and full of big plans on how he was going to improve K9 police work in South Carolina. Hearing Summer's cynical view of how police dogs were valued clearly showed how much good he could do with the COA.

But not if he was buried under reports every day.

Still, his father's "good job" was worth a whole lot. Would it balance out the scale? He wasn't sure. His good opinion soothed some of TJ's fears about how much of his success he owed to the Shepard legend.

"I think we're on top of the situation." TJ didn't meet his father's eyes because he knew that was not the answer Tom Shepard hoped for. Tonight was not the right time to get into a discussion of why TJ was wrong about feeling worn down by the work. Chief Shepard was looking for his next leader, and leaders did the job that had to be done.

Even if they had to catch up on sleep when they managed to retire.

Bee stuck her head around the doorframe. "Quitting time. Mom called to say she has dinner ready, and we better be home before the last serving dish hits the table." She pointed at TJ. "You're coming, right? It's meat loaf but there will be mashed potatoes, too."

Since TJ would rather go to bed hungry than face meat loaf, Bee was doing her best to sweeten the offer.

All of the Shepards that still lived in Horizon got together a couple of times a week for his mother's meals. During the day, she ran the high school from the principal's office, but in her spare time, she enjoyed experimenting in the kitchen.

During times like this, his mother wanted them all to gather around the table.

She was as invested in keeping the Shepards safe as his father was in protecting Horizon.

But the weight of his father's stare convinced TJ that the meat loaf was a solid excuse to skip this meal. The more time they spent together while he was feeling this way, the odds increased that he'd be too honest about how little he enjoyed this part of the job.

Getting through the storm without additional family drama was his priority.

He didn't want to disappoint the chief, but he also didn't want to spend a lot of time listening to how he was the right man for the job. As far as TJ could tell, he was the only successor his father had considered.

That didn't bolster his confidence in his own ability.

TJ said, "I'm beat. I'm going to pick something up and head for home."

Bee pursed her lips. "Brave, Tommy. I'll make your excuses to Mom." Her wicked grin was proof that whatever she said, it wouldn't put TJ in a good light. His mother wouldn't believe it, most likely, but heading it off made sense.

"I'll call her," TJ said as he stood from the chair that had molded to his backside after hours of reports, phone calls and meetings. The way every muscle protested was new, and he didn't enjoy it.

Days out in his patrol car or working with Lucy never left him feeling so…old? No, not old. He wasn't old, even if he felt ancient.

"I heard through the grapevine that you got Dr. Patel on track," Bee said as she bent to scratch Lucy's head. The retriever had been on duty in the Command conference room all afternoon, too, but Lucy had been able to rest her eyes. "Charlene called to say that Dr. Patel contacted her directly to see if she could help out. The plan was to pick up the cats she needed to foster this afternoon."

TJ sighed as he remembered his fleeting hope

to stop by the animal hospital again before the storm. Unfortunately, his father had made other plans for his afternoon, and it was too late to go see Summer tonight. Dr. Forsyth had kept a small apartment at the clinic, and TJ assumed that was where Summer was living. Finding the answer to that would be simple enough.

If Bee didn't already know, she could make a phone call to get the information without using department resources.

Involving his sister would open him up to endless teasing and a promise to repay with an unspecified favor at some point in the future.

TJ didn't have the energy for another skirmish with prickly Dr. Patel that night anyway.

"When I stopped by, Dr. Patel said Hank and Hattie were headed out to help her with the animals, and I called Boogie to get him over to put on the hurricane panels." TJ shrugged as Bee narrowed her eyes at him.

"Did Dr. Patel *ask* for you to call Boogie or..." She let the question trail off, but they both knew the answer.

"I'm glad I was able to help." TJ chanced a direct glance at his father. The chief was assessing TJ's words, expressions and movements and developing a theory. That was clear in his slight frown.

Time to go.

"See you both in the morning," TJ said as he

motioned Lucy to follow him and hurried toward the lobby.

"Night, TJ," the officer manning the front desk called out. He waved a hand, but did not relax until he was down the steps and on the sidewalk in front of his patrol car. The wind had increased as night fell. The cooler temperature might weaken the coming storm, but rain was definitely in the air.

When Lucy was loaded into the back seat, TJ slid behind the steering wheel. "What do you think, Lucy? Pizza?"

His partner was always in, no matter which take-out choice he made.

The people at Palmetto State Pizza on the square made special accommodation for his K9 partner, namely in the form of cheese handouts under the table.

On a nice night, he might walk the two blocks, but with the threat of rain building, he was happy to find a front-door parking spot. The pizzeria's windows were shuttered. This far inland, there was less danger of damage, but he was glad they were taking precautions.

"Smart people are probably already at home at this hour and in this weather," he muttered. Lucy snorted her agreement, but that didn't stop her from sitting forward. She knew where she was and was always alert for cheese.

Then he remembered Bee's promise to let his mother know he wasn't coming and pulled out his phone. He wasn't surprised when she answered before the first ring went through.

"My baby, are you on your way?" his mother asked. A rattle of silverware made him question whether his father and Bee were going to make it "before the last serving dish hits the table."

When he didn't immediately answer, she added, "I want to hear all about your trip over to Columbia. When you mentioned that it was the annual state meeting, I got curious."

TJ smiled. "Curious" was one way of putting it. His mother had internet sleuthing skills that would put CIA agents to shame. When she got "curious," she started digging up information.

"The grants that COA is putting together are impressive, TJ, but it was the work they're doing to lobby the legislature to step up protections for K9 officers that really got my attention," she added.

"Yeah, me, too," TJ said tiredly. He really didn't want to think about how his excitement had deflated in the face of life at Command.

"If we discussed it at dinner, I bet your father would be interested," she said slowly.

TJ took that to mean his mother would be in his corner to back whatever TJ wanted to do next because she knew how much he valued the work.

But it didn't mean that she understood that what he wanted would directly conflict with his father's plan. The mismatch hadn't been fully outlined to

TJ, either, not until he'd been assigned his role as second-in-command.

Where she would fall in that disagreement was less clear.

"Not tonight, Mom." He waited for her to respond, but the expectant silence was a trick she had always used brilliantly. No one could out-wait her, not her students or her children or her husband. "I need a break. Some quiet time. Today was…"

His mother was easy enough to talk with about most things, but TJ was afraid she'd be as disappointed in how little he wanted to sit in his father's chair as the chief would be.

"It was a long day," he finally said.

"Hmm." His mother knew there was something important he wasn't saying. She always had. "Okay. I'll be headed into the station to check on you tomorrow, Thomas Junior. The schools are closed, so I can direct all my attention to you and your sisters. How about that?"

TJ laughed because his mother never changed. She might go along with him for now, but she wasn't going to forget that he wasn't telling her everything. "How about that?" was her favorite way of showing that she was onto him, even if she wasn't pushing it yet.

He could tell her there was no need to come to the station.

He might remind her that he was fully grown

and employed as an officer of the law with some critical duties in the face of the storm.

But she would just play her own card, the highest-ranked one in the whole deck. She was his mother, and she would do exactly what she needed to do.

Besides that, if he spent too much time arguing with her, Lucy might figure out how to open the back door on her own. Free cheese had already been delayed for too long.

"As long as you aren't bringing meat loaf leftovers, I will be thrilled to see you." TJ grinned at her spluttered objections. "Love you."

She was giggling when they hung up. That touch of normal life made it easier to relax his shoulders as he slid out of the patrol car.

He and Lucy trotted across the sidewalk to the pizzeria. After opening the door for her, he was in the middle of a very goofy "Who wants a treat?" conversation when he realized there was a small audience waiting just inside.

The crowd included the owner and chef, Leo Marcell, who was ready with a cheese cube in hand, couples at three tables, and Dr. Summer Patel.

While Lucy sat beautifully to accept her treat, TJ awkwardly cleared his throat. "Hey, I'll have my usual, Leo." Then in a wasted effort to regain some of his cool, he motioned at the windows. "Glad to see you're taking precautions."

Leo paused in entering the order for TJ's supreme pizza with all the meats and most of the veggies but not a single, solitary mushroom ever. "Uh, of course. We aren't closing, but we aren't taking risks, either."

Before TJ knew what he was doing, he gave Leo a thumbs-up.

It surprised them both. Neither one of them used thumbs-up.

Leo blinked before nodding. "Okay. Have a seat there next to Dr. Patel and we'll get it ready."

TJ offered his credit card, signed the receipt and crammed his hands in his pockets before they could offer any other sign language without his consent.

Then he turned to face Summer Patel.

On the plus side, her face was a little more open than when he'd met her earlier that day.

Not being stuck on a roof might have something to do with that.

As he slowly moved to take the seat next to her, he desperately auditioned conversational openers in his head. None of them seemed good enough, and he'd dug himself such a deep hole that afternoon that he wanted it to be right.

Consequently, he waited too long, and the silence spun out between them.

Thank goodness Lucy never experienced social anxiety.

She came to lean against TJ's leg, her focus completely on Summer.

"Hi, Officer Lucy," Summer said and reached out to offer her hand for Lucy's sniffs. "Hi…TJ."

Gratified and amused as he watched the quick flash of emotions across her face, TJ said, "Good evening, Summer." It almost sounded as if he was confident of his ability to speak to her. He really wasn't.

It was becoming ever more evident that something about Summer Patel scrambled the paths of his brain that made conversation easy.

The way her face cycled through varying levels of concern reassured him that she wasn't sure of her conversational skills, either.

"Yo, TJ," Leo said and raised his hand. "Catch. Treats for our girl."

Days, weeks, months in the future, he would look back with gratitude that his ability to catch soft lobs of cubed cheese that normally landed on Palmetto State Pizza salads never left him, no matter how close Summer might be.

Words were messy, but letting her be pelted with cubed cheddar might cause an actual altercation.

His shoulder rubbed against hers as he made the catch in what he believed to be a highly athletic manner.

Then he held out his hand to Summer. The cheese instantly caught Lucy's attention.

He added his reliable charming smile as he met Summer's stare.

"Our girl? I think he meant Lucy." Summer's lips were twitching. "She's the best girl and the one who gets cheese treats, right?"

TJ paused.

Then he noticed the curve of her lips matched the sparkle in her eyes.

She had made a joke.

With him.

The giddiness that swept through him would be concerning, but it felt too good to laugh with her. Some of the weird tension that always accompanied his interactions with her disintegrated while Lucy glanced anxiously from his hand to Summer and back.

"Yes, I am aware," TJ said through chuckles, "but I thought you might want to give her the treats."

"I do." Summer nodded as she took the cubes from his hand and offered one to Lucy. "And I'm really glad I ran into you tonight."

TJ had to fight to keep his eyebrows in their normal position. Displaying any shock at her words would derail what was becoming their most successful conversation to date.

But *really* glad?

He could see being relieved to see him.

Possibly even a *little* glad.

Really glad was new territory.

One of the things he had learned about talking with Summer Patel was that he should slow down. Jumping in too fast always led him in the wrong direction, so he leaned back in his chair to wait patiently for whatever might come next.

It wasn't a hardship. Slowing down gave him time to study her face.

When they'd met earlier, her stress had been clear in her tight lips and the small vertical line that creased her forehead. Tonight, some of that was there, because obviously the storm was still on the way, but something had changed. Her face was more expressive, and her eyes were warmer.

He liked it.

"I owe you a big thank-you." Summer licked her lips, and he wondered if saying the words had caused physical pain. Then he realized this might be the best night of recent memory.

All because of this brief meeting that lasted long enough to make a pizza.

There was nothing unusual about the moment, but he couldn't shake the feeling that something big had changed.

CHAPTER SIX

SUMMER WISHED SHE'D had more time to figure out what she wanted to say to TJ, but this chance to do the right thing was too good to pass up. Words were never a problem for her, but here she hesitated.

Overreacting to TJ Shepard had become a habit, and breaking it was going to take some effort.

It didn't help that Summer hated being wrong more than almost anything.

Unfortunately, the one time she would have welcomed TJ's brand of help, it wasn't coming. In their other encounters, TJ had rushed in, said something that immediately irritated her, and set the course. Tonight, he was watching and waiting.

That made everything harder.

"Thank you." She nodded because that was a good start.

"You said that already." TJ's lips curled as he studied her. "For what?"

That was more like the TJ she knew. It made it easier to think.

"Well, I jumped right into digging out the list

of emergency fosters, which was a big job since every bit of paper that came into the shelter ever was piled on top of the single desk in the office without rhyme or reason," Summer said, determined to show him that she'd had her reasons for needing the assistance she was grateful for. "And when we managed to find it, we immediately started making calls to volunteers, so it was a huge relief when Boogie showed up out of the blue to help with the panels over the windows, even though I didn't ask for your help."

When she realized she was doing it again, asserting her independence in some knee-jerk response when he hadn't really threatened it, Summer added, "But this one time, I appreciate you ignoring what I said."

TJ frowned and didn't immediately answer, so she continued, "Because I had everything under control. I told you that."

None of this was sounding very grateful, was it?

Before she could regroup to try again, he rubbed his hand down his face, and Summer realized he was exhausted. "Long day, I guess?"

He nodded. "Yeah. So many reports. Phone calls. Meetings. I'm not at my best tonight. I'm glad Boogie got the hurricane panels up. And did you get all of the animals evacuated successfully?"

Summer's first instinct was to tell him not to worry about it, that it was her responsibility and she'd take care of it. He had other things to worry about, and she was on top of the situation.

Then she realized that was more of the prickly defensiveness that had gotten her in this spot in the first place. With her staff, with her volunteers, and with the police officer who had helped her in spite of all that.

Other people would exchange the same information as a way of passing the time, making friendly chitchat. None of this had to be a judgment of her abilities.

So she tried something different.

She decided to be…open.

Transparent.

If moving to Horizon was about starting over, that seemed like a habit to at least explore.

Maybe it could replace fighting with TJ.

"Most of them. We were able to get all the cats out to temporary fosters this afternoon. Three of the people on Jewel's list were not available, either because we couldn't reach them or because they've moved away." Summer inhaled slowly. Putting that out of her mind for a brief moment had been nice. "We have three dogs left at the shelter tonight." She winced. "Big ones."

"Uh-oh," TJ said slowly, "not big ones. You're going to need some space for them."

She nodded sadly. "Yeah, they're the hardest to adopt under normal circumstances, too. The Great Dane is a senior. He just needs a quiet spot to rest, you know? That leaves the boxer and the puppy that is obviously a Newfoundland crossed with a brown bear." She held her hands out to show the size. "Big. Hairy. Energetic. Feet the size of dinner plates."

When she and the Browns had waved off the last emergency foster, those three dogs had been settled quietly in the shelter's large indoor pens, but they needed a place to go.

TJ bumped her shoulder with his to get her attention. "Got a solution for that?"

Summer studied his face. If she was guessing correctly, he had some suggestions, but maybe he was trying to make his own new habit. Was he asking her if she wanted his help before marching in to take over?

Because if he was…

The fluttery sensation in her chest caught Summer off guard.

She didn't flutter under normal circumstances.

Instead, she'd spent entirely too much time arguing to convince people to listen to what she wanted to say.

Having the space to decide was new.

She liked it.

"Well," Summer said as she ran her hands over her jeans, "Hank and Hattie were going to make calls tonight, and Charlene at the Sandlapper offered to help, but she's already fostering three cats. Adding three dogs on top of that seems like too much to ask." She tilted her head to the side. "Worst case, I can move the dogs into my office and care for them myself. I think I'll be okay."

The way he was chewing on his bottom lip was her warning that he had a suggestion.

"Or..." he said slowly, "you're going to move inland for the duration of the storm yourself, so we need to find a hotel or place to stay that will also accept three dogs. That's the worst case, but you have to find a place to shelter."

That stopped her in her tracks.

Leave her clinic, the place she'd just invested quite a large portion of her life in via a business loan? That seemed wrong.

"But—"

"I know Dr. Forsyth told you he only left twice in his time here," TJ interrupted and held up a hand, "but you have no idea what it's like to sit through a storm like this all on your own. I can find a list of references to support my claims here if you don't trust my expertise..." He shook his head. "Leo? Could you tell Dr. Patel here what you would do if you were living out on the Island? Stick it out or evacuate?"

Disappointed at how TJ's initial question was about to veer back to their well-worn track of arguing, Summer firmed her jaw. When Leo shrugged, she bit back the urge to explain forcefully that she didn't need to be made a special example of here in this pizzeria. He said, "Me? I'd probably come into town for a couple of nights. The storm will be bad enough, even if they're saying it probably won't take out buildings, but the sound. It's relentless, Doc. Wind and pounding rain. If the lights go out, you do that in the dark." He put both hands to his apron. "Sitting through that all alone has got to be even worse."

TJ stood. If she read his intention correctly, he was going to go to the occupied tables and solicit their opinions as well.

That would be a step too far *past* the step too far he'd already taken.

Summer grabbed his arm and pulled him back down into the seat next to her.

"There's honestly no need to have everyone in this place confirm your opinion of how stupid I am, TJ," Summer whispered in his ear, angry and hurt and reminded all over again that insisting on her independence was the only way to avoid this.

As unusual as her flutters had been a second ago, this frustration was too familiar.

She froze when he leaned closer to whisper, "There's not a single cell of me that believes you're stupid, Summer. You don't trust my advice. That part puzzles me, as of the two of us, I'm the only one who has actually lived through hurricanes, but this is too important to go along to get along. I need to know you're safe. Please come into town tomorrow and stay until the storm is gone."

I need to know you're safe.

Summer fought the shiver of awareness that swept over her. His voice in her ear was powerful. It grabbed her attention.

Some of her irritation eased as she leaned back to study his face. However bad TJ's skills of persuasion might be, Summer believed his heart was in the right place. It showed in his brilliant hazel eyes, which were entirely too easy to read as close as they were in that moment.

And she really hoped she wasn't being swayed by how handsome said face was.

If he had said any part of that first, before turning it into a public display, she would have understood and accepted his advice.

Wouldn't she?

The fact that she wasn't certain reminded Summer that this was the pattern she was trying to break.

Summer leaned back. "I appreciate your concern. What I don't get is why I'm the lucky target. Do you publicly shame everyone into doing what you want out of concern for their safety?"

TJ tilted his head back and rolled it on his shoulders. "Public. Shame."

Summer crossed her arms over her chest and tried to ignore the twinge that resulted at hearing him repeat her words.

Was that an exaggeration? Immediately, her fairer half shouted, "Yes!"

But the stubborn side of her couldn't back down.

Someday, when she was better adjusted to life in Horizon, away from her family, she would be able to. That was the plan.

As it was, Leo saved them both from any more awkwardness.

"Dr. Patel, I've got your pizza ready." He held out the box and smiled.

Summer stood, eager to escape the awkward bubble she and TJ had made, but she couldn't make herself leave without saying anything.

"I..." She cleared the frog from her throat nervously. "I really appreciate your advice, TJ. I will definitely think about coming into town." There. That seemed very adult, an easy way to soften the way too harsh boundary she'd just set ablaze between them.

His curt nod made her think he would need something bigger.

"Call 9-1-1 if you need any assistance, Dr. Patel. Lucy and I are here to serve Horizon." TJ ran his hand down Lucy's side and did not meet her eyes.

The "Dr. Patel" landed as a direct hit.

"If you have any trouble finding a place, Doc, let me know," Leo offered. "My house is filled to the rafters with kids, but we'll make some room. Everyone here is ready to help a neighbor when we have storms like this one."

As Summer accepted the pizza and smiled politely at Leo behind the counter, she had to accept that she had set the terms. TJ was only agreeing to them.

She didn't want his help, so he wouldn't give it anymore.

That was what she'd been working so hard to establish. Right?

Why did it feel so very wrong?

The raindrops splattering on her windshield did nothing to improve her suddenly low spirits as she navigated the dark, wet roads back to the Island. The water flowing under her normally fine bridge had risen, and she wondered if volunteers would be able to make it out to the shelter to pick up the three remaining dogs in the morning.

And if TJ was right and she needed to leave, was that window of opportunity quickly closing?

On the way up to her apartment, Summer paused to see if Russell Crow had anything to say ahead of the storm. He'd been quiet while Boogie was there hanging the storm panels and the volunteers had been streaming in and back out. When there was only the sound of the growing wind and splatter of rain, Summer muttered a quick hope that the rooster had moved somewhere safer for the duration of the storm.

"That chicken has better survival instincts than you do, Summer."

When Summer was inside, she set the pizza box down on the cramped kitchen counter. On a normal day or night, she could see the shelter across the large yard through the dormer window, but the hurricane panel protecting the glass blocked her view.

While she was still going in mental circles about the best choices for the three dogs at the shelter and herself, her phone rang. She immediately relaxed, certain that TJ had somehow tracked down her phone number and refused to give up on her safety.

His stubborn persistence might crash against her own stubborn resistance, but she needed advice, and he was her best option.

Then she saw the display. “Mom…hello.”

“Sunshine, what are you doin’? Get home now.” Her mother’s voice was pure Georgia as always, but there was a thread of worry underneath it. “I have been worried sick for days, ever since I realized this storm was headed right at you. Staying there is foolish, Summer. Get yourself in the car and start driving.”

Summer crossed her arms over her chest as she paced in a tight circle. Asking why it had taken days to call and check on her if she’d been so worried wouldn’t accomplish anything.

Her recent spectacular boundary-setting with TJ made her hesitate to stir up any more confrontations.

“If you aren’t coming this way, I’ll hop in the car and drive right to your front door,” her mother added. “Ought to get there right about the same time Agnes does, which is an even worse plan, but you're forcing my hand here."

The urge to dump all of her worries in her mother's lap was nearly overwhelming. Packing up three huge dogs and heading for Atlanta would be a quick solution, but the aftermath would be so very complicated, no matter what damage the storm caused. Running to Atlanta when things got difficult would make the strings harder to cut.

Besides, coming to Horizon was about illustrating how independent she was, how capable she was of making her own decisions, even if they were ending an engagement that both her parents wanted. Telling her mother she should have offered help sooner would be counterproductive.

So would begging her to come or showing up on her doorstep with three dogs in tow.

The thump of the panel covering the kitchen window reminded her that she had some decisions to make. Quickly.

"I've been swamped getting the clinic and shelter ready for the storm, Mama." That was not exactly a lie, even if most of her preparation had taken place in the last twelve hours. "But I'm watching it. The Horizon Police Department has been really helpful. That's life in a small town, I guess. Neighbors looking after neighbors, especially when they're new to town and there's a hurricane on the way."

Leo's words had stayed with her, but hearing

the words out of her own mouth caught Summer's attention the way no one else would have been able to do.

Because that was exactly what TJ was doing, trying to help a neighbor.

How much of their communication difficulty was his fault?

Summer had the growing certainty that the biggest heap of it was hers.

Straightening that out would be a job for a sunny, clear day.

"You should never have left Atlanta, Summer," her mother said. "Dixon was beside himself when we had dinner last night, worried this storm would get you before you had a chance to come back around and realize this wedding was the right thing all along. Your father…" Her mother sighed. "Well, you know how he is. Come home tonight and we can get all of this straightened out."

She absolutely knew how her father was. And her mother.

For that matter, her fiancé and the ways in which they did not fit together were even plainer.

That was why she was in Horizon.

"The next time y'all have dinner, tell Dixon I'm fine. He needs to move on with his life." Summer wanted to explain that he could still be the son her father needed, but he was never going to be her husband. But she didn't have time for the argument that would follow.

"Love you, Mama. I'll call tomorrow to let you know where I'm staying." Then she hung up the phone. Her mother hadn't gotten to the part where she offered that, if Summer would sell the clinic and move back, they'd take care of whatever was left of the loan afterward and get her set up with a new job if she insisted on it. After all, Dixon had said more than once he'd be happy to have a wife who didn't work.

Dixon admired her father. His idea of their marriage matched Summer's parents': her father was a successful doctor, and her mother kept the house running.

But Summer loved her job.

To build a relationship with Dixon, she'd made compromises all along. His career meant Atlanta had to be their home, so she'd left Auburn, changed her focus and returned home. Everyone in her life had been so happy with the move that it felt right.

And she'd chosen to do it herself, even if now she could look back to see how consistent pressure on all sides had influenced that choice. Her parents loved her. She believed Dixon loved her, too. Going along with them had made life easier.

But how anyone could know Summer even a little bit and suggest that she give up the career she'd worked so long to have…

It had made her choice to end their engagement black-and-white.

He didn't know her, and neither did her parents. They loved her and believed they knew what was best. Taking the easy option offered along with their assistance was so tempting, but she'd learned over a lifetime that the conditions in very fine print were too costly.

As long as she would turn herself into someone else, they would happily solve all her problems.

But if the storm did damage that she couldn't repair, this gamble would turn into a big loss. Her finances were stretched thin and so was her support.

Would she buckle under the strain? Failure was always a threatening undercurrent, and this storm had elevated it to the surface.

Her stubbornness usually made it impossible to give in.

Summer hated that she was wavering here.

Losing her ability to trust her gut would be terrible. Going home now would be a short-term solution, but it would also be a setback in reclaiming herself.

"The storm is temporary, Summer. Don't make a decision you'll regret because you're afraid. Boogie said he could fix any damage, and if you can't trust a man named Boogie, who can you trust?" she muttered as she entered a search for motels inland on her phone. The news reporters had said evacuating only five or ten miles away from the coast would be enough for safety. For Horizon, the list was short, so calling three motels and two small bed-and-breakfasts didn't take long at all.

Especially since they were all fully booked at this point.

"Okay," Summer drawled as she braced her hands on her hips and evaluated her choices. "In the morning, you'll see if Hank and Hattie had any luck finding another emergency foster. You will load up the dogs and take them to the foster yourself." The Browns were never going to fit any one of these dogs in their rubber ball of a car, so they'd need saddles to ride them unless Summer took care of the transport. If she wasn't here, waiting for the storm to hit, she'd be concerned over Russell Crow's safety, too, so she added "find a tricky rooster and carry him to safety" to her mental to-do list.

"That will get you off the Island and everyone out of danger, even if you have to drive to Columbia to find a hotel room. Not Atlanta, but not here in the path of the storm, either. Tonight, you will go and get the dogs and move them in here." Because Leo's words were making more sense the longer she sat alone in her small apartment, listening to wind and rain and wondering what was happening to the rising water outside in the dark. Having company would make this less scary, even if it was a stranger in the hotel room next door.

Being alone made every bit of this harder.

Too much time to think would leave lots of

room to replay the cringe-worthy moment of allowing the melodramatic words "public shame" escape her brain through her mouth and having TJ Shepard hear them.

Worse, he'd been hurt by them. Reading TJ was getting easier. Everything he felt was in his eyes. Remembering the lack of warmth in them as she'd left the pizzeria would keep her up even if the storm wasn't on the way.

The long night would give her plenty of time to think of what she'd say the next time she ran into him.

TJ REGRETTED LETTING Summer walk out half a second after the door closed behind her. He met Leo's stare across the counter, but there was no easy way to admit he'd mangled another encounter.

Leo's mournful sigh captured the atmosphere perfectly anyway.

The ding of the oven interrupted whatever he might say, but when he came back to the front counter with TJ's pizza, his face said very clearly that he wasn't going to let the awkward moment pass by without remarking.

After the day he'd had, the last thing TJ wanted to hear was advice on managing Summer. It couldn't be done, at least by him. In the morning, he'd get someone else to check on her, make sure she had a good plan. She could be mad at him for it, but she would be safe.

TJ stood and reminded himself that he'd already tasted shoe leather once. Silence was his best defense here.

"I don't know, man." Leo slid the box across the counter. "With the whispering, I was picturing a little rom-com in the atmosphere. You. Her. Cute dog. This place. Pizza in the air." Leo made a small rainbow with a wave of his hands before making a heart over his chest. "But you didn't stick the landing."

TJ huffed out a laugh. It wasn't truly funny, but he'd been on the same page as Leo. He'd been a second from getting Summer's personal phone number before the urge to make sure she listened to his advice took control.

Maybe making such a big deal before she'd even had an opportunity to argue with his advice was a mistake.

He shook his head.

It had been a mistake. Obviously.

The real question was whether he'd learn from it and do better.

And whether Summer would speak to him after he'd given her his version of the cold shoulder. Icy politeness was his nuclear option, but he hadn't hesitated to use it here.

"We have trouble understanding each other," TJ said as he picked up the pizza box. "Eventually we're going to run out of fresh starts, so this rom-com may be destined for a tragic ending."

Leo cleared his throat. "I've seen a bunch of couples through here. It's one of the finest date night restaurants in town, after all."

TJ swallowed a smile. He appreciated a man with confidence, and Leo had it. Palmetto State Pizza was a nice place, but date night? TJ realized it had been so long since he'd needed a place to bring a date for dinner that he wasn't certain how the pizzeria ranked.

"One thing you should be aware of." Leo leaned one elbow against the counter. "Now, I'm not saying you're headed for any kind of Romeo and Juliet situation, but you have a mushroom mismatch here." He nodded grimly, as if he was delivering terrible news. "She's all about adding them, and you don't want them touching anything. It's not that you can't overcome this incompatibility. There are ways—ordering two pizzas, for example. It's just something to be aware of."

TJ nodded because there was really no other answer that would get him out the door without more conversation. It had been a long time since he'd read any Shakespeare, but he was pretty sure that Romeo and Juliet had actually liked each other before everything fell apart.

He and Summer couldn't even make it as far as Step One.

But at least they also wouldn't die from whatever developed between them.

Maybe.

"See you, Leo. Be careful tomorrow." TJ waved and led Lucy back to his patrol car. When they were dry and safe in his small apartment two blocks on the other side of the police station, TJ moved the paperwork he'd gotten from Red Kelly at the state meeting off the couch. It outlined how to enter a race for one of the elected positions in COA and an application to be considered to serve as part of the Ethics Committee if he won.

Then he plopped down, turned on the TV to have sports play-by-play fill in the silence and cover up some of the noise of the wind rattling the windows, and tried to relax the tight muscles in his shoulders and neck.

"The last thing I need is to start tomorrow with a headache, Lucy."

She rested her head against his knee and sighed.

He methodically ate the first piece of pizza without noticing much, while he replayed his conversation with Summer in his head. The regret was impossible to ignore, but it was the worry over her safety that would keep him awake.

CHAPTER SEVEN

At the shift change the next morning, TJ finished his first cup of coffee before the briefing started and was wishing for a bigger mug by the time the chief made it through all the updates that had come in overnight. It had been a long night, and caffeine was his lifeline.

Hurricane Agnes's arrival was imminent, as evidenced by steady strong winds and the ominous clouds roiling just off the coast. All of the state's emergency services agencies had moved into place, and the storm's path was showing estimated times for landfall.

TJ had been in this place before, preparing for emergency response, but the weight that came with the waiting felt different this time.

His mother had made good on her threat to show up at the station that morning, but she'd come bearing blueberry muffins and his youngest sister, Lila. They made easy conversation with the officers in the room, most of whom had been through Horizon High School during his mother's tenure, and handed out muffins. Since his sister had a preference for bright colors and bold patterns, she literally brightened the room. Today's outfit was a top with bright yellow polka dots and deep purple jeans.

All three of them were lifting spirits in the station house because police officers loved blueberry muffins almost as much as doughnuts.

"You all know this, but we're heading into the most challenging time, the waiting," his father said as he wrapped up his report. "We'll be in Command while you're out today, awaiting your situation reports and monitoring conditions. Zone assignments are the same as yesterday, except..." He paused to glance down at his clipboard before turning to the map. "Roberts, I need you to swing out though this zone along the coast, the Island here. Shepard will be my backup in Command, but we want to drive by and offer any last-minute evacuation support before the storm hits." He pointed at the screen. "Approximately six hours with rain and winds increasing. Monitor your surroundings and make good decisions based on your safety. I want everyone back to the station in advance of landfall. You have your assignments."

"We serve," the officers in the room answered before the shuffling of chairs and feet signaled their exit.

Before TJ could pull Roberts aside to make certain she planned to stop in at the animal hospital,

Bee waved a hand in front of his face. His plan had been to keep it as quiet as possible, since calling Dr. Patel out again would draw attention he didn't want. He also understood now that Summer wouldn't appreciate any whiff of "public shame" involving her.

When he glanced around to find Roberts, she was already gone.

TJ met his sister's stare. Bee asked, "You okay today? Look a little tired."

He nodded. "I am. Both. I'm okay but I'm tired. Sitting in a conference room chair wears me out."

"Yeah. The chief's been doing this for decades, but even he seemed exhausted last night. You should have heard him trying to explain his theory of resting when he had time. It was 'someday,' but Mom was determined he would name a date." Bee's small smile of sympathy alerted him that he might be sharing too much if he wanted to avoid a discussion of his future, but Lila interrupted before he could figure out what to do about it.

Lila threw her arm over TJ's shoulders. "Now that I've done my part to keep the town safe by lifting the morale of our public servants, I'm going home. I need a nap."

Bee tilted her head. "Did you bake any of these muffins?"

Lila shook her head. "No, but my presence is powerful. You see how eager everyone was to get to work?"

Bee raised her eyebrows. "Hard to argue with proof, little sis."

"Before I go, I need to know what is wrong with you." Lila waved a hand before he could answer. "Don't give me that."

"I haven't said anything," TJ said slowly, "and I'm too tired to have a heart-to-heart about whatever it is you think you see."

Lila pursed her lips. "Uh-huh. Why so tired? Tell me or I'm getting Mom involved."

TJ huffed out a breath. That had always been her weapon. As the youngest in the family, she hadn't needed much more, but at some point, they would reach an age when it didn't work anymore. Right?

"I had a run-in with Summer Patel last night. She was having trouble finding enough emergency fosters, and she had no plans to evacuate. That worries me." TJ crossed his arms over his chest, satisfied that he'd relayed the situation without adding extra emotion.

Even though the emotion had contributed heavily to keeping him awake all night.

Bee squeezed his arm. "And now you're stuck here instead of headed out to the Island to make your case about why she needs to leave."

There wasn't much to add to that, so TJ nodded.

"Call Roberts and tell her to get Dr. Patel into town," Lila said with a shrug. As if the answer was simple. If he could trust any other officer to get Summer moving, he could relax. Maybe Roberts would have better luck, since she hadn't repeatedly clashed with the doctor already, but TJ wasn't sure anyone could convince Summer. Not even his going to extremes at the pizza parlor had done the trick.

"And you don't want to tell the chief that you'd rather be out doing the job than stuck in Command," Bee added. TJ wasn't surprised his sister was reading all the signs correctly.

"Gross. Who would want to be stuck here all day instead of out and about?" Lila asked before patting Bee's shoulder. "No offense."

"Offense, Lila. Offense taken." Bee narrowed her eyes, and TJ briefly wondered if *he* should get his mother. His sisters had been meaner fighters than his half-brother or any of his friends when they were growing up. "But Dispatch is the part of the job I love, so being here means I'm exactly where I need to be. That's not the same for TJ."

Lila nodded as if that was perfectly clear.

So TJ questioned how his father, who had taught them all everything they knew about observation, could miss what Bee knew without TJ saying a word.

"An incoming hurricane means it is not the time to rock this particular boat," Bee added.

Lila sighed. "Okay, I guess I'll take your word for it, even though I, a semiprofessional boat rocker, have never found one time better than another." She hugged TJ. "There's only the right time. If this isn't it, I will step up to help you. I am wonderful in that way."

TJ stared at her and forced his lips into a straight line. It was hard. She really was adorable in an annoying kid-sister kind of way.

"I will head out to the Island. If Dr. Patel still needs an emergency foster, I will help with that. I will also ask her to wait out the storm with me. I have a pull-out couch that will be uncomfortable, but at least it will be dry." Lila brushed off her hands as if the matter was simple and she'd handle it.

TJ immediately shook his head. "No way. It's too dangerous. I don't want her out there, and I won't be sending my baby sister out to the Island with a hurricane on the way." The reaction from either of his parents would be so terrible he didn't even want to imagine it.

The way Lila's chin immediately firmed was a warning.

He should have recognized the signs in Summer because he'd been watching Lila square up her whole life.

Bee pulled both of them into a hug and said, "You aren't sending her, TJ, and Lila is smart enough to check the bridge before she gets into trouble." She squeezed them hard. "And all three of us are smart enough to know that we never tell Mom or Dad about this."

She held on long enough for the message to get through before stepping back.

"You are the smartest of my brothers and sisters, Bee. I've always said that." Lila gave them both a brilliant smile. Then she narrowed her eyes at TJ. "And you've always been smart enough to know when to go along. Do we have an agreement? Zip your lips?"

The headache that had been building blossomed into a full-on pain.

Lila had that effect on him. "Fine. Be careful."

Her long-suffering sigh would have made him smile except it attracted the attention of their mother. The way her eyes landed on them had never failed to straighten his spine. Whether he was innocent or guilty, he was ready to confess everything.

"I'm headed out!" Lila waved her hand at her parents. "Let me know if you need any more help with benevolence before the storm." She shrugged on her bright pink raincoat and sailed out into the lobby.

She'd made her escape before their mother could start asking questions.

"You've got to admit, she has flair," Bee murmured. Then she caught his gaze. "And she knows every bit as much as you or I do about hurricane safety. Besides, she hasn't annoyed Dr. Patel at every single encounter, so I like her chances of persuading the doctor to come into town much better than yours."

TJ knew it was a good point, hard to argue with.

"People who didn't have to live through the *Pitch Perfect* years really like her," Bee said with a slow shake of her head.

"How many times did we watch that first movie?" TJ asked as he remembered the way Lila would repeat word for word every bit of dialogue.

"And the singing. So much 'Since U Been Gone.'" Bee widened her eyes. "At the top of her lungs with no *warning*."

Her dismayed tone shook a laugh through the tightness in his chest. Bee was always the one who kept them on an even keel.

"Give her an hour and then check on her," he said. Bee immediately agreed. "Forget about not telling the chief if she's not back in town at that point. I'll go get her myself."

"Leave Command?" she asked in a scandalized tone.

"There are some things that matter more than keeping my job." TJ wasn't sure he really believed it, but hearing the words come out of his mouth felt right.

"Even if it's the job you love instead of the one being thrust upon you," Bee said as she turned to head for Dispatch.

Instead of waiting for his father, TJ moved into the conference room and settled into his spot behind the laptop he'd been hunched over the day before. Lucy followed at his heels and settled down in her post under the table, close to the action.

He was reading through the reports from all the state agencies when the chief walked in. "No changes to the track or timing." TJ moved the phone closer to dial. "Do we start with the mayor this morning?"

"She's on her way down. Rainey wants to be in the middle of the action as the storm rolls in." His father met TJ's stare. It wasn't hard to read what the chief thought of that. He was never a big fan of having bystanders in the way of the work. "Want to tell me what kind of plot you were hatching with your sisters?"

The immediate need to tell him everything had to be controlled. "No plot. Just some unusual affection in the face of the storm."

His father crossed his arms over his chest.

To wait.

The tactic might have worked except the mayor breezed in. "No one told me there were blueberry muffins. I would have been here sooner." Rainey Blackwell was dressed for storm response, in khakis, a denim shirt and heavy boots, but something about her always spelled expensive. The outfit might be appropriate for work, but she was camera ready in case news reporters showed up in town.

"Where can I set up?" Rainey held up her laptop case with one hand and waved the other hand, which was holding a muffin and a lidded coffee cup.

The chief pointed to the last empty corner of the room. "Ground rules. This is the police department's Command. I am in charge here." The chief waited for her to agree. "When I am not in this room, Officer Shepard is second-in-command."

Rainey sipped her coffee before answering. "You got it, Chief." Then she turned to TJ, one corner of her lip curled in a smirk. "And Chief Junior."

When his father's chin snapped up, TJ wondered if he should call his mother again.

"Do you have a problem with my Command setup, Mayor? Maybe you'd be more comfortable in your own office upstairs if so." His father's grim expression backed the firm tone.

Rainey raised a shoulder in a breezy shrug. "Wouldn't dream of disrespecting your storm command, Chief." She sniffed. "But," she drawled, "your long-term planning may need some discussion. After the storm. I've asked my assistant to schedule some time for us to do that. In my office. Upstairs."

Long-term planning? Was she referring to the chief's plans to name his own successor? And if it wasn't TJ, who did Rainey have in mind?

Horizon's police chief was appointed by the mayor with the approval of the town council.

Rainey had always backed TJ's father. Anything else would have been political suicide in Horizon.

"I look forward to it," his father said before yanking his seat out to settle behind his own laptop.

At his gruff response, TJ immediately lowered his head to stare down at the laptop monitor. He did not want to get caught in any crossfire. The tense silence in the conference room was broken only by the dings of emails coming in, whooshes of responses going out, and the occasional hunt-and-peck typing required to write them. The small television set up in the corner was muted, but it was easy to see the slow progression of the rain bands ahead of the storm.

Their radios crackled before Bee came on. "All officers, be advised all patrols along Oceanside Parkway and specifically neighborhoods along Duneside Road should be on the lookout for a large brown German shepherd mix. Answers to Skye. We have a panicked eight-year-old begging for any help. Abby Wheeler has called her grandmother, who happens to be sitting next to me in Dispatch, to beg for help finding her dog. Contact Dispatch for further instructions if you spot Skye Wheeler, a three-year-old German shepherd mix. Over."

When TJ glanced at the chief, he expected disapproval. They didn't make it a habit of putting out calls for lost animals, but the storm changed the rules.

Instead, his father was watching him. "The shelter has been evacuated, hasn't it? We'll need a plan to hold the dog if it turns up."

After clearing his throat, TJ said, "Dr. Patel was working on it. Roberts will need to confirm."

His father turned back to scrolling through reports on his laptop.

The urge to pull up his radio and send the directive out to Roberts was hard to ignore, but Lila's deadline was near.

TJ was on the verge of doing something excessive to break the icy silence in the room when his cell phone vibrated. Intensely aware that his father would seize the opportunity to ask questions TJ didn't want to answer at that point, TJ raised his coffee cup. "I need a refill. Anybody else?"

Rainey immediately waved her own in the air, so he moved around to pick it up.

His father shook his head and poked the bridge of his glasses to move them up his nose.

Relieved and anxious, TJ stepped aside as soon as he cleared the doorway to check his message.

Made it to Dr. Patel's without any problem. The water is still rising, but the bridge is okay. I met one of the emergency fosters coming out as I was going in, and Dr. Patel was getting ready to load up her car to drive inland as far as she had to go to find an open motel room.

TJ tried to relax, but the bubbling dots that indicated Lila was still typing made it difficult.

Bee joined him, stepping close to ask, "How's it going with the chief and the mayor in close quarters?"

TJ didn't take his eyes off his phone, but shook his head slowly.

"They really aren't selling this to you as a dream job, are they?" she asked with a sigh.

Lila's next message came before he could find a way to answer that without saying too much.

I scrapped those plans. Dr. Patel is locking up and coming to stay with me. You're welcome. I'll let you know as soon as we're both safe and sound. Meanwhile, I'm in love.

TJ's eyebrows shot up. In love? With Summer Patel?

He wasn't much of a believer in love at first sight, but even he'd been knocked off his game by Summer.

"Hmm, two Shepards in love with Dr. Patel is going to make family dinners super awkward," Bee said in a teasing voice.

Hitting her with his meanest side-eye was definitely showing more of his hand regarding his own feelings about Summer than TJ was truly comfortable with, but it was automatic.

Lila's next text contained a selfie. She was absolutely drenched, but her smile was brilliant. In the way, way back of her SUV was an absolutely enormous Great Dane. He was black or dark brown, but he had the bushiest gray eyebrows TJ had ever seen on a dog.

Meet Duke. He's going to take up more room than Dr. Patel!

Bee texted back, Very distinguished gentleman! Keep us updated.

TJ rolled his shoulders before answering. Thanks, sis.

"Maybe that will make it easier, getting through this storm watch." Bee squeezed his arm. "I hate to see this exhaustion on your face. Soon we'll be back to normal, right? Being stuck at the station won't last forever."

He met her stare, but neither one of them said the rest of the sentence that hung there.

Being stuck at the station won't last forever *unless you become the chief.*

TJ grabbed the coffee cups. "First, caffeine, then reports."

Bee nodded. "Excellent plan." Then she hurried back down the short hallway to Dispatch.

When he returned to the conference room,

Rainey and the chief had moved closer to the television and turned up the sound. TJ lowered the volume on his two-way radio to listen.

"At this rate of speed, Hurricane Agnes is expected to make landfall in the next couple of hours. The winds are strengthening and rain continues to fall, raising water levels in these zones. Worsening conditions mean anyone still in these areas should be evacuating." The weatherman's expression was grim as he added, "Sheltering in place to ride out landfall may be the best option even now."

TJ clenched his phone, willing Lila to send another message that she and Summer had arrived at her apartment. Returning to his seat in front of the laptop with the unending barrage of emailed reports felt almost impossible, so he paced over to where he could see the large map of Horizon across the squad room.

"Dispatch, what's the situation report on the patrol officers?" his father asked through the radio handpiece attached to his shoulder. "Over."

"Chief, all officers have moved inland to the first high water perimeter," Bee answered. "They are waiting for orders to return to station or proceed to assignments as necessary. Incoming calls are slow right now, but we're prepared for an increase as the storm lands. All communications are functioning as expected, and we are monitoring the state's emergency management transmissions to assist as needed. Over."

"Roger, Dispatch," the chief replied before stretching his arms out to the sides.

TJ stared hard at the large clock on the wall as he watched the minutes roll over. Summer had had more than enough time to drive the ten miles to Lila's house, even in the poor conditions.

The satellite images on the TV were showing bands inching closer to the coastline.

Before he could figure out what to text, Bee sent a message. Lila, everybody safe?

TJ forgot about his father's observation and picked up his cell to watch the dots while Lila typed. If the answer was good, he'd be fine here. They were almost through the waiting stage, and there would be actual jobs to do. That would make everything easier.

Dr. Patel isn't here yet. I'm worried. Should I go back out to the Island?

He was already standing when Bee's official voice came through the radio on his shoulder. "Chief, we've got a report that Dr. Patel may still be on the Island. Can I get an order to send a patrol car out to check on her? Over."

Bee was carefully avoiding that their report was from Lila.

"Hold, Dispatch," his father said immediately. "Roberts, check in. Over."

The smart thing to do was wait for Roberts to report on her view of the situation, but the time was ticking too loudly in TJ's ear to wait. "Lucy, stay." He waited until she settled down in her spot under the table then stood.

"Where are you going?" his father asked.

He met his father's stare as he moved around the table, headed for the door. "I'll be back with Dr. Patel ASAP."

He didn't hang around to find out his father's reaction. After running through the lobby and then the pouring rain, TJ heard his father through the radio in his patrol car. "Officer Shepard is on his way out to the Island now, Dispatch." There was a scratchy pause before his father added, "Officer Rodriguez, please report to Command. We need a 2IC while Shepard is out on this call. Over."

TJ turned up the windshield wipers and made a sharp U-turn before Mark Rodriguez answered, "Copy. On my way."

He missed the radio chatter as the pounding rain beat down on the roof of his car.

When he made it to the bridge connecting the Island, water was moving swiftly under it, but the bridge was still clear. Debris blasted through the air, whipped by the trees along both sides of the road. Garbage cans rolled across the street and every light pole was shivering in the wind gusts. The words "shelter in place" were on a loop in his brain.

Relief settled over him for a brief moment when he saw Summer's SUV parked next to the animal clinic. If she'd been lost somewhere between here and Lila's house, his chance to help would get much more precarious.

Right now, he had to get Summer back in the car immediately so they could get to town.

Even if he had to carry her kicking and stuff her in the back seat.

"Do not yell. Do not yell." He repeated the mantra to himself as he rolled down the gravel driveway. A fight would only slow their evacuation, and it was crystal clear that there was no time for delay.

As soon as he parked, he jumped out of the car and trotted toward the side door of the animal clinic. He slid to a stop at the sight of Summer standing in the pouring rain, the weak beam of a flashlight sweeping the flowerbeds closest to the door. When she saw him, she yelled, "What are you doing here?" She had one hand covering her eyes while the other turned the flashlight in an arc to light up the area in front of the clinic. "Go back!"

Before he could grab her to stuff her into the patrol car, full-on caveman tendencies in overdrive with the urge to get them both to safety, a tree branch cracked too close for comfort. Summer screamed, wrapped her hand around his wrist and yanked him inside.

CHAPTER EIGHT

SUMMER BRUSHED WET hair off her forehead to stop the water pouring into her eyes as she watched TJ do the same, amazed that he was standing in front of her. The fact that he'd answered the call she'd never made almost seemed magical. Ever since it had become clear that she was going to be waiting out the storm on the Island, TJ had been in her head, alternating between saying "I told you so" and saving her in some miraculous manner.

Had her brain melted under the strain?

She'd been loading up to leave, finding and capturing Russell Crow the last item on her list, when an emergency had upended everything. She'd been racing against the storm ever since.

Even if she'd decided to call for help, Summer wasn't sure when she would have had the time to stop to do it. She might have had time to catch her breath and call Lila Shepard before the storm hit if the rooster would just cooperate for once.

There was nothing magical about this situation, and she was glad to see TJ anyway.

But she needed to get him out of there.

"What are you doing out here in this storm? You have to get back into town," she said as she tried to urge him toward the door. "Is Lucy in your patrol car? Get out of here!"

TJ planted his hand against the door and shook his head. "Of course not. She's safe, but you aren't. I have to know why you aren't at Lila's house, but I don't want to hear another word from you until you are in the car," TJ said slowly.

If she was reading him correctly, he was too angry to open his mouth any wider. The expression on his face was new. Not even their argument where he'd said "public shame" so coldly had caused this.

"I can't leave the clinic," she said before realizing that they were wasting precious time. There was only one way to convince him to go now, so she wrapped her hand around his wrist again and started towing him into her exam room. "I had an emergency come in, an injured dog. The young couple who hit her helped me get her on the table and sedated before I sent them away. I did quick surgery, but I can't move her from the clinic right now in case I need my equipment, medicines. I need to stay here. Please leave now."

Summer waved a hand at the dog laid out on her exam table. The German shepherd had been hit by a car, but her wounds were cleaned out and stitched up. When the general anesthetic wore off,

Summer would need to give her something additional for the pain and to stave off infection. She had to be in the clinic until she was certain the dog was shaking off the anesthesia as expected.

He didn't have the same restrictions.

"We're fine here. You can go. Stop fighting and get back to town." Summer reached out to take his hand again, determined that he would listen this time.

Instead, TJ braced both hands on his knees, and it was like watching a balloon quickly deflate, all the air escaping silently. She was on the verge of trying to push him back out into the rain when he put his hand to the radio on his shoulder and said, "Dispatch, this is Shepard."

A woman immediately answered, "Go ahead, TJ. Tell me you're back in town already. Over."

He shook his head. "I'll be sheltering in place at the Horizon Animal Hospital. Dr. Patel has had an emergency surgery and can't move the patient yet. Please let the Wheelers know that Skye has been in an accident, but she's at the clinic here. Over."

"You can't stay," Summer said. The pressure in her chest was building as guilt and the desperate desire to get him out of there combined.

He didn't answer as the woman on the other end of the radio said, "Copy."

Summer hadn't given up on arguing, but TJ held up a finger to stall her.

Then a man said, "Shepard, be safe."

"Ten-four, Chief." TJ leaned his head back to study the ceiling for a long minute.

Summer sighed unhappily. "Should I pass along a status update on Skye?"

He pulled out his cell phone, punched a button and handed it to her.

Summer held the phone to her ear in time to hear the woman who had been on the radio say, "This is an extreme way to get out of being stuck in the station house, Tommy."

Tommy?

Summer cleared her throat, "Um, hi, it's Dr. Patel. If you get in touch with Skye's owners, please let them know that she was hit by a car. The driver pulled over and picked her up to bring her here. She's got a leg injury, most likely a bad sprain, and had some wounds that needed stitches, but I didn't see any sign of internal bleeding. After surgery, she's stable. She's sedated now and resting easily, so I'll continue to monitor her for pain as she comes out of the anesthesia. If the family would like, they can call tomorrow for an update."

If the phones were still working.

If the clinic was still standing.

And if TJ Shepard didn't give in to the urge to put her out of his misery for dragging him into this mess.

"I'll relay the message, Dr. Patel. I'm Bee, one of TJ's little sisters. You met the other one earlier today," the woman answered, her voice extremely professional. "She's the one who alerted us that you might need assistance."

A little cold.

And Summer remembered she should have already let Lila Shepard know that she wasn't going to be riding out the storm with her. She'd arrived as Summer, Hank and Hattie were loading up two of the remaining rescues with the volunteers the Browns had managed to recruit overnight.

After Lila had been so kind to insist on taking Duke the Great Dane home with her and making up a nice, dry couch for her to wait out the storm, Summer had left her in limbo…and now she'd added endangering their brother, so Bee and Lila were both going to cross her off their "friend" list.

That was depressing.

"I've been in surgery, and the storm…" Summer shook her head. Now wasn't the time for apologies. "I'll be sure to text Lila and let her know that I'll be sheltering here."

Summer had really liked sunny Lila, even if the storm had robbed them of the opportunity for proper "getting to know you" time.

The nervous roll of her stomach was surprising. She'd never spent much time worrying about how to find or make friends, but messing up here felt major. She wasn't sure how many Shepards there were altogether, but it seemed she had some kind of ingrained inability to make an easy introduction.

"Tell TJ to check in. Everyone will be worried until the storm passes," Bee Shepard said.

Before Summer could find the right words to apologize or swear she'd send TJ back to safety if she could, Bee ended the call.

Heavy guilt settled over Summer's shoulders. As she offered him his phone, she asked, "Is it really too late to go, TJ? Is the bridge under water already?" She wanted to urge him to check the wind, the rain, but his posture was easy enough to understand. He wasn't moving.

If anything happened to him because of her…

"Doesn't matter. I can't leave, not without you." TJ picked up a towel off the stack she'd piled up before Skye's surgery and ran it over his hair. When she'd managed to sedate the dog, she'd grabbed everything she might possibly need for whatever injuries she discovered to make sure it was within close reach. She never wanted to try emergency surgery without a vet tech's assistance again.

She'd managed to help Skye, but her fingers were still shaking.

The adrenaline of the emergency would wear off soon, and then she would be left with only the fear.

And TJ.

Soaking wet, he was evaluating the room, the lobby and the hallway that led to the breakroom and the back stairs up to Summer's apartment.

"So we're going to make the best of this. We're in an interior room here. That's good. Windows are shuttered." TJ pointed to the ceiling. "What's on the second floor?"

"My apartment. It's small, but there's room enough for all three of us. If the water comes in." Summer bit her lip because the threat of flooding was terrifying. In this storm, the water was the biggest danger. "The furniture is more comfortable there, but for now…" She motioned at the dog sleeping off the anesthesia she'd used while sewing up her injuries. "And some of the machines in here, the medical refrigerator, some of the lights, are tied into the generator."

TJ nodded. "When the electricity goes, we'll have some light."

Summer gulped at the way he said "when."

As if there was zero doubt in his mind that the lights would go out.

Being stuck in complete darkness would be terrible.

"I was going, TJ. I promise. This isn't me being stubborn or whatever. I was leaving. I understood what you were telling me. I just… I couldn't leave her." Summer ran her hand over Skye's silky ear.

"Of course not." TJ shook his head. "You couldn't leave her any more than I can abandon you here alone. We are on the same page there, Summer." He crossed his arms over his chest.

That was a relief.

But he still seemed pretty angry.

"What I don't get *now* is what you were doing outside. In a hurricane." The precise pauses in his words convinced Summer that he was doing his best to control his emotions.

She definitely appreciated that, but sometimes, it was better to have something louder to work with. Her initial response was to explain to him that she was an adult who could make her own decisions, even when it was raining. That would be so much easier if he raised his voice.

That would provoke her to respond in kind, and they would be back on familiar ground.

Then she remembered that they were stuck together until the storm passed.

And it was her fault he was here in the first place.

Maybe an explanation could make all of that time together a little less tense.

"After I induced anesthesia," Summer said, "while I was waiting to begin surgery, I heard Russell Crow. He didn't sound as obnoxious as he normally does, but he was also obviously still nearby." She shoved a dripping hank of hair off her forehead. "As much as I'm learning to loathe him, I couldn't leave him out in the storm if there was any other option."

TJ didn't answer as he scrubbed the towel through his hair.

"I'm guessing we aren't talking about the actor,"

he finally said slowly. "That's the rooster I heard when you were on the roof?"

"Not the actor…" Summer blinked.

Then the ridiculousness of the situation overwhelmed her and the uncontrollable giggles she'd been battling for two solid days escaped.

TJ didn't join her, but his shoulders relaxed a fraction.

Skye didn't join her, either, but she blinked sleepy eyes open, so Summer moved to stroke her head carefully. "Hey, Skye, how you doin'?"

The dog sighed from her soul before licking Summer's hand and closing her eyes again. Summer waited until she saw the dog's sides rise and fall slowly. Sleep was good. Skye needed it to heal, and Summer needed the dog to remain calm so that she could attempt to find some calm for herself.

Then she realized TJ was still waiting for an explanation.

"Yes, that's the rooster who has adopted my animal clinic for unknown reasons. He's an escape artist who enjoys taunting me from sophisticated hiding spots." Summer held out a hand. "On the one hand, he's obviously a skilled survivalist, so I should leave him to the wilds and Hurricane Agnes." Exhaustion provoked a deep sigh. "But on the other hand, he's just a bird. There's a storm. It's kinda my job to save him?"

Instead of explaining to her how silly the impulse was, TJ nodded in understanding.

That small agreement hit Summer hard.

Her parents would have lectured her on taking stupid risks.

It was easy to imagine the scorn her ex-fiancé would have shown at taking any risk for a chicken. He was a surgeon who refused to wash dishes because he might injure himself. She had assumed the same reasoning applied for why he didn't cook, clean or open doors. Those things had been simple enough to live with for the sake of keeping everyone around her happy.

If Dixon had managed to understand how important her career, her work and the animals she helped were, Summer might never have walked away.

She couldn't compromise on those things because they were who she was.

Russell Crow was testing her limits as much as her ex-fiancé had right now.

Even her internal critic had some powerful words about being outside in a storm on another futile search for an ornery rooster.

But she had done it because it was the right thing to do.

It seemed TJ Shepard got that.

Whatever he misunderstood about her, he got this part.

Nothing changed in that moment, except everything between them was different for Summer.

Understanding the piece of her that no one else in her life did had to change everything, didn't it?

Then she realized she might be TJ's version of Russell Crow, the annoying creature who refused to follow directions and had to be rescued anyway. Saying any part of that aloud would have him worried for her sanity, wouldn't it?

She might have tried anyway, but the lights flickered.

TJ straightened. "So, TV? Radio?" He glanced around. "Flashlights, batteries, candles, water, snacks…"

Summer licked her lips, reminded again of how little she knew about getting through storms like this. "All upstairs, since my plan was to not be anywhere near here at this point. Why don't I grab us both something dry to wear before we pull it all together?"

"Good plan," TJ said before the lights flickered again. "I'm thinking we better hurry."

"I hope scrubs are okay," Summer said as she hurried down the long hallway into the tiny supply closet where the clinic's spare scrubs were stored. While she dug through the piles of shirts and pants, she tried not to think about being so close to TJ for the duration of the storm.

How she felt about him might have shifted, but his irritation with her hadn't changed.

Her original plan for life in Horizon had been to prove her independence, her ability to make her own life and the plans she had for it come true.

Finding herself suddenly so interested in having more of TJ's brand of help because it came along with a man who seemed to really see and accept this piece of her would take some adjustment.

The close quarters of this storm meant some of that adjusting had to happen with the man in the room.

She finally found a matched set of scrubs for each of them and forced herself to close her eyes and breathe in and out. It was tempting to run through possible conversations in her head. Being prepared for any eventuality was her preference.

"At some point, you're going to have to learn that what happens next is not under your control, Summer." She shook her head. "Seems like being stuck in a hurricane with a wounded dog, an annoyed man and a renegade chicken would be the lesson that sticks."

Then the lights went out.

Summer clutched the scrubs to her chest as panic threatened to take over.

Her racing heart pounded in her ears.

Control was an illusion.

Darkness was scary.

Independence was overrated.

She needed to find TJ now.

As TJ peered through the pouring, blowing rain under hunched shoulders that did absolutely nothing to block the water from his face, he muttered to himself. "A chicken. You are outside in a hurricane looking for a chicken, TJ."

When Summer had left to go get dry clothing, he realized the moment to hunt for Russell Crow was fleeting. The rain was terrible. If he was going to do anything to address the worry on Summer's face about the animal she wanted to rescue from the storm, it had to be right then.

If he had hesitated even a second, it might have occurred to him that he'd been angry at Summer for taking foolish risks when he'd found her outside, and it didn't make any more sense for him to be picking up the hunt. He wasn't invincible, either.

But when she'd explained how she'd ended up there, with the injured dog and the missing rooster, he'd understood her choices.

In the same place, he would have done the same thing.

And if he'd been unable to locate the irritating chicken, he would have worried throughout the storm. There was no doubt in his mind that Summer would spend the same time and energy on Russell Crow unless they made sure he was safe.

So TJ had grabbed his damp towel before pulling his flashlight off his duty belt.

Then he had stepped outside to do a reckless

assessment of where he thought a rooster might hide and headed out into the downpour. The press of wind reminded him immediately that he was making a bad decision, but once it was made, everything got much clearer.

Moving fast was smart, because he needed to get back inside ASAP, but it also fit the pounding adrenaline that urged him to hurry.

He went down the line of shrubbery Summer had been searching when he drove up and turned the corner of the clinic to see an outside staircase that led up to the second story over the clinic. Thinking like a chicken wasn't easy, but he tried to keep it simple.

"Get out of the rain…under the stairs maybe." TJ ran across the yard, waving the flashlight as he went. The movement he saw out of the corner of his eye stopped him in his tracks. He'd almost convinced himself that something was loose on the building and caught a gust, but then he saw a thin neck and a tennis ball–sized head. "Russell Crow, I presume."

His answering squawk didn't indicate impending cooperation, but TJ decided the time for negotiation was over. Did he know anything about the proper handling of angry, scared roosters? No, but that was what the towel was for. After he hunched his shoulders to slide under the stairs, he set the flashlight down on the ground, took the soaked towel off his shoulder to wring out as much water as he could, and then slowly approached the bird.

Settling the towel over the rooster was much easier than TJ had expected, so he decided Russell Crow was exhausted and ready to accept his fate, whatever it might be.

"It's a rescue for now. We'll have to see what the rest of the night holds, Russ." TJ hitched the rooster under one arm and picked up his flashlight. As he was hurrying across the yard, he paused to study the driveway and road leading away from the clinic. Water was visible, running down the street and pooling across the gravel. "Looks like the bridge is under water."

He was concerned the clinic would be next.

When he was underneath the protection of the small overhang near the door, TJ scanned the yard. The clinic, his patrol car, Summer's SUV…they were all on higher ground than the shelter or any of the outbuildings. If flooding was a problem, they were in the best place they could be.

"That will have to be enough," he muttered as he opened the door and then shoved it closed against the storm.

The thick darkness of the clinic's office was his first clue that things had changed while he was fighting for Russell Crow's life. He could see the weak glow of light that had to be coming from the exam room where the backup generator had kept the lights on. Everything else was black.

Before he could make his way there, Summer came racing into the waiting area.

"Outside! What are you thinking?" she demanded.

His angry retort was on the tip of his tongue, but it was unnecessary.

Summer spotted the rooster under his right arm.

All of the responses that immediately boiled up, some sarcastic and some just flat-out irritated, were wiped away when she threw her arms around his neck…carefully because there was an unpredictable rooster at his side, but the intent was clear.

Summer Patel hugged him like he was a hero returning from war.

Because he had rescued the chicken she hated.

Why did he suddenly feel invincible?

The dramatic change in direction from fighting to friends knocked him off balance, but he anchored himself with one arm around her shoulders.

"Thank you," she said, her face pressed in the bend of his shoulder. Her skin touched his, and he could feel the quickness of her breaths and the tension in her body. "Thank you for coming, TJ. Thank you for finding him. Thank you for being here."

He'd known there was something different about Summer Patel, and her effect on him.

Hearing her say this, having her arms around him…

TJ could never have imagined this feeling.

Nothing about the world had changed. There was still a dangerous storm raging outside.

The electricity was out and the water was rising.

He was soaking wet.

There was an agitated chicken under his arm. The towel wouldn't hold him indefinitely.

Right there, in that moment, this woman and her gratitude made him feel different about himself.

He'd done the right thing coming here and risking his neck to retrieve the rooster.

This was like the satisfaction that came from hearing a classroom of happy kids chanting his name, but multiplied by a thousand.

He would have stayed there until the sun came up.

But then he realized Summer was crying.

CHAPTER NINE

Of all the ways Summer had embarrassed herself with TJ Shepard, sobbing into his wet shoulder while he held a drenched chicken under his arm had to take the first-place trophy. When things were less awful, she might spend some time brainstorming what could be more humiliating than this, but she never wanted to endure whatever might be worse.

If she could just stop the tears, she might recover, but that was out of her control.

Where was her control anyway?

The reflexive panic she'd felt at being plunged into darkness brought all of her doubts about her ability to survive this storm alone to the surface. Every worry she'd had about the choices she'd made to get here tangled with her fear of the storm, freezing her in place.

Then seeing him there, holding a weird towel-covered lump under one arm, had swamped her defenses.

Flinging her arms around him to hold on for life

had been a choice, but she'd never made it. The need to be close to him had taken control.

"Hey," he said in a low voice next to her ear that surprised a shiver out of her. "We're okay, Summer. I know it's scary, this wind, but we're okay."

Then he stopped talking and tightened his left arm around her shoulder to pull her closer.

She lost track of how long they stood there, but eventually the tears stopped. He held her tight, without speaking, until she stepped back.

"I know you're being sweet," she said through an ugly gulping noise that would haunt her sleepless nights with cringe, "but I'm not sure I can live with the memory of that meltdown between us." She wiped her face with her damp shirt and realized she'd left him standing there in wet clothes while she pulled herself together. "And eventually the lights will come back and you will see my embarrassed flush, bright red nose and swollen eyes."

TJ sighed. "Fingers crossed. I hope it's soon. I'd hate to miss all of that."

Summer laughed through a jagged exhale of breath. He squeezed her shoulder with a warm hand, and she was grounded again.

"We do so much better with fewer words, don't we? I'm really impressed. You didn't tell me to just stop crying," she said as she took two big steps back. Being too close to TJ raised the temptation to plaster herself to his chest again to unmanageable levels.

"Maybe I'm learning?" TJ didn't sound convinced, and that made it easier for Summer to let go of some of her embarrassment. "But if you have a plan for a temporary home for your rooster, I do think that should be our next step. I'm not an experienced rooster wrangler, and his beak looks too pointy for comfort. I'd hate for your next surgery to be on me."

"'Rooster wrangler?'" Summer asked as she motioned him to follow her through the exam room and into their surgical area. After pulling a dog carrier off a stack in the corner, she shoved a clean blanket inside and carefully placed Russell Crow on top. Then she closed the door with profound relief. Everyone was accounted for and together. "I don't think rooster wrangler is the official title. Do you mean chicken tender?"

When he didn't immediately react, she turned back around to see him frozen, one hand ruffling his hair, while a confused frown wrinkled his brow.

"Chicken. Tender," Summer repeated, certain that might be the funniest joke she'd ever made in her life. The fact that she'd managed it under the current conditions filled her with pride. For some reason, she wanted him to be impressed by it, so his response was even more upsetting than falling apart in his arms without a hint of warning. "Is that play on words too *fowl*?"

Then his lips twitched.

The first snorted laugh surprised them both, but then TJ let loose, deep laughter shaking his shoulders. His amusement turned the occasional flutters she'd been suffering around him to a steady warm glow inside. It had been such a long time since she'd felt it.

"Wow. From tears to what might be the corniest joke I have ever heard in one move." TJ shook his head. "I am impressed, Dr. Patel."

"I would worry that I'm losing my mind, but I'm pretty sure the damage is already done at this point," Summer said. "There are dry scrubs over there." She pointed at the heap on the floor where she'd dropped them when the lights went out. "If you're done being all heroic and everything, you can dry off."

TJ bent to pick them up. "Done being heroic? Never." He pointed at Skye on the exam table. "For my next feat of strength, I'm thinking of carrying your patient upstairs. Can she be moved?" His face was serious as he added, "Please tell me you have an interior staircase. The wind and rain will make getting upstairs difficult if not impossible if we have to go outside."

"Move her already? It will be tricky. I don't want to reopen any of her wounds." Summer tipped her head to the side. "We talked about staying here. With the generator?" They had, hadn't they? The emergency lights weren't strong, but her apartment would be completely dark.

She'd also be cooped up with TJ, Skye and Russell Crow in a tiny, personal space.

Considering her weakening protective barrier, it seemed better to keep it businesslike.

"We did." He nodded. "But the way the water is rising…" He stopped and smiled. "Well, I think the storm surge is beginning, and based on the water levels, I want to move…" He exhaled. "Up. We should go up. Now. The water rises fast, and I don't want us to be caught off guard. Having to move her in a rush will be even harder."

The way her heart immediately sped up jerked Summer to attention. She couldn't afford another meltdown. Neither one of them needed her to be anything other than solid here.

Before she could lurch into action, he wrapped his hand around her arm. "It's not time to panic," TJ said firmly, "but we'll finish preparing upstairs. Help me figure out how to do this safely and point me in the right direction."

His conviction reassured her. It was a relief to have someone else take the lead.

And as soon as she survived this hurricane and had a minute without impending doom hanging over her head, she would absolutely examine why that was true, since it was an about-face in her opinion of TJ Shepard's directives.

For now, he was making total sense.

Summer nodded. "Okay. Yes. We'll do that. There's a staircase at the end of this hallway."

She hurried around the exam room to pull out the soft-carry stretcher and gurney they kept on hand for busy surgery days. When she was ready, she motioned at TJ. "You lift her head and shoulders, shift her over to the stretcher. We'll go on three."

His confident nod eased some of her worry. "One. Two. Three." They seamlessly shifted Skye over to the stretcher with only a single annoyed huff in response. The anesthesia was holding strong. "Up the stairs we go."

They each grabbed handles on either side of the soft stretcher and started walking. Skye's eyes opened as they jostled her, but she only sighed heavily, as if being disturbed was a monumental inconvenience.

"Sorry, girl," TJ murmured. "We've got some stairs to climb, but we'll get you a comfy spot to rest in just a second."

Moving up the stairs was a slow process.

While Summer shone the flashlight ahead, TJ took each step carefully and kept up a running stream of comforting nonsense for Skye's reassurance the whole way.

At the bottom of the stairs, Summer had been grateful beyond everything else that TJ Shepard had showed up for her, even though he'd ignored all her loud protests about her independence and driven her a little crazy through it.

By the time they made it to the top of the stairs, Summer realized that the significant warm and fuzzy feeling was expanding in the center of her chest, and it was directly tied to the man who was pressing a kiss to Skye's head as he waited for her to build a comfortable nest of pillows and blankets in the center of her living room floor.

After he settled the dog in the middle, he tucked a blanket around her carefully.

And Summer knew she was in big trouble.

Liking him this much while they lived separate lives in Horizon would have been manageable. Nothing about her plans for independence would have to change because crossing paths with TJ would happen so infrequently. Eventually, he'd do or say something to return them to normal hostilities.

But she was afraid that riding out this storm together was going to leave too much opportunity for her to embarrass herself. Letting that warm fuzzy out would expose her, weaken her, so keeping it under control was going to be important.

"I'll run down and rescue Russell Crow again." TJ grinned at her, the very picture of "everything will be okay" for the moment. "Be right back."

"And the scrubs. If you want dry clothes," Summer called to his retreating back because she felt like she had to say something approaching normal even if nothing felt that way at the moment. She'd also need to go down to get painkillers and food, but that could wait a minute.

Her first priority was Skye. Summer knelt down

next to the dog and gently eased back the blankets. No bleeding. The stitches were good. The dog was resting comfortably.

She and TJ had made a good team,

"Okay, Summer, you managed to work together for ten minutes. It's a record, not a love story." Dampening this fuzzy warmth growing against her better judgment seemed important.

Distance might help her return to her previous view of TJ as someone who was annoying but generally okay and handy in an emergency, but they would be stuck together in her one-bedroom apartment.

So that left busyness.

"All right, candles, radio," she said as she turned to the closet that also served as a pantry and started pulling things off shelves to stack them on the counter that separated her postage stamp–sized kitchen from the living room. "The candles are all scented and have names like Fresh Breeze and Sweater Weather, so we're in for a sensory experience. I also have another flashlight." She clicked the button to switch it on and off again. "Extra batteries." When TJ came back upstairs, she was digging through the box she'd designated her apartment's junk drawer. Her search turned up a few batteries that should fit the flashlights.

And then she was out of busy ideas.

"What else?" she asked as she turned back to TJ. Russell Crow's carrier was on the floor at his feet. He'd leaned one hip on Summer's most comfortable armchair, right next to Skye, to shine his flashlight toward her. Having his undivided attention made her nerves spike again. "Fire. We need fire."

She moved over to the kitchen cabinets to pull down a tiny matchbox. When she'd moved in, she hadn't understood why anyone would have matches when there were much easier ways to start a fire. The answer was clearer as she stood there in the dark with no idea where to find the long utility lighter she normally used.

As Summer lit two of the candles she'd stacked on the bar, she heard water start in the bathroom. Her immediate thought that it wasn't safe to take a bath during a hurricane was chased by the memory of hearing a radio announcer add an emergency water supply to the storm preparedness list.

Because she might be stuck here without power or water for days.

If she made it through the storm otherwise unscathed.

"What am I doing here?" she muttered and wobbled on weak knees over to the chair TJ had vacated. Sitting down felt right. She might never stand up again.

"Do you mean what are you doing in this living room, as in what do you need to take care of next?" TJ asked from the doorway to the bathroom. He had changed into scrubs and was carrying his belt and radio in one hand. "Or what are you doing in life in general?"

Summer huffed out a breath. The urge to cry on his shoulder was building again.

Her knees did feel like they were returning to a solid state, though.

Which was nice.

"I meant Horizon specifically. Why does anyone live here when this can happen?" Summer tangled her fingers together and forced herself to stay put in the chair. Flinging her arms around TJ would make her feel better momentarily, but when they both survived, things might get weird. "I've invested everything in this place. What happens if I lose it? How could I make a mistake like this?"

Confessing her fears aloud took some of the building pressure away.

It also immediately reminded her that those were inside thoughts. She didn't let fears like that out of her mouth under normal circumstances.

He knelt down in front of her and took her hands in his to straighten them out and warm them with easy pressure. "It has been years since we've seen direct landfall like this, Summer. Not sure what brought you to Horizon in the first place, but you just got so lucky to be here for it."

She could see his smile in the gloomy darkness and wanted to trust him.

Her doubts about how she, or really anyone,

could plan anything for life here weren't answered, but that was a problem for after the storm.

Since she had a big business loan to cover, her long-term planning was centered around this clinic, and if she'd made a huge mistake…

Well, the list of things she had to figure out after the storm was growing too long.

"Honestly, all it took was a broken engagement, a need to leave town and a very persuasive vet who only evacuated twice in the time he lived here, and here I am. The only luck I'm really sure about at this point is that you're here with me." Summer gripped his hands. "Leo was absolutely right. Going through this alone would be impossible."

TJ leaned closer, and Summer wrestled the urge to slip her arms around his waist until the moment turned awkward.

"I have so many questions, Summer, but I have on dry scrubs." TJ waved a hand theatrically to show his new outfit. "You need to change, too. Then we'll figure out where to go from there. Small steps will get us through this."

Summer nodded. He was right. Everything he said made so much sense now.

"I'll take this." She grabbed the flashlight and moved to her dark bedroom to find something dry. Flipping the light switch reflexively when she stepped inside had her muttering, "No electricity, Summer."

Standing in front of the dark closet gave her a chance to let her heart rate settle.

It was hard to decide on the right outfit for hurricane readiness. Scrubs were her uniform, comfortable and easy to grab, but she decided on jeans and a T-shirt. If the worst happened and this was all she had left, it was a good all-purpose choice.

Imagining being left with only the clothes she was wearing almost froze her in place again.

"Unplug all your electronics while you're in there," TJ called from his spot in the living room, and the return of the voice, the bossy one he'd used as an officer of the law, set her teeth on edge.

"Get over yourself, Summer. Do not start a stupid argument about his delivery. He's here. You're not alone in the storm. He has a good heart and experience. Hold on to that and let the rest of it go." It was good advice, so she stopped to think about the silly chatter he'd murmured to the sleeping dog he'd carried up the stairs and the way he'd insisted on a cozy bed to put her down in.

That scattered some of her annoyance with his bossy voice.

Why was she like this? She'd had enough of orders and pressure to conform, but he was the expert here. Learning from more experienced teachers had never been a problem before, but something about TJ was different.

For some reason, it was important that TJ thought she had it all together.

"Maybe you ought to figure out why his opinion matters, Summer." She shook her head. Some things were so much clearer when she said them out loud.

If she was honest with herself, she'd decided at some point that everyone had to believe she was self-sufficient. In control.

"Not even you can control a hurricane, Dr. Patel," she said as she picked up her flashlight.

Being grateful for his presence while also getting annoyed at his bossiness left her in this mixed-up place that wasn't good for either of them, especially in close quarters while a storm raged. She had to get a grip on her own reactions.

After she'd unplugged everything in her bedroom and bathroom, she decided the other thing she could do to maintain their truce was to follow the same instructions on the first floor while she gathered up painkillers for Skye and food for Russell Crow.

Space would help reset her equilibrium.

She had always needed some quiet and time alone to recover during high-stress periods.

This storm definitely met the criteria.

Even if the thought of going alone sent another quiver through her knees.

"I'm headed downstairs." Summer waved the flashlight. "If you're hungry, you can check out the refrigerator and freezer. We should probably clean them out anyway since the power is out.

I will also dig around in the clinic breakroom. Whatever is there I will claim as the spoils of war, due to emergent circumstances."

She turned on her heel but stopped at the pitch-black doorway.

The memory of the panic she'd felt when the lights had gone out stopped her.

Talking herself out of it silently took some work, but she didn't want TJ to hear her lecturing herself on silly fears.

It was completely irrational.

Nothing had changed downstairs. She knew the layout.

The storm was buffeting the building, and it would be very much the same on the bottom floor.

TJ would be close enough to hear her call if she needed him.

She'd almost resolved to step down into the dark stairwell when TJ said, "Hey, Summer?"

Relieved to have any reprieve, she said, "Uh-huh?"

TJ picked up his flashlight and turned it on. "Would it be okay if I come downstairs with you?"

The relief that swamped her battled with her stubborn urge to prove she was absolutely fine, but before she knew which one was going to win the war, he added, "If we're both working, we can get it done much faster. I solemnly promise to follow all your orders."

Summer cleared her throat, painfully aware that

he'd tacked on the last part to humor her and grateful enough to accept the effort as he'd intended it. "Don't think I don't know what you're doing, Officer Shepard. Humoring me."

His low chuckle rippled through the darkness and settled low in her abdomen.

"Is it working?" he asked as he moved closer to her.

A sensible request combined with that voice? It was working entirely too well, but Summer wasn't going to admit that.

CHAPTER TEN

As TJ followed Summer back into her dimly lit exam room, he realized he was smiling. Considering the situation, that was weird. The wind was a constant moan, muffled only by the beating rain. Here, the storm's noise was muted, but if they needed any reminder of the critical situation they were in, all they had to do was pause to listen.

But being here together…

Well, it didn't make things better, but he was happy at how well it was working out. Asking if he could join Summer when he'd noticed her hesitation had felt like a breakthrough. It had been on the tip of his tongue to stop her. If he'd demanded a list and told her to settle in next to Skye, which had been his initial impulse, she would have jumped down the stairs into the darkness to show him she could.

Her agreement had been easy enough.

Letting him know that she saw through his scheme was 100 percent Summer. That was what made him smile. Her unexpected humor, even in the face of all of this, was attractive.

Maybe the storm would give him the opportunity to learn better how to deal with Summer's prickly outer shell. Every glimpse he got of the warm woman made him like her more. Spending more time with that Summer when they weren't under the threat of a massive storm or squared off for battle could be sweet.

Right. Just as soon as he survived a literal hurricane and then navigated the storm of either reordering his life to match his father's expectations or…

TJ wasn't sure how to keep the analogy going. If he refused to step into the chief's job, would that mean his ship sank? Or that his life was under water?

"Can you take the breakroom?" Summer asked as she reached the center of her exam room. The emergency lights powered by the generator gave everything a blue glow. She was already unlocking a heavy metal door. "I'll grab some painkillers and dog food for Skye, while you unplug things in there and grab anything edible."

Her voice was strong, and she'd regained some of her certainty.

What a relief. He understood her fears, but this was going to be so much easier for her if she had a plan. The way she naturally evaluated the situation and what needed to happen before outlining next steps decisively was also familiar. The chief of police had the same manner at the morning shift change. His mother ran her kitchen and the town's high school with that confident tone.

TJ felt more confident because of her.

Over the course of nearly four decades, his parents, both leaders who were certain of their own abilities, had built a strong marriage and family. Did they butt heads? Of course, but they'd somehow found a way through all of that. None of the Shepard kids doubted that their marriage would last forever, even if they weren't always speaking to each other over the dinner table.

Instead of opposites attracting, his parents were more like two rocks that made a spark when they collided.

Maybe an incurable mismatch in pizza toppings and minor skirmishes over who would take the lead didn't mean he and Summer had irreconcilable romantic differences.

Were they less Romeo and Juliet and more "variety is the spice of life"?

The inconvenient timing of seeing and understanding the real Summer when he wasn't sure he was fully clear about the real TJ was a problem, but he wanted to keep going.

This was Summer's domain. Following her lead was easy. What all this meant about who they could be together was a problem to solve after the storm.

"Good plan. I'll ransack the breakroom. If you

need me, yell." TJ headed into the small kitchen area and methodically worked around the perimeter, unplugging appliances, opening cabinets and drawers, and piling a half-empty box of crackers, a bag of what appeared to be leftover Halloween candy and three apples on the small table in the center of the room. Summer's "In my defense, I was left unsupervised" tote bag was on one of the chairs, so TJ took the tools out and shoved the food inside before slinging it over his shoulder. The refrigerator yielded a large pitcher of water and a six-pack of energy drinks that he wouldn't touch on a normal day.

"These are desperate times, TJ," he said as he swung his flashlight around for a final check of the room.

"Talking to yourself?" Summer asked from the doorway.

His heart slammed against his chest as adrenaline pumped through him. Why was he startled? There were two of them in the building and he knew she was in the next room. The darkness, the storm… Maybe he'd just been too deep in his head.

At least he hadn't shouted like he was under attack by the boogeyman. That would not instill the level of confidence he was going for.

"It's a habit." TJ tried for an easy tone, as if he was completely comfortable. They were in this together. He didn't need his partner worried for his backbone because he panicked when she appeared as totally expected. Pretending that talking to himself was absolutely normal wasn't difficult with Summer, either. It was something she did, too. "Not a bad habit, necessarily, because I am a very interesting conversationalist."

Her low chuckle pleased him enough to let the smile return.

"My solo conversations are more about letting the critical inner voice have a say, but I get what you mean." Summer waved her flashlight around the room. "Looks like you got everything."

TJ stifled the smile at her official approval. "Yeah, we have slim pickings here, but at least we have dog food if worse comes to worst." He highlighted the bag at her feet.

"Yeah, I'm not sure Skye is ready for food yet, but we're probably going to need something for Russell Crow soon."

"No chicken feed?" he asked. "I thought that's what chicken tenders preferred."

Summer laughed. "In desperate times, even the best chicken tenders can make do with the highest quality dry dog food. Russell Crow eats bugs under normal circumstances. He may be spoiled for his old life with a comfortable carrier and fine dining delivered right to his door," Summer said. It was hard to see her face in the darkness, but TJ could hear the smile in her voice. "I much prefer this quiet rooster to the one startling me into new gray hairs."

"What flavor? It's not chicken, is it?" TJ asked slowly and knew the instant she turned her head to stare at him. Even in the shadowy room, he could feel the weight of her stare.

"Hmm, that would be..." She bent and picked up the bag. "Oh, no, salmon and brown rice."

"Well, that's a relief," TJ said as she straightened.

"Are you ready to go back upstairs?" she asked.

Before he could answer, a low crack outside was followed by a crash that shook the building. For too long, it sounded like the world was ending.

TJ wasn't sure how it happened, but Summer was in his arms and repeating, "Oh, no," on a loop under her breath when he realized the world continued to spin. The storm pounded the building. Whatever happened outside, they were still there.

"Hey, we're okay," he murmured as he ran his hands over her back. He said the words in his own looping response to her "Oh, no" until she caught her breath and nodded. "When you're ready, you need to go upstairs and check on Skye." Then he remembered that he was trying to learn a better way. "Right? If she woke up, she'll be scared." There was almost no way the crash hadn't startled the dog.

"Okay, I'm ready. Let's go." Summer picked

up the bag of dog food at her feet and turned toward the stairs.

"I'll be there in just a minute." Even in the darkness, TJ could see her slam to a stop in the hallway. "I'm going to check outside. From the doorway. I'll be safe. I promise."

Summer exhaled a loud, angry breath and resumed her march upstairs, but she muttered the whole time. "I want to tell you exactly how stupid I think that plan is because what difference does it make what happened outside as long as it is outside and the storm is still raging and we are fine inside, but I don't want to waste the time arguing with anyone who thinks it's a good idea to go outside in all of that..."

It was muttering, in that it was angry and spoken to herself, but the level was cranked to eleven, so it was more like a shouted lecture, and the way she hit the word "outside" every time was impressive. It died off when she made it to the apartment.

"This still seems like progress. Obviously, she cares," TJ said to himself as he moved to the clinic's heavy front door. It was protected by an alcove that he hoped would shelter him from the wind a little.

Stepping out into the storm, even with the shelter, was evidence that Summer was absolutely correct. It was a stupid idea.

Wind battered him immediately, slamming the tote bag he'd forgotten was slung over his shoulder into his side and back. Rain fell in sheets, obscuring the yard, but it was easy enough to see the water had risen rapidly. The clinic's driveway was gone, covered in water.

He might have been worried about his patrol car getting carried away in flood waters, but the source of the crash was impossible to miss.

A large tree had fallen and slammed across the hood of his car before rolling to land on the ground in front of it. In the dark and blowing rain, it was difficult to gauge the full extent of the damage, but the shattered windshield, crumpled hood and side panel hanging low enough to divert the water flowing under the car were clear enough. This car wasn't moving anywhere anytime soon.

"Oh, boy," he said slowly as the implications of wrecking his patrol car on a call he'd never been ordered to undertake settled across his shoulders. "That is going to be a difficult conversation."

TJ retreated inside and locked the door before leaning against it. Explaining this to the chief was going to be tough. Worry about his father's reaction settled as a hard knot in TJ's stomach, but he attempted a silent pep talk. Whatever the damage was, it could be fixed. It was just a car, not a life. It could be replaced. All things considered, the storm damage appeared to be minimal at this point.

All of those things were true.

But the image of his father's face as he'd left

the conference room that afternoon was a powerful counterpoint to every one of those points. He'd been disappointed that TJ left.

Maybe even angry.

Learning about expensive repairs to a patrol vehicle driven by an officer who didn't follow orders would not improve that.

"You can't change any of it, either," TJ said. Shaking off the mental image took a second. Maybe he could get advice from Summer on making big life changes when the people around him disapproved. She had never hesitated to stand firm on her own judgment.

Sometimes that certainty left her facing a raging storm.

Exhausted, TJ gathered the rest of his haul from the breakroom and scanned the exam room as he passed through. If the water was coming in, they had done everything they could down here. Summer had plugged her cell phone into one of the outlets along the counter lit by the emergency lights. "Smart." It made sense to try to keep one of their cell phones charged while the generator was operational. He could hear the low hum of the small refrigerator as well. After her patients' safety, keeping those medicines stored properly was critical to Summer's clinic. He hoped the generator was on high enough ground to avoid the rising water.

Everything else was dark and silent.

He checked the charge on her phone to see it

was at 90 percent before switching it out for his on the charger. Since he had his police radio to make contact with his family, it made more sense for Summer to hold on to her phone. Her family might try to call for updates and panic if they couldn't reach her. Most of his would be gathered around the police scanner anyway, so his two-way radio would work to communicate with them.

As long as the battery held its charge. TJ made a mental note to watch the battery life.

Picturing her irritation at overriding her decision to leave her phone downstairs made him hesitate, but he decided it was an opportunity to practice his communication skills.

"We'll call that growth again. And you've been gone so long that she's probably convinced you've washed away," TJ muttered. Maybe her muttering had stopped. The delay had restored some of his calm.

He needed it.

Summer was depending on him to be certain and calm.

The memory of her tears had stuck with him, and he didn't want a repeat at this point.

They still had a long night ahead. He needed confident Summer, so confident TJ was who he would have to be.

SUMMER KNEW IT was silly to worry about TJ. He was a grown man who had weathered hurricanes before. He would step outside, look around and come back in. But as she bustled around her apartment to make sure Skye was content and set up food and water for her and Russell Crow, all she could think of was how devastated she would be if he was hurt or worse.

She wasn't certain how many days she'd known Officer Shepard, but she was afraid his safety mattered more to her already than Dr. Dixon Brooks's ever had. Since she'd been convinced she could love him enough to marry him, that was a lot to absorb. It had taken three years of dating long distance and six months of lots of dropped hints after she'd moved back to Atlanta before Summer had agreed.

With more distance and the clarity of this life-and-death storm, it was becoming clearer that Summer had really loved making her parents happy and her picture-perfect life with Dr. Dixon Brooks more than she had loved the man himself. He'd been successful, with a career that helped others, and he'd fit into her family seamlessly. If Mr. Right could be custom ordered, so many of her friends would have chosen Dixon. He didn't fit Summer, though.

On paper, every decision that led her to the altar was logical, but now she could see that she'd missed the first big step: marrying the right person *for her*.

It was impossible to say that TJ was that man

at this point, but it was also impossible to ignore how having him here with her felt.

Caring about him as a fellow human being made perfect sense. She wanted his safety as she would any of her neighbors.

That didn't explain away this weird feeling that she wasn't really herself until he was nearby. Could she blame that on the storm? The unusual circumstances were warping her emotions.

It was the only answer that made any sense. Otherwise, there was something really rare happening here. Her whole life, she'd tried to make decisions based on logic, the kind of sound reasoning she would need to argue her way into getting agreement for what she wanted to do. With TJ, logic was taking a back seat to this innate connection.

Fighting with him made sense.

Missing him, worrying about him, watching for him to appear didn't.

Unless she could blame the storm outside.

"Don't be ridiculous, Summer. Hurricane Agnes did this, not love," she whispered to herself as she sat down next to Skye. The candles had been distributed on the end tables in the room to create a glowing circle. The battery-operated radio was playing at a low volume, but it was within easy reach if Summer wanted to turn it up. Russell Crow's carrier was on the edge of the furniture, close enough that he was definitely included in their protected circle without disturbing Skye. She'd done everything she could do. All that was left was the waiting.

When Skye shifted to lean against Summer's side, she ran her hand carefully over the dog's head. "No one falls in love in three days."

Summer wanted to be relieved to have a logical explanation.

As soon as TJ was back, she would get right on that.

CHAPTER ELEVEN

CONVINCED HE COULD present the right attitude, TJ hurried up the stairs to find Summer had joined Skye in the cozy nest on the floor. She'd been busy rearranging things, and the whole atmosphere of the room leaned closer to romantic escape than shelter against the storm.

But maybe that was more about TJ's state of mind than any real intent on Summer's part.

Skye was curled into a tight ball with her head resting on Summer's leg.

"How's the patient?" TJ asked as he set all his hunted and gathered food and drink on the counter. After grabbing his radio, he piled the rest of the loose cushions from the couch next to Summer.

"She was pretty anxious when I got back up here, but her legs aren't cooperating yet. The anesthesia's still working. When I sat down next to her, she started to relax." Summer ran her hand over the dog's head. "I'll stay down here with her, but you should stretch out on the couch. The radio says the center of the storm is nearing land, so we've still got a ways to go before this is over."

Her tone was very…professional, distant. TJ figured that had to do with his insistence on going outside. He wasn't convinced it was an improvement over the loud muttering.

Being polite certainly wasn't as nice as laughing at her silly jokes.

TJ moved to the cabinets in search of glasses and poured them both water from the pitcher he'd pilfered from the breakroom. "See? It has taken only one storm and you already sound like a seasoned hurricane survivor. You've learned all the lessons. You might as well be a local at this point."

She huffed out a laugh. "I'm repeating what I heard the radio announcer say. I've always been very good at learning whatever I needed in time to pass the test."

"Meaning you forget it as soon as the test is over?" TJ unpacked his tote bag. "That doesn't sound like the Summer I know."

Her snort made him smile. "The Summer you know? From all our extensive chats?"

She had a point. They'd mainly butted heads. Why was he certain he knew things about her that he'd never even fully considered? He might not be able to answer questions about her favorite band or least favorite vegetable, but something had convinced him he could predict where she would fall on the things that really mattered.

TJ shrugged. "You can learn a lot about someone when you argue."

Her quiet "That's very true" convinced TJ it was a loaded answer. There were other people in Summer's life that she'd argued with and discovered things she didn't like.

"Hungry?" TJ asked instead of telling her she should eat something. Another sign of progress.

"There's leftover pizza in the refrigerator. Grab that," she said by way of answering. TJ noted that she wasn't saying yes or no to his question. He smiled as he opened the refrigerator to take out her mushroomy leftovers.

For some reason, her stubbornness bothered him a lot less in that moment.

It was easy to imagine having a similar back-and-forth about dinner a thousand times, but neither of them was treating it like a battle at this point. Minor skirmishes could be invigorating.

Summer opened the pizza box and laughed as Skye craned her head in interest as she took out a slice of pizza. "You're feeling better, aren't you, girl? I gave her some food and a painkiller, so I'm not sure she remembers she's recovering from an accident." After a big bite, Summer said, "Tell me how bad it is." She straightened her shoulders. "Outside. I can handle it."

Then he remembered he had some medicine of his own to take.

TJ grabbed his two-way radio off the counter

and moved to settle in next to Summer in the nest of pillows on the floor. "I should make a situation report to the station. Two birds with one stone." He stretched out his legs. "Shepard to Command, over."

His father's answer was immediate. "This is Command. Go ahead, Shepard."

TJ felt the weight of Summer's stare as he said, "I just did a quick survey of the water levels along the front of the clinic, toward the road and the bridge. The water has risen to fully cover the bridge and driveway, but it doesn't appear there's danger of breaching the building itself yet. The electricity is out but the clinic's backup generator is running, so we have emergency lighting downstairs and power to Dr. Patel's critical equipment, including my cell phone for now." When he offered Summer her cell phone back, she didn't immediately argue with him, but clenched it with both hands. He hoped that meant she appreciated having it, but he was certain she would have something to say. Hoping she was distracted, he added, "There is a tree down across the driveway." Leaving out the state of his patrol car was a gamble, but nothing would undo the damage at this point.

Maybe this was all he needed to report. "Dr. Patel and I are safe on the second floor with food, water and a battery-operated radio to track the storm. We also have a dog and a rooster at this party. Over."

Summer's quiet laughter made him smile.

There was a pause, but TJ had no doubt his message went through.

Needing a moment to come to terms with Russell Crow's presence made perfect sense.

"Copy, Shepard. Monitor the battery life on your radio closely. If it's necessary to power off, notify Command in advance. At sunrise, we'll expect another sitrep. At that point, the storm center will have passed, and the rain bands should be weak or dissipating. We'll gauge the extent of the storm damage. Emergency crews will work on restoring power as soon as it's safe to operate, and the mayor has requested a visual bridge inspection by the county road crew engineer tomorrow. We will keep you and Dr. Patel apprised of developments via your ongoing check-ins. Over." His father's voice was firm, professional. TJ understood that he was speaking with the Horizon chief of police, not his dad.

"Copy, Chief. Dr. Patel has her cell if there's an issue with the radio. Over." TJ squeezed the radio tightly, wondering if his father or Bee would add anything personal to the message.

"Ten-four, TJ. Over and out," his father said finally.

TJ inhaled slowly as he turned off the radio and set it on the couch behind him.

"Wow. That was very..." A triangle of cold

pizza floated in front of his face. "Eat something. You need it."

He took the pizza from Summer and aimed his flashlight down at it. "Mushrooms. And they're everywhere." Since his other choices were not inspiring, TJ picked off the largest chunks he could see and created a little pile inside the pizza box.

"Mushrooms are delicious. You're removing the best part," Summer said.

TJ could hear outrage and a smile in her voice.

Then she added, "Thank you for switching out the phones. I told myself I didn't really need it, and keeping it charged made sense, but I am more comfortable having it here. Just in case."

Relieved that they'd managed to avoid this particular skirmish, TJ said, "Leo warned me that we were a star-crossed couple after our meeting at Palmetto State Pizza. Juliet wants fungus on her pizza, while Romeo is clearly correct that it's a crime."

Summer scooted around to face him. "Romeo and Juliet, huh? We were really giving off tragic vibes, I guess."

TJ took a small bite of the pizza as he wondered what she thought about that. Relieved to find the bite mostly unobjectionable since he couldn't see what he was eating, he settled in to finish his slice.

"The wind is quieter. Is this the eye of the storm?" Summer asked.

"Definitely calmer, but we aren't through yet."

TJ sipped his water and took a second slice of pizza. Removing the mushrooms kept him busy for a second and distracted him from his concerns about his father's answer.

"So, your dad… He seems…tough. When I met him at the station as I was paying off the ticket I was so unfairly issued, I was impressed at how professional he was. He definitely maintained that on the radio," Summer said casually. "His tone reminded me of my dad's when he's particularly displeased with me. Like now. I almost called him about the loose roof-thingy before you showed up, but I remembered he doesn't know much more about construction than I do, and he's not really speaking to me right now."

Not speaking to her? TJ tried to imagine his father cutting off communication completely, and the picture wouldn't form.

"Right now, during this very storm, I'm supposed to be learning all the ins and outs of a storm command center. Locked into a conference room to monitor the situation at my dad's right hand. Otherwise, I won't be ready to step into his shoes. Since he's ready to retire and hand over the keys to the chief's office, he's not happy with my decisions." TJ winced as he remembered his father didn't even know about the smashed squad car yet.

"Oh, boy, even if I manage to keep you from being swept away in a hurricane, I have to live with destroying your career trajectory and possibly your relationship with your dad." Summer whistled softly. "I've always been good at making messes, but this might be near the top of the list. Not first, but maybe second."

When he realized he wasn't the least bit bothered about his career trajectory, TJ said, "You might have done me a favor. Paperwork was killing me slowly but surely. My career, the part I love most, is still on course. Lucy is safe at the station house, either manning Command without me or snoozing in Dispatch under Bee's feet. When this storm is over, we'll be back to writing parking tickets with the best of them." TJ bumped her shoulder when she seemed about to protest, but she withheld her usual firm explanation that Horizon would do better to improve signage than harassing innocent visitors.

"Death by paperwork sounds terrible," Summer said.

TJ inhaled slowly. "It really does, but he's ready to hand over his command to someone. For him, that someone is me, and the time is soon."

Something about the darkness and the storm around them made it easy to talk to her.

"You don't sound convinced," she said quietly. "Because you aren't sure you can do the job or you aren't sure you want to?"

TJ wanted to explain it all, just lay out all his concerns for Summer. Her objective opinion could be helpful.

Summer waited for his answer before squeezing his hand. "Or maybe a combination of those things."

He turned to study her face in the darkness, amazed at how well she was reading him with only a little to go on.

"I've actually been in this same spot more than once, TJ. If it's the second one, just tell him. You told me how much you loved working with Lucy. You should do what you love. Don't make yourself miserable for someone else."

Russell Crow decided to make his presence known, but this subdued murmuring sound was much easier to listen to than his strident crowing from TJ's first encounter. TJ interpreted his clucking or grumbling or whatever this particular sound was labeled to be curiosity.

"I think that means he found the food I put in," Summer said as she leaned over TJ to stare into the carrier. "If I had met this quiet rooster first, I might not have plotted against him in my head."

"You still did the right thing, saved him from the storm and fed him salmon instead of chicken," TJ murmured as he inhaled her scent. This close, he knew she smelled like fresh rain and warm, clean laundry. There was no reason it should be seductive, but if scented candles were sold with this mix, TJ would be the first in line to buy.

As she plumped up the pillow behind her back,

Summer said, "Go ahead and laugh at me. I can take it."

The fact that he found her love-hate relationship with Russell Crow cute rather than funny was hard to explain.

Or maybe it was both, but the way he wanted to squeeze her close while they laughed together was brand-new for TJ.

"We've got a lot of storm left. Tell me about your dad. I'm guessing he gave you an order you didn't like? Why isn't he talking?" TJ asked. "Is he the kind of person who is sure he has all the answers?" Poking her was dangerous to their current truce, but a little bit of distance might save them both some heartache when the sun came up again.

He wanted to tell her everything, about the job and what he wanted most and how it didn't fit what his family expected, but it was much safer to be asking the questions.

Instead of responding immediately, Summer exhaled loudly. "Are you trying to say I am clearly a carbon copy of Dr. Jay Patel? We were doing so well, TJ. Well enough that I suspect you have an ulterior motive for opening the door to an argument."

He didn't answer. What could he say? She was right.

"But it's a long night. There's no TV and the news is all storm, all the time, so let's *talk*." Summer rearranged her pillows with a loud thump. "I was supposed to be a surgeon like my dad, but I disappointed him a long time ago by choosing veterinary medicine." She cleared her throat. "And he has always stated his opinions on what is best for me very firmly."

"That's what's causing the distance? Your job?" TJ asked. He tried to picture his father holding on to his disapproval for years.

She shook her head. "Oh, no, the job is not the worst of the worst. I have a long history of resisting what my parents expected and digging in until I figured a way through the consequences. My father argues, he lectures, he eventually shuts down but always comes back. This time, I was engaged to marry his partner in his practice. When it was clear that was going to be a big mistake that would only grow more complicated with time, I walked away. From the big society wedding, the man, their plans." She sniffed. "Moved away, actually. To Horizon."

TJ winced. "I could see that causing a rift."

"Yeah," Summer said, "his protégé was about to become the son he needed, the way to pass along the practice he'd built to the next generation, and his daughter blew that to pieces." She sniffed. "There's also the price tag of planning the summer wedding to outshine all other Atlanta summer weddings, and it's a long list of grievances we're working through."

"What made you walk away?" TJ asked and

wondered why he needed to know the answer. "And then move so far away?"

Summer shrugged. "My fiancé did the one thing I couldn't reason away. He made it clear my career was unimportant in this big life plan."

TJ whistled. "Yikes." No way would that work for this woman.

"And the constant pressure to change my mind, to go back to being the Summer everyone expected when I knew it wasn't right for me..." She rubbed her forehead. "Horizon, here I come." Then she sighed. "And now on top of putting you in danger, I've also jeopardized your relationship with your father and your career. No wonder you looked ready to murder me and then carry me away to safety when you got here. Why do I feel like that's a much bigger threat to our Romeo and Juliet storyline than our inability to order a single, perfect pizza?"

He appreciated her attempt at humor, but he couldn't let her beat herself up. She'd done what she had to do.

"I made my choice, Summer. Me being here is not your fault." As TJ said the words, they sounded absolutely correct. At some point, they'd gotten past the knee-jerk misunderstanding phase, too. He might try it, to get some distance, and she might let him get away with it, but she was going to call him out at some point.

"You were standing outside in the dark in the

pouring rain. I was afraid and I didn't have all the information." TJ sighed. "And I reacted without having all the information. I tend to do that around you for some unclear reason. That anger was more about fear for your safety."

Admitting his mistakes was never easy, but doing so in the dark with the background of wind and rain steadily battering the roof wasn't too bad. The two of them were all alone in the world at that moment. Telling her a secret, that he sometimes made mistakes, was easy.

"Thank you, Officer Shepard. For coming here. I'm not sure I would have made it through this without you." The atmosphere created a cocoon for them that must've made it possible for Summer to say things, vulnerable things, she might not have in full daylight.

TJ was almost certain that she would have come out on the other side fine whether he was here or not, but it was nice to hear her gratitude.

"I promise not to break down in embarrassing tears again that will drench the shoulder of your fashionable scrubs," Summer said dryly. He knew she was embarrassed by the momentary weakness after the electricity went out, but he believed that moment might have changed everything between them.

Summer shifted as if she intended to move away, but TJ wrapped his hand around hers and tangled their fingers together to rest on his leg. He waited for her to pull back.

Instead, Summer leaned closer, so that her shoulder rubbed against his. Their heads rested on the same pillow.

Something settled for him in that moment, like it should have made an audible click, when she rested against him, her hand warm in his. Whatever happened outside, they were okay together.

"Why a veterinarian?" he asked.

When she didn't immediately answer, he rubbed his thumb across her palm. If there was no storm outside, this would be the best date he'd had in a long time.

"I've always loved dogs," Summer finally answered, "but they didn't fit in the Patel household. I did manage to get my own guinea pig once I started working." She turned her head toward him. "I did that by sneaking it in the house and swearing the housekeeper to secrecy. I made it almost six months without my parents finding out." She shrugged. "One of the volunteer opportunities my mother insisted I take on was the local animal shelter. She wanted me to make fund-raising calls or… I don't know, organize a food drive. Instead, I helped with surgeries. There was a veterinarian at the shelter who put her heart into her work, a very chic, put-together woman who impressed my mother. I did really simple things, just as another pair of hands really, but the vet convinced me that

I had something that other people didn't. I didn't make this grand decision then, but when I went to college, it was always there in the back of my head. Okay, I will become a doctor. That's what my parents demanded, but for myself… I wanted to put my heart into it."

Hearing her say the words made TJ realize that that was what he'd responded to in Summer from their first encounter. Whether it was arguing with him or fixing the loose roof-thingy, she put her heart into it.

That was attractive.

"So, choosing veterinary medicine over orthopedics, leaving Atlanta and ending an engagement. Those are big decisions, but I'm not sure they count as messes." Many parents would understand that Summer was finding her way. He hoped his own would want him to be happy, wherever that took him and whoever he married or didn't.

"Well, we have a long history of me taking my dad's orders and twisting them," Summer said before yawning widely. TJ would have laughed at the pop of her jaw, but that would be another off ramp in their easy conversation and they were cruising nicely along.

"Yeah? A little malicious compliance?" TJ asked.

She shook her head, and he realized she'd rested it against his shoulder at some point. He liked that, too.

"Not malicious…just persistent. My parents wanted perfect grades. I made them, but I chose subjects they were not fans of. Doctors need a lot of science, right? I got the requirements in, aced them, but I added creative writing and interior design in my undergraduate days. In high school, extracurriculars were important to them, so I had a whole raft of after-school activities, but they included marching band." When Summer tilted her head to study his face to make sure he was following her, TJ nodded and tried not to think about how easy it would be to kiss her.

Before he could decide whether it would be a bad idea to do so, but only a reasonably bad idea instead of a doom-level mistake, Summer wiggled around to scooch down and stretch out in the nest of blankets and pillows.

Then she urged him to follow her lead.

TJ tried to get comfortable. It was much easier to relax when Summer rested her head against his shoulder.

Thinking about how that felt right made it hard to breathe normally, but she didn't seem to notice.

"I love my parents. I want to make them happy. Always have. I dated Dixon after they introduced us, and they were pleased. I moved back to Atlanta to be close to Dixon and to them. I agreed to marry him. All of these things thrilled my parents. The Patel-Brooks wedding was going to be front page material of my mother's favorite Atlanta magazine or she'd die trying."

TJ tried to imagine how much pressure she'd have been under to go through with the wedding. He'd never lived in a city the size of Atlanta, but having their whole social circle watching would have been heavy incentive to go through with the ceremony and hope for the best.

"What made you call it off?" TJ asked.

Summer was quiet for so long that he wasn't sure she would answer.

"Dixon told me I couldn't run my own practice," she said quietly. "Not that I didn't need to. We'd had that conversation before. A busy surgeon needs a wife like my mother, who can support his career and the family." She shook her head, and TJ felt it in the slide across his skin. "No, he told me I would be bad at the business side of the practice."

TJ hummed. "Please tell me you didn't believe him."

Summer grinned, the curve of her lips whispering across his arm. "Nah, I didn't, but it was evidence in black and white that he didn't know me well enough to marry, and I *did* know him as well as I needed to walk away."

The surge of pride TJ experienced at her words was another surprise, but it was easy to imagine being proud of Summer for a lifetime.

Then she added, "I'm just now realizing why I knew he was wrong for me, with this storm and everything. Dixon wouldn't have been here for emergency surgery, he wouldn't have stayed here to help his patient, and Russell Crow would be a goner if left to his mercy. Dixon would have made logical decisions at each step. We both know that I did not stick with logic at all, but I understand that it matters to me to find the right person, one who will fight for what's important to him and to me. That's not Dixon. He was happy for me to make all the compromises, big and small. The man I meet at the altar will understand and be ready to do hard things when they're the right things."

TJ closed his eyes as he absorbed her words. They landed in his chest with a hum, resonating like a mixture of recognition and a message. She was clear about the type of person she wanted, and he believed she was absolutely correct.

He just wasn't certain he was that man.

Would that man be struggling over choosing not to pursue the chief's job? He had a feeling Summer would say no.

"Are you sure it's not just cold feet? I hear that's a thing brides and grooms experience before the big day," TJ said and covered his heart with his hand. "Not that I would know."

She squeezed his arm. "Don't do my mother's job for her. That was her argument. Then the storm came up, and she's pretty certain I'm not as smart as she hoped I was." Then she sighed. "This storm is making me reconsider some things. Not Dixon exactly, but this clinic is my key to being firmly planted here. I don't want him to be right, that I'm not cut out to make business decisions on my own, but if I'm forced to go crawling back home to ask for help because of this storm..."

TJ didn't like how often Summer brought up the prospect of leaving Horizon.

Would making it through this storm and repairing whatever damage the hurricane had done convince her to plant real roots or pack up and move inland?

TJ stared up at the dark ceiling as he considered asking her what being planted in Horizon looked like for her. Was that for a lifetime? Or was this one stop that would lead Summer on to her next stop, wherever that might be but most likely a place without the threat of hurricanes?

After a moment, he decided it didn't matter. Even if Summer could answer the question now, so many variables could change the answer tomorrow.

"Does it sound like the wind is dying down to you?" she murmured. Her voice had taken on the drowsy quality of a woman drifting off to sleep.

Falling asleep would be the best for both of them.

"Yeah, and the rain is lighter, too." TJ stared down at the top of Summer's head. "Rest. When the sun comes up, this will all be over."

He knew Summer had drifted away when she

didn't immediately launch an argument in response to his order.

At the beginning of the day, he'd been exhausted after a long sleepless night replaying his argument with Summer at the pizza place in his head and dreading another day stuck in front of a laptop.

Absolutely nothing had gone like he'd planned, and as he blinked heavy eyelids and listened to a happy chicken murmuring in an animal carrier, a dog snoring, Summer's deep, even breathing and the dying storm outside, he realized it had turned out so much better.

All it had taken was ignoring a direct order, coming to terms with Summer and her stubborn independence, and a hurricane.

Nothing had been resolved, but everything looked different after twenty-four hours.

TJ closed his eyes and decided the morning would be soon enough to worry about getting his life on track. For now, this bubble was exactly where he wanted to be.

CHAPTER TWELVE

THE FIRST THING Summer noticed as she opened her eyes was a moist dog nose and very concerned brown eyes filling her vision. She wasn't sure how long Skye had been watching her, but the dog was locked in on Summer's face, waiting for signs of life. Summer yawned and laughed at the way Skye tilted her head in response. Skye would probably still feel some of the drowsiness from the anesthesia, but at the moment, she was alert and ready for something.

"And good morning to you, too." Summer scratched under Skye's ears. "Food or a trip outside? What is your most urgent request, hmm?"

Then she realized that her living room was still shadowed, but so much lighter. The window in the exterior door had not been covered by storm shutters, and weak sunlight made a small square on the floor next to Russell Crow's carrier.

"The storm has passed," Summer said as relief made her weak for a moment. She and TJ had made it. Whatever had happened outside while the winds and rain battered the clinic could be repaired. "We are safe."

The weight of TJ's arm draped over her waist registered as he said, "The crick in my neck may be permanent, but all things considered, I agree." The sleep in his voice, warm and rough next to her ear, wrapped around Summer like a comfortable blanket. The urge to scurry away fought the desire to wriggle closer to him. She wasn't sure which impulse would win, but TJ settled the issue by sitting up with a loud groan.

"When we were kids, my sisters and I made blanket forts in the living room to camp out overnight. I don't remember every muscle in my body hurting like this the next morning." TJ scrubbed his hands over his face, and Summer decided that if he wasn't going to make it weird by calling out how they'd slept, tangled up together, she wouldn't, either.

"Sounds cool, but did you have a chicken as a special guest?" she asked.

His rough laugh and the adorable way his hair stood up in the back were uncomfortably attractive. It was easy to be on guard against the handsome man in the uniform, but this guy with bedhead created by sleeping next to her, wrapped around her, completing the safe space that made it possible to rest through the dying storm… She was in danger of doing something out of character.

Like run her fingers through his hair and press a good-morning kiss to his lips.

TJ scratched Skye's ears and pointed at the faint square of sunshine on the floor. "That is a very good sign."

"It is, and please let me be the first to say how very glad I am that I didn't get you washed out to sea by being too stubborn for my own good." The fleeting thought that she couldn't check out her own bedhead made her gather her hair in one hand. "Do you think we should step out to see if we're still in South Carolina this morning?"

TJ sighed. "Yeah, let's check downstairs first, make sure everything is dry, and then see what happened outside. I need to call in to let the station know what we find anyway." He rolled up out of the nest of blankets and pillows and stretched long and tall, and it was really difficult for Summer not to stare. Hard.

"Is she okay to go down the stairs or…" TJ glanced over his shoulder at her, and Summer had the sinking feeling he caught her watching the muscles in his arms twist. Would she call that expression a smirk? Possibly, but he was a handsome man. He deserved to feel a little cocky, as long as he didn't mention her interest directly.

Summer knelt next to Skye and ran her hands gently over the dog's hips and legs to test for pain. Skye was patient but clearly ready to go out. "One minute, girl." After she shook out one of the painkillers she'd brought up, she mashed it into a treat that Skye snarfed immediately, no questions asked.

"Let's give her a chance and see how she does." Summer stood and ran her hand through her hair when TJ's back was turned. "Inside or outside staircase?"

TJ glanced out the window in the door. "Might be a good idea to take a look from the ground before we step out on this staircase. That's a big fall if anything shook loose in the wind."

"Smart. That's very good advice. We can let Russell Crow out, too." Summer laughed at the way his eyebrows shot up before picking up the rooster's carrier. "What? I can be reasonable when you are reasonable, too."

TJ held up his hands in surrender. "Okay, you and Skye lead the way. If she has trouble, I can carry her the rest of the way."

Summer was relieved he was here with her all over again. Carrying a dog the size of Skye short distances would be possible, but Summer would struggle to get her back up the stairs if it was necessary.

The memory of TJ's muscles convinced her he wouldn't have much difficulty.

They made a careful trip down the stairs and walked through each of the rooms to stop in the lobby. Russell Crow clucked warnings from his carrier, but he kept his cool as they went.

"I was lucky, wasn't I?" Summer asked as she

shone her flashlight into the dark corners on either side of the door. The electricity was still out, but there was no water standing anywhere inside the clinic.

"The clinic is placed well, and you made sure it was prepared. That's all we can do," TJ said, "although I was also here with you, and that's definitely lucky." His grin made her smile. She wouldn't say it and inflate his ego, but she agreed.

Summer grabbed a kennel slip lead to slide over Skye's head while TJ opened the clinic's front door.

Before he motioned her through it, he said, "You're going to see a lot of debris. Remember it can all be cleaned up. Everything can be fixed because we made it through the storm." He nodded slowly and waited for her to agree.

The suspicion that he was trying to prepare her for something terrible trickled through her brain, but she understood that agreeing with him was the only way to get outside to see for herself.

So she nodded, but thrust the lead at him.

Whatever it was out there, she was afraid she was going to need all of her wits and her reflexes about her. He sighed and then stepped back to let her out the front door.

Summer walked four steps along the sidewalk that led to the drive before slamming to a stop. At some point, a tree had clobbered TJ's patrol car. The front hood was crumpled in half like a crashed paper airplane.

She froze as she watched TJ trail Skye around the bushes that lined the clinic.

All the landscaping was still there. Good.

Large puddles spilled across the driveway, but the water had receded and the bridge was clear.

There was also a small boat in the front yard that didn't normally live there, and sand deposited during the storm made its own paths across the open area between the clinic and the shelter.

It was hard to tell how many trees had come down along the tree lines at the edge of the property, but clearing up the mess of leaves and wood debris seemed like the biggest job overall.

Whatever the real name of the roof-thingy was, it was now dangling precariously from the window facing on the second floor. The fact that nothing had leaked on the second floor was another stroke of luck.

But mainly, she was stuck on the tree that had fallen and smashed TJ's car, and if she had to guess, it had happened during the loud crash he'd gone out to investigate.

And TJ hadn't told her about it last night.

"All things considered, it's not too bad," TJ said brightly.

When she turned to demand an explanation, he and Skye had bent down to examine what appeared to be fascinating driftwood near Russell

Crow's inadequate pen where the rooster was already scratching to find breakfast.

She waited, hands on hips. Since he was doing the low-voiced conversational chatter with the dog and moving slowly to be sure she didn't hurt herself, it was difficult to maintain her irritation.

"I see your pose and I counter with one of these," TJ said as he rose slowly. He pointed at his face, where one eyebrow was raised. "Before you hit me with whatever is bubbling behind that furrowed brow, let me just say there was nothing you could have done about this last night." He stepped closer. "Except worry and feel bad. There was no point in telling you about it then because we were still going to end up here."

Summer crossed her arms over her chest as she paced around the patrol car. The view got worse on the other side, where the passenger-side front tire had been punctured by a broken limb, so she returned to her starting point.

The distance was enough to realize that he was right.

Just like he'd been right about everything every time, even if she hadn't appreciated his manner of delivery.

When his cocky grin returned, she had to force her lips into submission.

Being caught agreeing with him might be more detrimental to her equilibrium than admiring the flex of his muscles. "I only ask one thing," TJ said as he sauntered closer, one finger extended and a teasing gleam in his eyes. "If you want to repay me for my stoic heroism last night..."

Summer rolled her eyes, but said, "I'm all ears." The anticipation surprised her. What would he ask for? And what would she give?

Repaying the debt she owed him for putting himself in danger and refusing to leave her alone would take something big, a grand gesture.

Whatever he asked for, she would try to give.

TJ leaned over, as if he had confidential information to share. "The fact that this happened before my report last night? To the chief? That's a secret you and I keep until we are old and gray. When we see each other after a long time apart, we will share a nod to vow that this secret remains hidden."

Summer immediately nodded and put her fingers to her lips to mimic turning the lock and tossing away the key. "These lips? They're sealed."

The way he studied her lips stopped her in her tracks.

They were teasing like friends...weren't they?

His eyes were intense when they met hers again, and the confident grin had faded.

"We have a deal, TJ," Summer said as she offered him her hand. The breathless voice that escaped as she tried to pretend they were completely back to normal was surprising.

His lips slowly curled. "Almost."

Summer narrowed her eyes. "Hmm, I'm beginning to reevaluate our friendship."

"Friendship?" he said as he gathered up Skye's lead. "Is that what we have here?"

Summer nodded uncertainly. They were at least on their way to friendship.

Did he think it was something more?

Did she want more?

"Your second condition?" Summer asked.

"If the fact that I withheld the status of my patrol car in my situation report were to come out, there would be consequences." TJ's lips curved, so Summer was convinced he wasn't suggesting anything career-ending.

But since he worked for his father, it was possible the family consequences would be something TJ wanted to avoid. She'd experienced her share of silly missteps that provoked disappointed shakes of her parents' heads, so she understood the urge to avoid them if possible.

"I'm going to need my own leverage." TJ tilted his head to the side. "Something that will cause you to hesitate before spilling our secret."

Summer blinked. "Why do I have the feeling you already have something in mind?"

"I do," TJ said immediately. "After you were snoring away last night, your head pressed against my shoulder in what might be the cutest face-plant I've ever seen…"

An embarrassed laugh escaped her as he wrinkled his nose at her.

"Well, before I could fall asleep, I spent some time replaying in my head your confession about how you chose veterinary medicine," TJ said as he turned to lead Skye back inside. Summer watched them go, impressed all over again by how well TJ worked with the dog, until he motioned over his shoulder that she should be following.

The urge to argue or plant her feet firmly in the gravel was strong, but she was curious about whatever he was working up to.

He kept up an easy chatter as Skye led the way through the clinic and back to the stairway. When the dog hesitated at the foot of the stairs, he bent down. "Are they too much, girl?" He didn't try to coerce her or order her up the stairs. Instead, TJ bent down to pick her up and started climbing. He'd almost made it to the last step when he said, "Do you see my arms, Summer?" He flexed and moved into her living room.

His wicked laugh floated behind him, and it was nearly impossible to wipe the smile off her face. TJ was as irritating as any man she'd ever met, but he was also so much fun.

Before he could catch her goofy grin, Summer cleared her throat. "As far as I understand it, we do not yet have an agreement. Surely the chief is ready for you to report in. Better hit me with your final term before you run out of time." She would never tell anyone that TJ had hidden the state of his patrol car. What difference did it make to her? To anyone really?

But she couldn't deny that she was curious to find out what TJ was angling for.

He nodded. "Excellent point. Last night, you mentioned that you were in marching band." He shrugged. "I would like to see that." TJ reached down to grab his two-way radio and turned it on. Static filled the air for a second.

Summer blinked. "I haven't played the trombone in years, and I never had the best grip on the choreography even when I needed it for halftime shows. How are you picturing this in your head?"

"Video would be best," TJ immediately said, "but I will also accept a grainy group shot in the back of your yearbook. I want to meet young Summer."

Summer frowned. "I'm not sure your bargaining power is as strong as you think it is. What if I don't meet your second condition? What will you do about it?" The idea of introducing all-American handsome TJ to Summer at seventeen didn't thrill her. The obvious holes in his plan gave her every opportunity to just…not.

"Come on, Summer. We bonded. We're bonded." He motioned between the two of them to show that they were on the same page. "Don't break us up now."

"Fine," Summer finally said with a beleaguered

sigh. "There is a video. It is hidden in the wilds of the internet. In the interest of our mutually assured destruction and ongoing alliance, I will show it to you. Once."

TJ clapped as the Horizon chief of police said, "Command to Shepard, over."

Whatever celebratory dance he was working on ended as they both stared at the radio.

Then he pointed at Summer as if to make sure she was committed to their agreement before he answered. She offered him her hand for a businesslike shake and tried not to obviously react at the spark between them as his skin slipped against hers.

Arguing with TJ had been energizing, even before they'd come to understand each other better during the hurricane's dark hours.

This restless awareness, stirred by being next to him and satisfied only when they were connected like this, was something new. It was exciting, but she believed that also meant it could be dangerous.

Maybe showing him the video of the 2015 Lewis High School homecoming game would reset him to "friend" and cool off this flirting.

Summer wasn't sure whether she hoped it worked, but a deal was a deal.

CHAPTER THIRTEEN

Before TJ could convince himself to push the microphone on his two-way radio, he returned to the nest of pillows and blankets they'd created. Sleeping through a hurricane had not been something he would have predicted while he'd been cornered in the Command control room. Neither would being cuddled up next to Summer Patel, but waking up with her in his arms had felt exactly right.

As if it was where they were meant to be.

When Summer finished refilling Skye's food and water, she moved to the counter to pick up two of the apples TJ had confiscated from the employee breakroom. She approached him to hand one over, so TJ wrapped his hand around her wrist to urge her to sit down in her spot.

He wanted her next to him.

She awkwardly pushed her hair behind her ear and didn't meet his gaze, but she sat, leaning back against the couch.

Close enough that her shoulder brushed his.

They both took a bite of apple and chewed in companionable silence.

TJ knew he was postponing the inevitable.

He couldn't read what Summer was thinking. Was she feeling awkward after they'd woken up the way they had? Maybe she was mentally counting down the time until she could get him out of her space.

The brave thing to do would be to ask her.

TJ finished his apple and came to terms with the realization that he wasn't as brave as he'd thought.

Based on Summer's description of the right man for her last night and the way he felt about her this morning, that could be a problem. She was determined to settle for nothing less than brave.

He wasn't sure, but he had a hunch she would consider his wavering in the face of hurting his father disappointing, being too weak to do the hard, right thing.

It was a sign of her influence that he was starting to agree.

"I should start a list of all the repairs I need to make, figure out who to call," she said after she finished her breakfast apple.

"Give me a minute and we can do it together," TJ said before tacking on, "please."

Her narrowed eyes were accompanied by twitching lips.

Because she could tell he was trying to moderate his orders, but it was going to be a work in progress.

And maybe that was okay with her.

Seriously, if he was the only one who could see how well they were getting along…

Then he realized it didn't really matter if they were a perfect match in personality if their lives were going in different directions.

As much as he daydreamed about being a police officer somewhere outside of Horizon, he was never moving. He wasn't fully convinced that Summer believed she was staying here, even after they'd made it through the storm.

TJ pushed the button on his shoulder microphone. "Shepard to Command."

Immediately, his father answered, "This is Command. It's good to hear your voice. What is your situation? Over."

"Dr. Patel and I are both here, Chief. There is minor structural damage to the clinic and shelter, but I don't believe either building had a significant water incursion." TJ shook his head at the way Summer repeated "incursion" with her eyebrows raised. "Our initial review of the exterior shows trees down, sand deposits and some debris that will need to be cleared. The water level has receded below the bridge level, and the road is clear." TJ let go of the mic button to clear his throat.

"Here we go," he said to Summer before squeezing her hand. "Both animals are fine as well. The only casualty I have to report is to my squad car. A tree fell and smashed the windshield and hood and punctured the tire. Over."

He squeezed his eyes shut as he waited for a reaction.

Summer pressed her head against his shoulder in solidarity, and that was nice.

"Glad to hear there are no injuries to report," his father said.

Then he added in a dry voice, "Except to your department-issued equipment." The chief cleared his throat. "There are crews in the area working to restore power, and the mayor is on the phone with the city engineer now to get her headed out to look at the bridge. Sounds like a tow truck will be the next vehicle we send over, right after the power linemen."

TJ waited for his father to finish the transmission. The chief was a stickler for protocol, so waiting for him to add "over" was important.

"Shepard, return to Command ASAP. Your mother is here and she worries," his father said finally. "Over."

TJ smiled because it was easy to picture his mother hanging over his father's shoulder insisting that her message go out over the radio. His father might have resisted for a minute, but there was no doubt she would win a battle like that.

"Copy, Chief. Over and out." TJ tried to relax

his shoulders. They were in a tight knot around his ears. Before he could, he heard, "Shepard, this is Dispatch."

TJ exhaled slowly. His sister could go in any number of directions from here, but only an official Dispatch communication would meet his father's professional standards. Bee might have a little leeway, but TJ had just reported a wrecked squad car so he was walking a very fine line. "Go ahead, Dispatch."

"Officer Lucy Shepard would just like you to know that she slept well, even if it was on the inferior bed provided to her in the Dispatch office. Like your mother, she would like you to report to the station ASAP. Over."

"Copy, Dispatch. Thank you for passing along the message from my partner. Over and out." TJ dropped the shoulder microphone on the couch behind him and pressed his head to the couch cushion with a sigh. "Glad that's over."

"He seemed to take the news well," Summer said as she ran her hand up his arm, and TJ was convinced that he'd found the superior way to deliver bad news.

It was hard to focus on anything when her skin slid over his.

"As well as could be expected. Face-to-face, I'll get to see the frown, the stern consideration, but this wasn't terrible," TJ said as he glanced down at her. "It sounds like we aren't too far away from rescue."

She nodded. "Yeah, good news." Then she reached down to grab her phone. "But there's still time for me to pay your blackmail demands. One moment while I hunt the video down."

TJ almost told her he didn't need to see it after all. It had been a silly impulse driven by his curiosity and difficulty falling asleep. He'd spent too much time considering young Summer, a serious student with marching band for a hobby.

He'd wanted to know more about her, all of her, but nothing really mattered except the Summer sitting next to him.

The Summer who'd woken up in his arms was becoming clearer and clearer to him every minute they spent together.

"All right," Summer said and held her phone up in front of his face. "Behold 'Uptown Funk.' Be on the lookout for the trombone players."

TJ took the phone from her and hit Play. She didn't move away, but he tangled his fingers through hers just in case.

The video started with a wide shot of what looked to be a much newer, nicer football field than he'd played on in Horizon. He could hear the music before the band, decked out in red-and-gold uniforms, reached the center of the field, and the camera work was a little jerky until the band was fully in the frame. For a minute or so, the whole band was framed, and he could see their choreography was high-school sharp and their movements in sync, but it was hard to be sure where a trombone might be.

The person operating the camera had the same thought because there were a couple of zooms in until a young Summer Patel filled the center of the screen.

Then and now, her forehead was wrinkled by the single-line frown of concentration as she played the notes, the slide moving in and out as she marched. Eventually the video panned back out to show the band and dancers on the field had created the outline of a lion. Whoever had captured the performance didn't hit Stop until the band completely cleared the field.

When it was over, TJ put the phone down but he didn't hand it back to Summer.

She didn't say a word, but her raised eyebrows made him think she was trying to brace for impact.

"Impressive," TJ said and nodded as her expression turned suspicious. "I mean it. I could never do it, keeping up with the choreography and the music at the same time. Did you go to college on a music scholarship?"

Her defensive shoulders slowly lowered. "No, academic. Band was one of those things I did because I enjoyed it. Traveling to the games on the bus. Pep rallies. All of it made me feel like I was part of the team."

TJ realized that said so much about Summer. She liked the team part, and she did what she could to carry her weight. She wasn't afraid of hard work, and she would push herself to keep up. Her expectations for herself were high. Had he ever worked as hard to achieve his goals?

"Who took the video? They might be your biggest fan." TJ returned to the video and hit Play again.

"My dad. He was never on board with any of my plans, but he eventually came around. Every single time. He never missed a football game that I marched in, even if he wanted me to be a cheerleader or homecoming queen instead of marching in the horns section." Then she shrugged. "Actually, that was more my mother's desire than my father's. He was set on me following him into surgery from the very beginning. Anything else was fine, but it was absolutely secondary."

That made TJ think about his relationship with his parents.

His mother had wanted them to do well in school, but that was more about behavior and being good people. His father had never once suggested his kids follow him into law enforcement, but every day, he'd modeled what he considered to be a worthy occupation.

We Serve.

"And young Summer did what she wanted. She marched." TJ offered her the phone. "I'm really impressed." He was. Even as a girl, Summer had tried to find what would make her happy and she'd done it, even if she'd had to fight upstream to do so.

Had he ever faced that situation in his own life?

Not until now.

Summer shrugged. "Young Summer did the only thing she could do. Have you ever tried to be a cheerleader to make your mother happy? It's miserable. If you don't have the talent, even working twice as hard as everyone else on the team leaves you the weakest link. Young Summer, moderately-aged Summer…" She wrinkled her nose at him. He got the message that she wasn't "old" Summer yet. "I have to be good at whatever it is or I just…can't. I can't be happy." She shook her head. "That's why all of this with the storm and finding my way in Horizon, it's so stressful. I don't feel good at this."

They'd spent a long night together under stressful circumstances, and he was more impressed by her than ever.

If she had one foot out the door, turned back toward Atlanta or some other place that might fit her better, he would be a fool to pursue anything more with her.

That didn't mean he was a quitter, either.

Especially since he was so good at seeing what other people should do about their problems.

Did her independence leave any room for anyone else at this point? She'd been fighting to make her own decisions her whole life. Would she be able to change that or would it be easier to walk away?

"I guess you were immediately good with the trombone when you picked it up. Never had any trouble remembering the music or the notes," he said without staring directly at her. He had the idea that avoiding a direct challenge might make it easier for her to follow him.

She scowled. "Of course not. I was never great in band, honestly. I had to practice twice as long as everyone else. Every time I tried out, I was amazed to make the cut, and I get your point. I did learn a lot about hurricanes and preparing for them. When the next one comes, I can get the storm shutters up. I can get supplies ready. I can even make sure I have a hotel lined up in case I need to leave." She bumped his shoulder. "But what about an emergency? What then? Do I kidnap another police officer and force them to sit with me?"

TJ asked, "You want to replace me?"

She stared up at him. "You'll be chief of police, right? Running Command from my living room is going to be tough."

It was impossible to argue with that point, so TJ held out her phone. "Thank you for sharing. You didn't have to. I know we've got a solid agreement, with or without leverage."

She sighed as she took it back. "Once I've cried on a man's shoulder, what's a little high school embarrassment?" Then she said, "Can I have your phone number? I don't know when, but I'm probably going to need it."

He didn't love the disgusted tone about needing to call him in an emergency, but it was secondary to the fact that she asked. After he rattled off the number, he said, "Send me a text so I have yours."

She nodded and punched some buttons before slipping the phone back in her pocket.

"Okay, what do you want to do while we wait?" she asked as she stared up at him. "I need to get the repair list started, check out the interior at the shelter, but maybe I'll wait for the power to be restored."

Since everything was changing, TJ found it impossible to look away. They'd gone through the storm together, but the real world would soon cross the bridge to the Island. He didn't want to let this go.

"Honestly?" TJ said slowly, uncertain if he was about to make the worst decision of his life or the best. "I'd really like to kiss you."

Her pupils dilated.

That was easy to see because he was locked in.

Her gaze shifted to his mouth before she licked her lips. Then she tilted her chin in a quick nod and moved to meet him halfway.

When her lips touched his, everything else

faded. Summer was soft against him, her arms wrapped tightly around him. His focus narrowed to her mouth, the hitch in her breath and the curve of her bottom lip. The second kiss was deeper, slower and twice as dangerous. By the time he leaned back, they were both breathless.

Her slow blinks convinced him that he was not alone in the new world he'd landed in.

"Whoa," she said in a breathy voice that perfectly fit his own reaction and thrilled him at the same time. He was glad they were in this together.

Being tossed into the deep end alone would have been scary.

"Yeah," he agreed.

Before he could get his brain to cough up something intelligent to get a conversation started, the lights flickered back on around them.

Summer pressed a hand to her lips and moved away. "I…"

TJ anxiously waited to see how she'd fill in the blank, but a horn honked from her driveway, sending Skye into excited barks. Russell Crow entered the chat with a strident crow from outside.

"Rescued by the honk." TJ squeezed Summer's hands before he stepped back. "Time to digest…" He waved between them to encompass the kiss, the nest of pillows, their new relationship. "Tomorrow. Tomorrow?"

He waited for her to nod her agreement.

Then he leaned down to press another kiss to

her lips. She was laughing when he stepped back, his hands raised high. "I couldn't help myself. Tomorrow is a long way away. There's no telling whether you'll still like me then, and I couldn't let this moment disappear."

It was harder to head for the staircase than he expected, but he forced his feet toward the doorway.

When she said, "I'm still going to like you, TJ Shepard," he turned back to meet her stare.

"I just don't know what happens next," Summer said.

Since he didn't have any answers, either, TJ decided to get to work.

Figuring out what to do first was easy enough if he focused on the outside world. Get the squad car towed to town for repairs. Line up help to get the downed trees cleared and the debris removed. Call Boogie to schedule the repairs the clinic would need.

Maybe he should have gone over the list with Summer, but there was no way he was going to let any of this go. The clinic was important to Summer's success in Horizon.

She'd explained clearly how success drove all of her decisions. Failure at the clinic meant failure in Horizon, and she would never stand for that. He could be the kind of man who supported her career easily by helping to restore the clinic. In time they could come to terms on how to work together with her need for independence.

To have that time, he'd get the clinic back to normal ASAP.

He also had to find the right way to tell his father he didn't want to be Chief. In the same spot, he knew Summer would do that, and overnight, he'd learned how much he admired her commitment to herself. He could learn to do the same.

The decision was made. He just had to figure out a way to communicate it the Shepard way.

CHAPTER FOURTEEN

ON THE THIRD day after the storm, Summer braced her hands against the tired muscles in her lower back and surveyed the wide expanse of lawn between the clinic and the shelter. So much had changed in such a short span of time.

When she and TJ had stepped outside the morning after the hurricane, she'd been overwhelmed. On top of the weird, scary and cozy night that had changed everything between the two of them, there had been the devastation caused by high winds and water to take in, including the wrecked car, six full hickory and oak trees pushed out of the ground and bits and pieces of countless others, and enough sand to build her own beach. TJ's cheerful "Not too bad" had been her only hope that the damage could be fixed.

The tow truck had removed his car first thing.

The rest of the day had been a wild mix of people in and out, and phone calls from the Wheelers, who were desperate to find out how Skye was, followed by their arrival to pick her up when the roads were clear. Watching the dog reuniting with her family had reminded Summer of why she did what she did. Her job mattered and she was good at it. Getting stuck in the clinic had been scary, but she'd made the right decision for Skye and the Wheelers.

After checking in with Kima and Natalie, her office manager and vet tech, Summer had made the difficult decision to reschedule all the routine appointments for the week. She'd had no idea how much time and work went into recovery from even minor storm damage, but everyone had needed days to reset. Kima's daughter was at home while the elementary school cleared up the mess of flooded classrooms, and Natalie was on call if any emergencies popped up while helping her parents clear out their attic after a tree fell and caused roof damage.

Everyone was fine. More than ever, Summer understood that was the most important piece. They would get back to normal business next week.

On day two, the small boat that had landed in her front yard was also efficiently removed. Seeing it aground next to her driveway, which was very dry land under most circumstances, made the record-scratch sound in her brain.

Boogie Howard had been a lifesaver with the boat.

He had spent half a day repairing the loose fascia, which was what he called the "roof-thingy" when he described the work. He'd shown up after volunteering for cleanup at the elementary school. Since Summer had never called him, she'd been surprised to see him roll in, but there was no need to ask why he was there.

Boogie had actually recognized the boat, which Summer had learned was a johnboat. After he called the owner, he'd helped the guy load it in the back of his pickup truck, and eventually the boat docking in her driveway would be a distant memory.

There were so many people working on the storm recovery with jobs she'd never once imagined in her life.

And they all did this like it was just a job, a Monday, any day ending in *y*.

TJ had gotten away with calling in reinforcements before. Clearly, he knew he could do it again whenever he liked. Honestly, the relief made it tempting to get used to his brand of bossiness.

To make sure he didn't get away with the infringement without consequences, she texted him as soon as Boogie left for his next job.

Either Boogie and I are on the same psychic wavelength or you sent him here. Without me asking.

Summer had hesitated but decided against adding, "Thank you." Keeping TJ on his toes was fun.

Guilty. You're welcome. His answer made her shake her head, but her lips curved with amusement completely against her will.

I'll let it slide this time if you'll share an embarrassing fact about your high school experience. It's a part of our negotiations, after all.

Summer mainly wanted to keep the conversation they'd started alive, but knowing something about young TJ could be fun.

The dots that showed he was typing had gone on for so long that she'd almost been convinced he was going to end the conversation, but eventually he answered.

Fine. You're probably the only person in town who doesn't already know this story, but when I was a senior, I was class president. The student council sponsored a blood drive for all the juniors and seniors, and I was very first in line. I wanted to show everyone it was easy, so simple, nothing to worry about! Instead of following directions and resting while I ate the prescribed cookie, I jumped up and immediately fainted. In the cafeteria. At lunchtime. I didn't break my nose but might as well have. The bruises lasted forever.

Did it make perfect sense that even in his embarrassing high school stories TJ had been doing something good? It really did.

It didn't surprise her that he had been a leader even as a kid. He was easy to trust. Maybe he'd misjudged his own invincibility, but he'd stepped up to do something he believed was important to convince others to do the same.

That made him easy to admire, too.

Her ploy had been successful. Ever since then, they'd been texting back and forth. The conversation wasn't as satisfying as being face-to-face, but Summer was happy to have the connection to TJ.

She hadn't spent a lot of time analyzing that feeling.

Hurricane Agnes had felt like the end of the world when the lights went out and TJ was outside, but it was obviously just a blip to Horizon and anyone who made their lives there.

Would she be able to adjust to these storms so that she knew and trusted they would come, but her life would go on like the day before?

Summer wasn't convinced, but the efficiency of Horizon's recovery operations was impressive.

Today, she was going to get both feet planted in the shelter's business as the emergency fosters returned the dogs and cats and Jewel discovered the new state of her office. Hank and Hattie had bounced in bright and early to make sure all the pens were ready.

As Jewel's pickup truck rolled down the dry driveway, Summer opened the door to the shelter office and smiled at Hank.

He was sorting again, this time from the pile that had gone into the trash can.

"Morning, Dr. Patel..." He stopped and cleared his throat before she could correct him. "Morning, Summer, I thought we might ease Jewel into things with a few smaller piles, instead of one big trash bag."

Hattie leaned one shoulder against the doorway to the workroom and added, "Plus we put food and water out in the kennels, so it's easy to get all the animals settled." Then she lowered her chin and her voice. "Sure am glad you're here. I'm anxious to see Jewel's reaction."

Hank wrinkled his nose in agreement, so Summer decided all three of them were on the same page there. Before she could find the right encouraging words or praise for all their hard work, Jewel burst through the door with what Summer had decided on their first meeting was her normal method of operation.

"Good morning, and I am glad to see your beautiful faces." Jewel flung her arms out to embrace the world. "I've been watching the news as we traveled home, just worried sick. I don't know if you know this, but it's easy to lose track of the real world when you're staying in paradise." Jewel clasped her hands together. "I didn't even know the storm was on the way until it was already over, but you didn't let me down."

Jewel fluttered through the office to hug Hank and Hattie before settling for an awkward shoulder pat for Summer. "I'm back now, and I'm ready to get back to the business of finding all these babies a home, Dr. Patel. I have so much energy. I want to do an adoption event every single week! Soon as we clear our shelter, we can help Charleston, Columbia. I had slowed down, but two weeks away… Whew, I'm raring to go!"

Summer wasn't sure how to respond in the face of so much energy. Holding an event every week seemed really ambitious. Helping other rescues was a big goal, and Summer loved setting goals, so she didn't want to discourage Jewel.

But Hank and Hattie had just been through a storm and evacuation. They were both smiling, but the expressions were more like stoic determination.

They were facing getting all the animals settled back in.

Even though they were clearly dedicated to the shelter and its mission, they needed more help to accomplish anything like Jewel's dream.

And no one else in the room had been on vacation for two weeks. They were running on energy fumes here.

The urge to tell Jewel she needed to get her shelter life in order first was strong, but she knew very well that dousing a person's excitement was a mistake. If they didn't have Summer's contrary personality, they might give up completely.

That enthusiasm fired her own, so she couldn't lose Jewel, either.

Instead of telling her about the mess she had to clean up first, Summer thought fast as she wrapped her arm over Jewel's shoulders.

The move surprised everyone in the room, Summer most of all.

Then she realized what she was about to do would top the gesture, and it was such a new plan, as it had just popped into her mind that moment, that it scared Summer.

But she was going to go ahead with it because it was the right thing to do.

"Jewel, I love it. I love that you have set this goal for the shelter." She squeezed Jewel's shoulders.

"Thank you, Dr. Patel," Jewel said. "I've been coasting along lately. This goal? I've always wanted it but couldn't get there. Dr. Forsyth, he was pretty happy with the status quo, but as I was watching the news and worrying about what the shelter would look like when I made it back home, it was very clear that all we have is today, you know? These animals need us to be going full speed every day."

All we have is today.

Summer blinked as she concentrated on those words for a second.

They were the confirmation she needed.

Whether she settled into the rhythm of Horizon or not was still to be determined, but she knew what she wanted for today.

"Call me Summer, Jewel." She nodded when Jewel's mouth dropped open. "Because we're going to be partners in this goal. I understand what you mean about today, but I want you to think about what we need to do today to get ready for tomorrow."

Jewel frowned. "Well, we'll get all the animals settled and back into the routine first. We're going to need some paperwork, too, because at least one of those emergency fosters is going to adopt a new member of their family."

"Really?" Summer asked. That was a development she never expected.

"Oh, yeah, foster fails are inevitable in situations like this one. I wouldn't be surprised if more than one family can't face returning their fosters today." Jewel pursed her lips. She was clearly the voice of experience at that moment.

"That's great news." Adopting out a cat or dog to someone who had answered the shelter's call for emergency help was a silver lining she hadn't expected.

Hank sniffed loudly. "Don't know if you noticed, Jewel, but we've done some rearranging." He patted the bare wood of the desk. The gleam made Summer think he'd come in early to polish it, too. "I made up some packets with the paperwork we need already. They're stacked on the shelf closest to the door." He pointed, and Summer counted five manila envelopes all ready to go for their next adoptions.

Jewel blinked. "Well, it's not necessary but..." She glanced at Summer first and then Hank. "I like it?"

Hank's shoulders immediately relaxed.

"We had to do some digging to find the list of volunteers. I just kept going. When you have the time, we can review everything and make sure we keep everything important. I've already set up files in these drawers. I threw your cookies away," he said quietly, as if he was trying to lower the volume of Jewel's response in advance.

Summer wasn't sure if she was picking up a little judgment in Hank's message because of her own feelings about the disorder, but his firm lips supported her interpretation.

So did Jewel's immediate reaction. "Everything was on the desk. Easy to reach. My system and the way I do things, *have* done things for more than a decade here, aren't good enough?" she asked.

Summer could hear defensiveness in Jewel's voice. She had been doing the job, and now someone was coming in to tell her that she should do better. Summer understood that response. Under criticism, she often went on defense, too.

But standing here, on the other side, Summer

could see the way through to reaching Jewel so clearly.

"They absolutely have been good enough, Jewel, and you have the successful adoptions to prove it," Summer said as she squeezed the older woman's shoulder. "But what if they only fit this goal, this shelter where it is right now, and not where you want to go with weekly adoptions and assisting other shelters?"

Jewel bit her lip as she considered that.

"You're going to need more help to get there." Summer straightened her shoulders. This was going to be difficult, but she was committed. "I have a proposal. Hank and Hattie will take on part-time paid positions to help with the shelter. We'll have to set up a budget and figure out how many hours make sense because money will be tight in the beginning. Hank will run the office while Hattie works with the volunteers." She closed her eyes before adding, "For three months, hire Hank and Hattie. Ten hours a week each maybe? That will free you up for planning and give you the support you need. You can't get where you want to go on your own, Jewel. They've both proven they have skills to help out."

Jewel tilted her head. "With what money, Dr. Patel?"

Yeah, that was the part that would hurt. This commitment would add to the strain of meeting the business loan payments, but putting the limit on the time frame made it possible for Summer to breathe.

Her forehead was still sweaty as she outlined her plan. "Call me Summer, Jewel. For three months, I'll cover it. I'll cover their salary if Hank and Hattie are in. Hank will make a plan for this office, organization and things to make this a place to welcome visitors." Summer turned a stern glance on Hank. "Improvements, small things, a can of paint? There will be a *small* budget." Because where she was going to find the funds for this was the biggest mystery of all. "During that time, you can work on fund-raising. I saw your list of donors. For this to work out long-term, it's going to take some of that enthusiasm you had when you walked in the door. If you can't see a way forward, maybe we need to rethink your goals."

Everyone watched Jewel evaluate that. When the silence grew uncomfortable, Summer added, "But no matter what, Hank is going to finish organizing this office. The state of that desk gave me hives. I will make a large cash donation to never see a stack of papers like that again."

As they waited for Jewel's response, Summer tried to picture what her own response would be in the same situation. She had a lot of experience fighting to hold her position even after someone had made an excellent argument against it. Spending time around TJ had given her more practice in admitting she was misguided.

Ill-advised.

Not 100 percent right.

Understanding that didn't change her opinion here because she was absolutely correct *here*. Jewel would understand that, or Summer would keep working until she did.

Jewel surveyed the improved office with Hank's neat stacks of files before saying, "All right. Three months isn't much time, and we've got a lot to get done." She clapped her hands. "Hank, in your plans for this new, improved office, I want a big whiteboard here." Her hands framed out a space on the wall that was currently covered with papers thumbtacked haphazardly. The lack of order to the curling yellowing pages meant that Summer had done her best to avoid looking directly at it. "And we're going to need a real computer setup. My laptop is on shaky last legs. Posting our photos to the animal adoption websites is a test of my patience and a higher power."

Summer ignored the hard knot in her stomach as the *cha-ching* of a cash register ran through her mind. The hit to her credit card kept growing.

She glanced at Hank, who handed her a list of things he planned to buy. "This morning, I made a list after I straightened all the leashes by the door." At the top, he'd written "whiteboard" and at the bottom was "laptop" with a question mark. "I'll work on a budget next."

Jewel straightened her shoulders. "And I will get some donations rolling in. May need some creative ideas, since I've always relied on the direct ask and those have been pretty sparse, but I'll figure it out."

Her uncertainty twisted the knot in Summer's stomach. Jewel's enthusiasm was the biggest determining factor to the success of the plan. Shoring that up would be Summer's job.

"I plan to greet Charlene, who just drove up," Hattie said. "Once I get her cats settled in, I'll see if I can't get some volunteers out here to help clean up the play yard. Dogs love sticks, but we don't want Summer here having to fix 'em up when the sticks don't love 'em back." She propped her hands on her hips. "And if the business is handled, I want details on how you and TJ ended up hunkered down together." The twinkle in Hattie's eyes was proof that the woman was teasing her. Hank's alert expression convinced her that she and TJ together had been a topic of conversation between the Browns.

Even Jewel had stopped fussing with the shelves Hank had organized to listen.

"He's every bit the hero you believe. I had an emergency come in, a dog that needed surgery. When TJ found out I couldn't leave, he stayed with me," Summer said.

Hattie's pursed lips were a very restrained reaction in Summer's opinion.

Hank cleared his throat. "Good as gold, every one of them Shepards."

Hattie nodded. "I heard through the grapevine that TJ's in a bit of trouble. Seems he didn't have permission to leave, and the car thing…" She widened her eyes to encompass what a mess it must be. "This might be the biggest scandal in Shepard history." Then she tilted her head to the side. "Or was it the fight with Dr. Patel about her parking ticket in Battery Park?"

That startled a laugh out of Summer. Either way, she was responsible for TJ's fall from perfect Shepard grace. The only question was which incident hit Number One on the list.

Never once in her life had she ever imagined she'd become infamous, even if it was just in Horizon.

"I owe TJ, for sure," Summer finally said. More than anything, she wanted out of this conversation. Talking about TJ was dangerous. She was afraid a goofy smile would surface. Escaping that office seemed to be the only way to prevent that.

Luckily, a lanky woman with a cat carrier in each hand had reached the door.

"Charlene, come on in here. Let's get these beauties settled in," Jewel said as she reached to take one of the carriers.

"Dr. Patel, good to see you in one piece," Charlene said.

Something about hearing the people who had pitched in to save the shelter animals call her "doctor" struck Summer as wrong. It never had bothered her before. In fact, holding on to the respect that came with the title she'd worked hard to earn had been important for most of her career.

But coming to Horizon changed things.

Respect set her apart, and it was becoming obvious that holding herself apart from the community that she'd need every time one of these storms came through would be a disaster. Nothing about being on a first-name basis with Hank or Hattie had changed the way they listened to her.

It had only made them less likely to evaporate when she spoke directly to them.

Overall, that was obviously positive.

They were also becoming the best friends she had in Horizon, so when she needed advice, asking them made sense. "I owe TJ and the Horizon PD a big thanks for keeping me in one piece. Any ideas on how I should give it?"

"Food." Hank didn't hesitate a second. "Everybody appreciates food, Summer."

His answer was basic, but it was solid. He had no doubt he was on the right track.

Then she realized she had the opportunity to kill two birds with one stone.

"What a terrible cliché," Summer muttered and then waved a hand as everyone in the room frowned at her. "Sorry. Thinking out loud. I do that. What if…" She paused to give her brain a minute to work. "We could host a community 'thank-you' with food. I'll invite the police department and Boogie. We'd bring in anyone who fostered this time around and in the past. Previous and future donors…"

Hank pursed his lips. "Sounds like you've got all of Horizon in one way or another, Summer."

Jewel propped her hands on her hips as she paced in a tight circle. "We could use it to beef up our volunteer list and request donations. Present our plans to expand the work we're doing. Always a good thing when you're holding out your hand for money to have something to show for it."

The imaginary price tag for the investments in the shelter had become a broken, spinning dial in Summer's head, but the plan felt right.

"Two questions, then. What kind of food can we do for a group that big?" *That won't bankrupt me?* Summer tacked on silently.

Charlene immediately said, "Frogmore stew."

Summer paused. She'd been expecting something more along the lines of grilled burgers.

"Low-country boil. Much better than a barbecue." Charlene crossed her arms over her chest. "And I've got the experience to make it happen.

The Sandlapper will be your first donor for the new Shoreline Shelter. You cover the cost of the ingredients, and I'll handle everything else, Summer."

She nodded firmly. Summer couldn't come up with any points to argue.

"What's the second question, Summer?" Hank asked. He was prepared to tackle it.

"How soon can we get this done?" she asked. Her mother had taught her the importance of sending thanks. It was good manners, and it had to be done as soon as possible.

Charlene pursed her lips. "Two weeks?"

Jewel visibly gulped, but nodded to agree.

Hank and Hattie exchanged a glance before nodding.

"Okay," Summer said as she did her best to catch her breath. "We're going to need some help with the fund-raising piece, but I know who to call."

She left the others to get on with the business of settling Charlene's cats in and headed back to her apartment. On the way, she pulled out her phone and hit the first number on her list of Favorites.

"It's about time you called your mother, Summer," her mother answered, skipping over the preferred "hello" completely. "I told your father if I didn't get more than one-sentence texts today, I was not taking 'no' for an answer. You will just wake up one day, and there I'll be, in living color on your doorstep."

Summer smiled as she climbed the outside stairs to her apartment. "Okay, and could you bring Dad when you come?"

Silence was her answer.

Russell Crow decided to remind her that he'd maintained his address under the outside stairs, but he was content with aggressive clucking. His crows had not resumed full strength yet.

"I was hoping you could help me with a fund raiser. For the shelter." Summer leaned her hip against the railing and glanced out over the lawn and the altered tree line outlining her home. "I'm saying thank you to everyone who helped me through this storm, and I want it to be a success. I need your help."

Inviting her parents to help was hard, but the shelter and reaching out to Horizon was important.

Her mother sniffed before saying, "You're in luck. I have just enough time for whatever it is you need, and your father owes me a favor. Tell me more."

Summer grinned.

She wasn't fully comfortable with her grand plan yet, because she was going to be trying a whole lot of new things and risking the failure that came along with it, but for the first time in a long time, confidence was stepping up. Maybe stubbornness could take a break.

Would TJ be pleasantly surprised?

It didn't escape Summer that he was the first

person on her mind or that his reaction was most important. She'd missed him since he'd waved from the front seat of the tow truck. Fixing that was the next thing on her to-do list.

CHAPTER FIFTEEN

TJ TRIED NOT to stare too hard at the large clock that hung on the wall of the conference room, but if he didn't make it out of there soon…

His phone vibrated to signal a text. After the long day, TJ was feeling reckless enough to check it while the chief was seated at the end of the conference table. He hoped it was from Summer. They'd been sharing mildly incriminating tidbits of their history over text, so in addition to the marching band video, he knew that she'd been on her high school Quiz Bowl team, but got only one answer correct at the state competition. Even then, as a part of a team, Summer had struggled with not carrying her own weight. To TJ, only scoring one wasn't so embarrassing, but the fact that it was about *High School Musical* had been the sticking point. Not math, science, literature… Zac Efron had been her single point on the board.

Why he found that adorable was another sign that he'd already fallen. Hard.

Summer was taking their exchanges seriously, and she wasn't holding back.

His father cleared his throat before he could read the message.

"Let's break down Command today before we leave," his father said, "because we can continue to monitor cleanup efforts under normal business processes." He glanced at TJ over his glasses. "There's no hard and fast rule about how long you need to have Command oversight with assigned leadership roles for special situations like a hurricane. The more you do, the easier it will be to determine how the external communications flow over the course of the event and to adjust case by case."

Ever since TJ had made it back to the station house, riding shotgun with Mike Stillwell from 24-Tow and his squad car on the back, his father had been doling out bits and pieces like this. The "notes for the future" came so often that TJ decided his father was trying to make up for lost time.

Not even ditching his assigned post and wrecking his patrol vehicle had diverted his father's intention to seat TJ behind the chief's desk. If anything, the chief was pushing harder.

And after three days of one-on-one instruction, TJ was more convinced his plan wasn't right for TJ.

He was also sure that convincing his father that it wouldn't work was going to be hard.

As hard as that falling tree crushing TJ's windshield and hood.

But repairing the crash with his father would take more than the two weeks the body shop had estimated to get his car back on the road.

Two solid weeks of desk duty.

His father hadn't even had to come up with a punishment for bucking his orders because that much time staring at a laptop definitely counted.

TJ jotted down a note about closing up Command to wrap up a special event. "We'll clear the conference room. I've read through the files you pulled on other storms, like Helene and Ian. Do you want me to work on a preliminary draft of the final report?" After all, he was going to have plenty of time at a desk to get it done.

His father didn't smile at the offer. The chief didn't smile often on the job, but it was easy to read the approval in his eyes. "Absolutely. We can work on the final together."

Before TJ could figure out how to open the door to the discussion of what might happen if he didn't step into the chief's shoes, someone rapped loudly on the solid wood door of the conference room.

"Both of the Shepards I wanted to see, and you're gathered together in this cozy conference room. What are the odds?" asked Red Kelly from the doorway. The director of the Coast Guard's Charleston K9 unit grinned, his broad form filling the space between the doorjambs completely. He was dressed in the Coast Guard's navy blues.

"Well, now, Kelly, I haven't seen you in months. What brings you to my neck of the woods?" his father asked as they shook hands.

As Red stretched across the conference room table to shake TJ's hand, he said, "Your mayor called in a favor, wanted a security response review of the Horizon Shipyard. I was on the team scheduled for the inspection. Since the storm damage was minimal there, we decided to go forward."

The chief propped his hands on his hips. "Yeah, Rainey mentioned that. She's been here working through the storm until today."

On the first day of recovery after the storm, Rainey and the chief had been busy fielding calls for assistance and requests for information. When they were busy, they got along well enough.

It was just when his father and Rainey had too much time on their hands that the air in the conference room grew thin.

TJ crossed his arms over his chest as he realized that his father had Red to thank for getting Rainey out of Command. He would wait until later to point that out. It wasn't that his father didn't like Rainey. He just didn't want the mayor in his business, no matter who that mayor might be.

Neither of them had addressed the subject of the chief's retirement.

"TJ and I talked in Columbia about some ways

he might plug in with the Canine Officers Association." Kelly raised his eyebrow at TJ.

"Oh?" his father drawled.

They had. Red had invited him to lunch to discuss the need for a representative for the eastern region. He'd been the one to outline all of TJ's qualifications for the office.

TJ had not yet had a chance to tell his father about any of it.

Before TJ could change the direction of the conversation, their radios beeped. "Chief, this is Rodriguez."

The chief pressed the buttons on his shoulder mic. "Go ahead, Rodriguez."

"Mayor Blackwell has an interview scheduled at the shipyard, a last-minute opportunity at the Coast Guard's invitation," Rodriguez said. "The news story is about plans there to beef up security in advance of the expanded repair contract. The Coast Guard has a representative on hand. I can represent the HPD as a visual presence, but I thought you might want to be present for the optics. Over."

"Optics. My favorite," his father muttered before speaking into the mic. "Be there in fifteen. Over and out."

"The chief's job is never done," Red said before clapping the chief on the back. "I ran into Emery last week. Your daughter is collecting commendations like I'm picking up gray hairs."

Red ran a hand through hair that was more silver than red these days. "Even over on my side of the Guard, we hear tales of her bravery. When I was younger, those high-speed, high-risk, high-reward sea boarding and interdiction maneuvers excited me, but canine security and narcotic inspection is way more my speed." Red shook his head. "You descend from a helicopter or board a suspicious vessel during rough seas once, and you never forget it. Emery's at a whole different level."

TJ nodded as he watched his father straighten his shoulders proudly. Emery was absolutely impressive enough that people who didn't even work with her heard stories about her. She'd taken up law enforcement but had given it a military twist by joining the Coast Guard.

If she hadn't, there would be no question who would step into Tom Shepard's shoes. If Emery had joined the Horizon PD, his father would have been happy to retire and leave the department in her capable hands.

For that matter, TJ would, too. Could he convince her to take the job?

"TJ, here..." Kelly shook his finger. "He's going places, too."

Was this an effort to make him feel better about his performance or...?

The chief immediately nodded. "He is. He's going to be chief of police." There was also no doubt on his father's face.

Kelly pursed his lips. "I could see that, but I'm kinda hoping to convince him to run for office of COA first. Sorta expected to have the paperwork in my email already."

TJ waited for his father to respond to that, but he was studying TJ's face, looking for clues to flesh out this story. At that moment, TJ didn't have any to give him.

"Well, Shepard here decided to change his assignment during the hurricane, so he was out of pocket for a minute. I expect he's been catching up since." The chief met TJ's stare and then patted Red on the back. "Gotta head out to make some 'optics' happen, Kelly. Don't be a stranger."

TJ waited for his father to return to his office before saying, "I'm still planning to run. I just..." He shrugged. "The storm did shake things up."

"What a difference a few days make, huh?" Kelly asked as he braced one shoulder against the wall. "Last I knew, you were pleased to tell anyone how much working with your K9 partner meant to the job. Talking about stepping up to chief of police is kind of a big deal. We didn't talk about that in Columbia. It will change things, you know."

"Yeah, it wasn't on my radar in Columbia. To me, the chief's retirement was in the distant future, because who can fill his shoes?" TJ didn't want to say he couldn't do it, but he wasn't certain that he could even if he wanted to. "Emery? Sure, but she's off doing superhero stuff."

Kelly's "hmm" caught his attention. "That sister of yours is something, to be sure, but Chief Tom Shepard is no fool. He sees you in the role, so there's no doubt in my mind that you're equal to the job. What does the mayor think? Isn't she the one who makes the decision to hire or fire around here?"

TJ nodded. "She does."

But if his father ran a campaign to get TJ appointed his successor, there was no way Rainey would go against him. In Horizon, it could be political suicide to appear to be facing off against Tom Shepard. As savvy as Rainey was and as many connections as she might have to negotiate for her own goals, winning elections was the only way to remain in her office upstairs.

He was no politician, but he had a hunch that publicly opposing a Shepard here in town would lead to defeat.

TJ was also aware of how that would sound if he said it aloud to an outsider.

Red Kelly might not have as much experience reading TJ as the chief did, but he wasn't having any trouble figuring out this situation. He tilted his head to the side. "I'd shake your hand and walk away so I could get to work on finding someone else to run for the Eastern Division's representative, but you aren't sounding like a man campaigning for a promotion." Red pointed at Lucy, who was in her spot next to the conference table, bored as she had been for three days straight at this point. "Have you considered what will happen to your partner should you step up to chief?"

Lucy straightened, aware that she was the topic of conversation. The way her ears perked up and her eyes locked on TJ's face indicated she was ready for an order, any order. He understood the need to get out of that conference room. TJ ran his hand over her back as he considered Red's words. "What do you mean?"

"Well," Red said with a loud sigh, "your K9 officer was provided to this police department through a grant from the South Carolina Canine Officers Association. Funds were raised to pay for her training and yours as her handler, and a committee of officers reviewed all the applications to choose you and Horizon for that opportunity."

TJ nodded. All true. He'd worked hard, too.

"If you accept a promotion into the chief's seat, how much time will your partner, this really expensive police equipment issued to Horizon for the purpose of improving public safety, spend doing the job she was trained for?" Red braced his hands against the chair in front of him. "When you're behind the desk here, who will be working with Lucy? She can't type reports or answer your phone, Shepard."

The word "equipment" stuck in TJ's throat immediately.

He almost missed the rest of what Red said because of it.

The memory of Summer saying police dogs had names like Bullet because they were weapons, not dogs, surfaced, along with the way he'd set her straight about his partner being his family.

Some officers viewed the dogs almost the same as their sidearms.

The best way to change that attitude and increase the protections for other dogs like Lucy was through leadership in the COA. The Ethics Committee was his target for that very reason. As a representative for his region, he could choose where he would serve.

To make this change, he'd have to change minds. Some of them would probably be just as difficult to work around as Summer, and he'd struggled with that.

But he'd also learned an important lesson from her. He knew it was the right thing to do, even if it would be hard. She had shown him what it looked like to take big chances to do what was right for herself.

The way to do that here was easy enough to picture.

He could win the COA election.

A lot of that certainty was based on the Shepard name and connections.

His father's support would move mountains in

an election involving members of South Carolina's law enforcement community.

He would force Emery to leave whatever risky operation she was on long enough to throw her weight behind him, too.

Bee was the kind of person who collected friends wherever she went, so she had some strings to pull.

Even Rainey, whose family connection had been diluted over generations but not completely erased, could probably be convinced to make some phone calls for him.

When he'd met with Red Kelly in Columbia, he had laid out a very simple road to a leadership position.

But TJ hadn't spent much time considering the impact of winning on anyone but himself.

Even after his father had started his training operation for the future chief, TJ's main worry had been about living through disappointing his father.

But Lucy's role here was even more uncertain. Who would become her partner? What would that officer think about her role?

And how many other K9 officers might be affected if TJ didn't step up right now?

If he was able to add a leadership role in COA, not much would change for Lucy. They would patrol in Horizon and work together to make sure other K9 officers and handlers could do so safely and successfully throughout South Carolina.

The chief of police responded to emergency events, but he didn't patrol Battery Park or answer traffic stops. When he worked parades, he was there for "optics" instead of actual crowd safety. He navigated town politics and ironed out public relations issues such as the new veterinarian in town calling for improved parking signage and outreach training for the police department's officers.

Headaches and paperwork, basically.

Lucy wasn't trained for any of that, and she definitely didn't deserve it. Since they weren't expected to answer any calls today, she was not wearing her bulletproof vest or badge, but there was no way to hide that Lucy was ready to go to work.

"I guess Horizon could identify another officer for training and send him or her back through the handler course. Lucy would be off the job for twelve weeks or so." Kelly crossed his arms over his chest. "Anybody else on the squad you think would be a good K9 handler?" He huffed out a breath. "That's a very police chief–like decision, choosing the person to follow behind you."

TJ stared out over the squad room as he evaluated the officers that filled the room during the morning brief. Finding someone to take his place as Lucy's partner would be easy enough.

Except for the crushing pain in his chest that might actually destroy him at letting Lucy go.

Yeah, that would be a problem in his day-to-day life.

Then there was the certainty that he would be treating Lucy a lot like Summer had suggested in the very beginning. He'd told Summer that Lucy was his family, not a weapon.

He'd made a dramatic speech about what Lucy meant to him and to his job. He could remember her grudging appreciation at the time. If he made the decision to become chief and was okay with giving Lucy to another officer, would that make him a liar?

Even if it didn't, Summer would see that he was compromising on this career that he'd built and loved. For what? It was easy to remember how she'd talked about her ex's opinion about her career. If he had dreamed of stepping up to chief, she might understand the decisions that had to follow for him to have that dream.

But Summer would certainly get making the decision to stick with what he loved most even if no one else did.

She would understand that Lucy changed everything.

It was impossible to believe she'd respect him ending up as chief because he'd been too unwilling to take a stand.

"No easy decisions." Kelly sighed. "Guess you've got some things to think through. Deadline to toss your hat in the election ring is in three weeks. I'll check back before then if I haven't heard from you."

He waited for TJ to agree and raised his hand in a wave. "Always nice to make it down to Horizon."

TJ dropped his head into his hands as he considered what to do next.

Talk to his father?

And say what…? *I don't want your job. Thanks but no thanks.*

Imagining his father's reaction to that made him desperate for a distraction, and he remembered the text.

Instead of Summer, Emery had texted, I hear you're warming the bench for a couple of weeks. She'd added the green-faced vomiting emoji to make sure he understood exactly how she felt about that.

"So I'm guessing Emery is also a 'no' on the job," he murmured as he typed. Turns out, tree beat squad car in the ultimate game of rock, paper, scissors. That was the way they'd always determined who got to do things first: take a shower in the cramped Shepard house, choose a TV show for the family TV, pick any chore other than folding laundry.

He and Emery both had fought to get laundry duty.

Bee and Lila had generally gotten stuck with the leftovers.

And Daniel, their mother's son from her first

marriage, had always been too cool to squabble over inconsequential things like who took the trash out. He had just done it, no argument needed. That discipline suited him and his career in the Marines well.

Instead of waiting for her to answer, he pushed the button to call her.

And he was relieved when she answered. "Bold move, ditching Command and your assignment."

TJ sighed. "Who told you?"

"Bee," Emery said with a laugh, "and Lila. They're concerned about you."

He wanted to close his eyes, but it wouldn't change anything.

"Apparently, they think you aren't interested in being the chief of police." She grunted and there was a loud clang. "Sorry, we're about to head out. Just packing up the boat now."

"I don't guess you have a desire to return to Horizon to take over the police department?" he asked, even as he tried to imagine her in the chief's office and the picture wouldn't come.

Her answer was immediate. Firm.

"No. Not for me." She cleared her throat. "I could see you in the chair, TJ, but that doesn't mean it fits you, either. We both like action, getting out to do the work. I guess I'm just saying I understand your hesitation here."

After hearing his father and Red Kelly praise

Emery so highly, her claim that the two of them were alike felt good.

"How do I decide? If I go for it and hate it, how do I get out? And if I don't go for it, tell him to find someone else..." TJ let the thought trail off. It hurt to consider.

"Yeah, it's tough. That's why you've let this go on and on and on," Emery said dramatically, a smile in her voice. "I'm teasing. I think you have to picture your life, what you want for it. You could keep your job now or move somewhere bigger to try different police work or step up to take charge of Horizon. What will make you happy? If that doesn't include the corner office in the Horizon PD, you know your answer."

Since the image that formed immediately had nothing to do with his father's job and more to do with a cozy nest of blankets and pillows and candles and Summer Patel and Lucy beside him, TJ was pretty sure he knew his answer.

"I was thinking of joining the Coast Guard. You could show me the ropes, right?" TJ asked, grinning at the way she sucked in a breath.

"TJ, no. You hate boats. You hate heights. Look for something closer to the ground, okay?" Emery laughed.

"My older and wiser sister with the good points for consideration," TJ said. "If I decide I want to run for an office of the Canine Officers Association, can I count on your endorsement and campaign support?"

She was the first one he'd said it aloud to.

He was anxious for her answer.

"Oh, now..." Emery stopped. "That is a game changer. That is a position that has TJ Shepard's name all over it."

TJ tipped his head down at the relief that settled when he heard her approval.

"You can count on me, TJ," Emery said as some kind of loud engine revved up in the background. "Find the way to go after what will make you happy. I'll help out any way I can."

The noise made it hard to hear, so he said, "Thank you, Emery. Love you! Be safe!"

Whatever she said was lost, but she'd ended the call. TJ turned to stare at Lucy.

Before he could get the words out, she stood.

"Reading my mind, are you, Officer Shepard?" TJ asked. "How about a foot patrol around Battery Park before we pack up Command? The report can wait until tomorrow."

CHAPTER SIXTEEN

AFTER A SOLID day of working with Jewel, Hank, Hattie and her mother via video calls on their plans for the thank-you-slash-fund-raising event, Summer was ready to get away from Shoreline Shelter for a minute or two.

They had made so much progress. Hank had taken his assignment and run with it. The walls were cleared and ready for a fresh coat of paint. The whiteboard had already been pressed into service as a very visible to-do list of items, each with a person assigned and a deadline. Through the process, she'd learned that Hank had retired from a long career as a successful construction project manager. He was putting all of that experience to work, and Summer was honestly most excited about the two filing cabinets he'd purchased secondhand from Hattie's favorite Charleston thrift store. There was so much work to do, but he'd seemed energized by it.

And it didn't hurt that he was coming in under the budget she'd agreed to.

Hattie had completed readmitting all but three of the rescues they'd sent out to emergency fosters. Two of them were living their best lives in their new homes after the foster fails Jewel predicted came true.

That left Lila Shepard and Duke the Great Dane.

Ever since the storm, Lila had been promising to bring the dog back to the shelter.

And every day, something came up.

Since Summer needed to speak to Lila anyway, to apologize for worrying her the day of the storm, she'd volunteered to track her down. Jewel had handed her one of the manila envelopes with the adoption paperwork. "Tell Lila to drop this back by when she has it finished." Her confidence that Duke was also already living his best life showed in the curl of her lips.

So, on Friday morning, Summer had a long list of things to accomplish in Horizon, and they all involved a Shepard in some form.

Making her apology to Lila seemed to be the easiest item to tackle first, so she parked on the street along Battery Park, not too far from the town hall and the spot of her original confrontation with TJ. Parking was challenging on the other side of the park, the original site of the town founded by Captain Emory Shepard.

Apparently.

She hadn't known that last part until Hank and Hattie's genealogy lesson.

Since she'd moved to Horizon, she had enjoyed window shopping along the narrow cobblestone streets that marked Horizon's oldest buildings. They ranged for a four-block square around the park. Lila's real estate office was in one of the two-story buildings that had originally housed Horizon's well-to-do before the Civil War.

Summer admired the heavy restored oak door as she stepped inside. The light tinkle of bells hung over the door announced her arrival, but there wasn't much need. Duke the Great Dane was stretched out in front of a beautiful antique desk, and he woofed a greeting while his tail beat solidly against the desk leg.

It sounded like someone was knocking.

Lila popped her head around the corner and smiled brightly. "Dr. Patel!" Then her face fell. "Oh, have you come to collect Duke? There was no need to do that. I was bringing him in today."

Summer pointed at the carved wood armchair in front of the desk. "Is it okay to sit here? I don't know my antiques."

Lila wrinkled her nose. "You don't know my budget, either. Sit away. That is a reproduction of a reproduction, but I like the lion heads on the arms." Then she waved her hand. "It fit the vibe, but if I told you how much it cost, you would start looking too closely at the rest of the furnishings. I go for atmosphere, the way I feel, more than anyone else's rules. This drives my mother crazy." Lila grinned. "That is a bonus."

Summer grinned as she bent down to greet Duke. He was perched on what might be the biggest dog bed Summer had ever seen. It was royal purple to match Duke's new collar, and Summer had a hunch that she and Duke both knew he was home even if Lila was still adjusting to the idea. "Is this a dog bed or a child's mattress?"

"A deluxe pillow-top mattress might have cost less," Lila said as she crossed her arms and leaned against her desk. Her casual pose made Summer think the desk was an inexpensive reproduction, too. "But he's had a hard life, and I wanted the best for Duke. I was planning to bring it to the shelter, too. For his next home."

"Right," Summer drawled as she pulled the paperwork from her purse and slid it onto the desk next to Lila's hip. "Well, if you change your mind and decide Duke is home already, fill this out. Jewel has waived the adoption fees for all of the emergency fosters who helped us out on such short notice, so you'll just need to drop this by the shelter." Summer crossed her legs. "Or I can wait and take it back for you. I'm not in a big hurry."

Lila's lips were twitching as she fought a smile, but she lost the battle quickly. "So at least I'm not alone. There were others who couldn't make themselves return to the shelter."

Summer tilted her head to the side. "Well, they

returned, sure, but they had already made up their minds. They just came back to finish the necessary paperwork. You win for being the one who fought it the longest." She bent down to scratch Duke's ears. "I admire your willpower. He's a handsome gentleman."

"Distinguished," Lila agreed with a sniff. "Duke Shepard. It has a nice ring to it."

Summer nodded. "And his surroundings, the furnishings, this bed…they all fit a Duke perfectly. I'd say it was meant to be."

Lila sighed. "I've been telling myself to do the smart thing, you know? I do not need a dog. I am running all the time, listing and showing and selling and just generally living. He might have a better option show up to the shelter tomorrow."

They both watched Duke stretch his long legs. He did not appear to be a dog worried about what he might be missing out on.

Lila picked up the envelope. "I'll just fill this out right now."

"Good choice," Summer said with a grin, "but that's not the main reason I'm here. I wanted to apologize for worrying you when the storm hit."

"You had an emergency." Lila waved her hand as she pulled a bright pink pen out of a desk drawer. "I get it. I'm just glad everything worked out." Then she leaned forward to rest her chin on her hand. "And you and TJ…" She waggled her eyebrows.

Summer shook her head with a laugh. Maybe she hadn't missed out by being an only child after all.

"I don't know how I'll ever repay him," Summer said, "but we want to have a thank-you for the community next weekend at the shelter. We'll have a low-country boil from the Sandlapper. I hope you'll come."

"Wouldn't miss it," Lila said as she filled out the forms in front of her. "But you and TJ…" She made the "continue" motion with one hand before focusing on the forms again.

Summer sighed. "It's not so much that I won't answer that, but that I don't have an answer, I guess. We…"

Lila raised an eyebrow as she dug in her desk drawer to pull out a checkbook.

"I was so happy to see him. I don't know how I would have made it through that storm all by myself." Summer studied Lila's face, anxious for any clues about what TJ might have relayed to prompt this question. "Did he tell you about the kiss?"

A loud rip accompanied Lila's hoot as she pulled the check out of the checkbook. "A kiss! There was a kiss?" Lila paper-clipped the check to her finished paperwork and slid it all back in the envelope. "Forget the waived fees. We'll call this a donation to the shelter. I love this for TJ. Last I saw my big brother, he was aging by the minute in the poky police department conference room. A kiss would liven him up!"

Summer realized she'd made an error. If she understood siblings, TJ would be hearing about this from Lila over and over. It would also spread to the other Shepards quickly.

And in a town the size of Horizon, it was easy to guess the kiss would be common knowledge by next week.

Begging Lila to keep it a secret was an option.

Summer decided in the next heartbeat that she didn't want it to be a secret.

"I guess your reaction means you aren't holding any grudges," Summer drawled.

"Against you?" Lila asked with a shocked expression. "No way."

Relieved, Summer relaxed in her seat. "With the way I squared off against TJ and then putting him in danger..." She shrugged. It was good to know there was at least one potential Shepard ally.

Lila waved a hand. "Anyone who can keep TJ in line has my approval, Dr. Patel."

Summer realized that whatever happened with TJ and the rest of the Shepards, she liked Lila a lot. "Please, call me Summer." As she stood, she added, "Bee's the next on my list to make amends. Got any ideas?"

Lila narrowed her eyes. "Iced latte?"

Confused, Summer asked, "Are you offering or...?"

"Nope, I'm meeting Bee at the Daybreak Diner, down on the pier," Lila said as she pointed generally east, "for a coffee break. She drinks iced lattes. That might be an ice breaker." She winked to make sure Summer picked up on the pun. "She's dragging the mayor out of her office, but Rainey's a good person to have in your back pocket, should you need anything in Horizon. Come with me."

In the past, Summer would have invented a reasonable excuse to avoid inserting herself into a group like this, friends who had their own inside jokes. It was never easy to get on the inside.

But something about Lila and today felt different.

"I'd love to." Summer smiled as Lila clapped.

After Lila attached a kingly purple leash to Duke's collar, she led Summer out and locked her office door. The walk to the pier was short, but it was sweet to see the way Lila deferred to Duke's pace. When they made it inside, two women were standing at the counter. The one in the police uniform had to be Bee Shepard. The family resemblance between TJ and his sisters was strong. Rainey Blackwell stood next to her, wearing a pantsuit Summer's mother would hang in her own closet if she could and four-inch heels.

"I brought Summer," Lila said as she waved at the woman behind the counter to order. "And I'll have my usual, Belinda. She's going to tell us about a kiss."

Summer felt her cheeks heat as Bee, Rainey, Belinda and at least four other people in the diner snapped to attention.

"Let's sit outside," Lila said as she took the cup Belinda slid across the counter. "Summer's buying this round."

Rainey immediately followed Lila out onto the wood deck that lined the back of the diner.

Bee's lips were twitching as she studied Summer's face. "My little sister is very generous. Unfortunately, that includes with other people's time and money, Dr. Patel."

"Please, call me Summer," Summer said. "To be fair, I did want to make a better impression on you. I would be happy to buy your coffee."

Bee waited for her to finish paying and motioned her toward the deck. "I appreciate the chance to get to know you better, Summer. I can be a little tough where my family is concerned, but there are no hard feelings. Everything worked out for the best." She paused. "Especially if you're kissing my brother."

Summer knew she had miscalculated by telling Lila, but how big a mistake it was became much clearer when she saw the way all three women immediately settled in, chins on hand, to wait for details.

A tug at the neck of her T-shirt did very little to eliminate the heat rising.

"We kissed. It was good," Summer said.

All three women inched closer.

"I would like to do it again." Summer sipped her iced coffee as the other three women exchanged high fives.

She glanced around the deck and was relieved to see there was no audience for the celebration.

Bee settled first and squeezed Summer's arm. "We're just happy for TJ. We may poke at him as little sisters are required by law to do, but he's got a good heart."

Lila nodded. "And he's pretty good at doing what he should do, but not always great about making himself really happy."

Summer was silent as she considered that.

Rainey leaned forward as if she was about to share a secret. "Saintly Shepards. That's what the haters call TJ and his family. On the one hand, I get it. They are obnoxiously good in many ways, but…" She shrugged. "They grow on you."

Bee cut her eyes at Rainey. "Rainey is a Shepard from way, way back. Don't buy her act."

"One of us, one of us," Lila said as she patted a hand on the table.

"I am," Rainey said with a hand pressed to her chest, "but I also know that, outside of Horizon, being a Shepard means a little less."

"But not nothing," Bee said in a singsong. "Especially in law enforcement circles."

Rainey's shoulder slumped. "Too true. Having a Shepard running the police department has been good for me, but retirement has always been on the horizon. I just wish your father..." She inhaled slowly before shaking her head. "Nope, we aren't doing that."

Bee and Lila didn't ask any questions, so Summer followed their leads.

But she really wanted to ask questions!

"TJ will be a fine chief of police," Rainey finally said with a firm nod of her head.

Lila and Bee remained silent.

"Even if I know someone who could take the job and run with it if he wasn't so stubborn," Rainey added before slumping in her seat. Summer saw Bee and Lila exchange a glance, but neither of them said anything.

As she watched the water in the bay rolling in choppy waves, she replayed her conversations with TJ about his job. If he had his sights set on his father's job, would he have been so quick to leave his assignment?

Any excitement he'd displayed about the job itself had all been related to Lucy and working with her. He'd mentioned how being stuck at a desk exhausted him.

Would he allow himself to be pushed into a job he never wanted?

She immediately hated the thought, but it was hard to dismiss. Family was important to TJ and all the Shepards. So was leading, doing the right thing for Horizon.

Would he sacrifice what he loved to do for that? How could she look at him the same way if he did?

"Have you talked with TJ about whether he wants the job?" Summer asked softly, aware that she was gambling with her newfound friendship with Bee and Lila. They knew TJ and their father better than Summer did. Surely if this plan to promote TJ was bad, they would say that.

"Hmm," Rainey said slowly, her eyes narrowed as she studied Bee and Lila.

Neither of the women met her stare.

"You always dress like you're ready for your front-cover photo shoot," Bee said in an obvious attempt at changing the subject, "but this outfit? It's on a whole different level. What's the occasion, Rainey?"

The mayor heaved a sigh. "Meeting with the chief. I set it up before the storm when I heard the rumors that he'd added a date to his retirement plans. Then I expected to go along with whatever he suggested. It's kind of the Horizon way, but now..."

Rainey's eyes met Summer's, and the urge to tell her to give TJ a way out was so strong. She might understand TJ's total inability to let her make her own mistakes during the run up to the storm better.

Summer decided it was time to go. Living to strengthen this friendship another day seemed prudent. "Does the chief have a preferred drink? I'm going to stop by the police department and invite everyone to the shelter's low-country boil next Saturday. Rainey, I hope you'll come."

She smiled brightly. "Wouldn't miss it, and I love to see you jumping into the community, Summer."

"He likes black coffee. That's it." Lila pointed in the window. "But if you pick up a piece of Belinda's coconut cream pie, he'll agree to pretty much anything."

After Summer bought a piece of pie and a cookie that Belinda threw in the bag with it because it was "TJ's favorite," she walked over to town hall. She asked the officer at the front desk if she could see either one of the Shepards, and he said, "Let me check, Dr. Patel."

Since they'd never been introduced, Summer had a bad feeling her reputation had preceded her, and it wasn't a positive review. Could she replace "Dr. Patel" with "Summer" and rehabilitate her image? Before she could test the theory, Chief Shepard walked into the lobby.

"Dr. Patel," he said and offered her his hand to shake.

So, no time like the present... "Please call me Summer, Chief." Then she held out the bag. "I was over at the Daybreak Diner. I thought you might like their coconut cream pie."

He narrowed his eyes, but did not hesitate to accept her offering. "You have good sources, I see. If I'm ever caught in a trap, there will be a slice of this at the center."

His minimal smile was warm, so Summer's confidence grew. "I owe a big thank-you to the police department, Chief."

He peered at her over the top of his glasses. "We appreciate that, but it's part of the job. No thanks required."

Summer could see TJ in his father's face and hear him in the words.

It was clear that Chief Tom Shepard meant every word. That was why his kids, his boss, Hank and Hattie trusted him.

Whoever stepped into his job would have big shoes to fill. Summer didn't doubt that TJ was made from the same mold, even if that didn't mean he had the same goals.

She also immediately understood how hard it would be to disappoint him.

"We're having a low-country boil at the shelter for everyone who helped out during the storm. I hope you'll consider coming and include everyone here in the invitation."

The chief pursed his lips. "Food is definitely the way to our hearts, Summer."

Hearing her name increased Summer's confidence.

"I hope I didn't get TJ in too much trouble. He really did everything he could to help in advance of the storm." She studied his impassive face. "I didn't know how much I didn't know until he was there, but I wasn't open to his constructive criticism before the storm. Having him there…" She sighed. "It made all the difference."

"TJ actually has the day off. I believe he and Lucy are probably jogging at the park," the chief said. "Any trouble he's in was of his own choosing." He raised a shoulder. "And very bad luck, with the car. He may wish he'd had more experience with this storm when hurricane season is in full swing and he's in the hot seat, but TJ's a good officer. He'll be fine."

It might be hard to disappoint Chief Shepard, but Summer would do it. In TJ's spot, she would have already explained that she loved what she was doing and had no plans to give it up.

She'd just say it and let the chips fall.

Or move hours away even.

Obviously, TJ hadn't done that.

It was simple. She could do it for him right now. One sentence, maybe two, to rip the bandage off and move on to getting things patched up.

But she'd set anyone straight who tried to interfere in her life that way, so she smiled brightly. "No one knows how committed TJ is to serving Horizon better than I do. Our first meeting will be recorded in epic poems, and all of that over a parking ticket. TJ won't easily give up on what he believes in." There, that was as close as she was going to get to telling the chief to back off. "I hope to see you at the shelter next weekend, Chief." She waved quickly and hurried out of town hall.

As she walked back through the park, she said, "It wasn't easy, but you managed not to interfere. That was the right thing, Summer."

Before she had a chance to answer herself, she spotted TJ and Lucy running near the wall that marked the boundary of Battery Park. On one side, there were ancient oaks creating a shady canopy over the brick walkways that circled a statue in the center of the park. She stopped to read the plaque commemorating Captain Emory Shepard, Revolutionary War hero and founder of Horizon. The town was founded in 1782 and originally called Liberty's Horizon after the ship Shepard commanded during the war and after.

"The next time I see Hank and Hattie, I need to drop this in conversation to show them I'm learning," Summer murmured.

She saw that TJ and Lucy had claimed a bench near the point of the park. It had a nice view of the choppy waters in the bay. As she crossed the park to meet them, she passed the playground that had been absolutely swarming with kids on her first visit. Today she could see it held a replica of a boat, one that might have sailed the high seas during the Revolutionary War. "Liberty's Horizon" was painted on the side. There were ropes to climb, a tall mast with stairs leading up to a small observation deck, planks to walk and portholes along both sides. It had to be a kid's dream.

Clearly, Captain Emory Shepard was still a big deal.

That kind of family history told her something about Chief Tom Shepard and his kids.

Family mattered to them.

So did tradition.

Unless something snapped TJ out of this, he was going to take his father's job. It was hard to imagine any other outcome. She couldn't understand giving up his own plans, no matter how close he was to his father.

That would be a mistake.

It would also change how she saw him.

Maybe she should have done more to help him get this decision right.

Then she realized she no longer had the cookie that Belinda had included for TJ.

Summer sighed as she neared the bench, but her regret floated away when a sweaty TJ Shepard grinned up at her.

The fact that Lucy was also grinning…

Well, it was honestly too much for Summer's heart to handle. It lurched and the world tilted, so she had to plop down next to TJ.

Staying out of Shepard business was the right decision, even if Summer itched to pull the right levers here. She wanted to tell him what to do, but she had to let him work it out.

His decision mattered too much for his life and the man she wanted him to be to do anything else.

CHAPTER SEVENTEEN

TJ HAD PLANNED to finish his run with enough time to drive out to the animal clinic to see Summer. It had been too long since he'd spent any time with her. When she appeared next to his bench, his heart had actually sped up. The songs and movies said it happened, but he'd never experienced it until Summer.

Having her next to him on the bench was sweet.

Even if she'd landed there with a thump.

"You okay?" he asked before taking her hand in his. "I was thinking about you and here you are. I'm happy to see you."

Summer licked her lips before nodding. "I'm really happy to see you and Lucy, but I had a sweet treat for you. I left it with your father."

An alarm sounded in his head before he shut it off. Had this been a chance meeting? Unless the chief had some public event TJ didn't know about, he was almost certainly seated at his desk. If that was true, Summer had gone looking to speak with him.

About what?

TJ leaned back. “Please explain.”

Their conversation where she’d insisted that TJ tell his father how he felt without worrying about the fallout had been in the back of his mind.

Surely Summer wouldn’t do the one thing that she hated more than anything.

Right?

“Now that Jewel is back, we’re making plans to hold a big low-country boil to show our appreciation to the volunteers who helped us out during the storm. You and the Horizon PD are a big part of that, so I wanted to personally invite the chief. I asked him to spread the word to the rest of the police department. I asked Bee, too. And Lila. And the mayor.” Summer crossed her legs as if she was really proud of herself. “It was a whole apology tour. I started with Lila, because I should have let her know I couldn’t leave the clinic before the storm hit. She invited me to grab coffee with Bee and Rainey.”

Then she winced, and he immediately went on alert.

“I messed up and told them about the kiss,” she said, “so you are definitely going to hear about that from your sisters. I guess I really do owe you a cookie now.”

TJ wasn’t certain where his anxiety that Summer had said too much about what he’d confessed during the storm came from. She was very clear about people staying out of her business. Surely she practiced what she preached.

"Is that all you talked about?" TJ asked as he tried to relax. He slipped an arm along the back of the park bench to wrap around her shoulders. The way her hair draped across it and slid across his skin in the gentle breeze off the water helped.

"You took that very well. I'm guessing you don't mind if all of Horizon knows you're kissing someone." Summer narrowed her eyes. "Because you are frequently making that kind of news around town?"

"Just hoping that the story that makes it around makes me out to be a legendary kisser," TJ drawled.

Summer sniffed. "It better. I did my part in the telling." Then she smiled. "I really like your sisters. Rainey's a little intimidating, but that's more about me than her. I think I could get used to this community thing."

Then she inched closer to rest against his side, and he decided nothing else mattered, not his family or career or even his next meal. He'd just sit here on this bench with her forever.

"I took your father a piece of pie from the diner as a peace offering and apologized for being so much trouble." Summer smiled up at him, and TJ knew his decision to never leave this spot right here was correct. "Think it will help? Maybe get you out of some hot water or anything?"

TJ squeezed her closer. “Not your job, Summer. You didn’t get me in trouble, so you don’t have any duty to get me out of it. But I think your idea of hosting the volunteers and the community is nice.”

She nodded once. “Very new for Summer Patel, asking for community involvement like this. I even called my mother for her assistance. I’m not sure which of us was more surprised, but it’s important to make this event a success.”

When she put her hand on his leg, TJ had the same lurch in his chest, accompanied by a flutter in his abdomen.

“Is she coming to Horizon to help?” TJ asked as he worked to put his scrambled brain back into gear.

Summer wrinkled her nose. “She is, and she’ll be forcing my dad to come along. It’s going to be a crazy week. Every appointment is filled, and Kima will be adding emergency visits on top until we catch up from being closed this week. They will be rolling into town next Friday. I hope they’re still here next Saturday and we’re still talking. I’d like for you to meet them.” Her cheeks colored. “Uh, that sounds…” She trailed off. TJ waited for her to finish the thought. “We aren’t a thing. Or at least we aren’t a ‘meet the parents’ thing, so it’s strictly voluntary. I would introduce you as the hero who got me through the storm, nothing else.”

TJ relaxed as he understood her issue. “You’ve

met every one of my family members in town but one. As soon as my mother is nearby, I'll introduce you to her, too, but you may hear stories about her beforehand. She's the high school principal, and for anyone except students like you or me, she makes a lasting impression." He waited for her to meet his stare. "If we aren't a thing, Summer, I don't know what we are at this point. I've never felt like this before."

She tipped her head back. "Okay. Good. Me, either."

TJ frowned. "You were engaged."

Summer closed her eyes. "I know. It doesn't make any sense to me, but the way I miss you when you aren't around… That never happened with Dixon. I think it could turn into a real problem, but I don't know what to do about it."

Relieved, TJ said, "You plant yourself here. I'm already rooted too deep to grow anywhere else. Maybe that problem isn't really a problem after all."

Her shy smile convinced him that she wasn't opposed to his plan.

"Now," he drawled, "there's the issue of the sweet treat that I am owed." He traced circles along her arm as he watched her face.

Summer would never be boring. He could see interest and confusion and a smidge of irritation cross her face before she said, "Owed?" She ended the word on a hard *d* sound, which was impressive.

"I will accept another gift in its place," TJ said. "I just expect it to be sweet, too."

The gleam in her eyes convinced him she knew where his game was headed. She tapped her lips slowly. "Whatever could I give you to replace it?"

They were both grinning as they leaned into the kiss. Their first kiss at the shelter had been hesitant, and the second rushed by the arrival of the crews after the storm.

This kiss was about who they were to each other, exciting sparks and the kind of security that he would spend a lifetime looking for. When it ended, Summer pressed her forehead to his shoulder, and he wrapped his arms tightly around her.

"Am I forgiven?" Summer asked. "For forgetting your cookie?"

When she leaned back, TJ said, "I would forgive you anything right now."

Summer raised a skeptical eyebrow. "Anything? What if I..." He watched her evaluate her options. "Ran over your foot with my car?"

"Depends." TJ smoothed the hair out of her eyes. "Was it an accident or on purpose?"

Summer laughed.

"Doesn't matter. When you run over my foot, a kiss will settle our debts." TJ shrugged. "I've got a whole 'nother foot, you know?"

Summer shook her head. "We've come a long way in a short time. I probably won't even be tempted to hit you with my car anymore."

TJ pursed his lips. "Well, the scenario is changing, but I still think we could clear the air with a kiss. After I'm released from the hospital, I guess."

Summer smiled at him before resting her head on his shoulder. That was how she'd gone to sleep against him. It felt right.

"I noticed your father is still making plans to hand off his job to you," Summer said. "Have you changed your mind about that?"

TJ tilted his head back to stare up at the leafy canopy overhead. "That's why I'm here. Lucy and I have good talks on this bench. I thought a run and some canine counseling would help me find the right words." He glanced down at Summer. "But no, every person I talk to… I get this confirmation that taking the job now would be a mistake." He held up a hand to count. "Red Kelly, the guy who is encouraging me to run for office in COA. My sister Emery, who might as well be a supercop at this point. Bee and Lila know something's up, even if we've never discussed it in black-and-white facts. Even my mom, when I danced around the subject indirectly, was hinting that she knew what I was thinking. It's like the only person who doesn't see all this evidence is my dad, the one guy who taught me all I know about actual evidence."

Summer sighed. "He doesn't want to see it. That's all. Believe me, I've lived this."

TJ stared out over the water in the harbor and

tried to grab some of the peace he'd come down to this bench for.

"Want me to do it?" Summer asked.

TJ turned to stare at her, inching back to put some distance between them. "Do what?"

Summer straightened. "Tell him you don't want to be chief. That's how I do it. Plain words." She bit her lip. "I might stop by the diner to get another piece of pie first, though. I still want your father to like me." Then she shrugged. "But it might be easier coming from someone else. Definitely for you, but easier for him to hear?"

"No," TJ said as he shook his head firmly. "I have to do it."

He wasn't sure what to think about Summer's offer, but it bothered him. She'd made it clear how important it was to her to find someone who could do hard things. Taking this from him to handle it… Well, it fit her character, because she wouldn't hesitate, but it didn't fit her description of the kind of man who fit her.

He was also relieved. It was clear to Summer that she shouldn't tell his father without his permission, at least.

Summer scooted back, and he heard his phone ding with a text, so he pulled it out of his pocket.

It was from his mother. Dinner. Tonight. No excuses. No meat loaf.

TJ sighed. If the universe wanted to hand him the perfect opportunity to rip the bandage off, this was it. If Bee and Lila were there, he'd have a friendly audience. His mother seemed supportive, even if she didn't understand the whole situation.

There would be food on the table.

Things would never get out of control when his mother had fixed dinner, would they?

Summer was watching him closely, so he said, "My mom. She's cooking, so the clock just started ticking. Arriving late is a thing you do not do when dinner is involved."

"And I have to get back to the shelter to see how the office is coming along. I'm hoping I missed all the painting, but most specifically painting the ceiling." Summer wrinkled her nose. "I can't handle paint dripping in my hair."

TJ tugged a strand of her hair. "I'm sure they can use your skills. You looked pretty good on the ladder."

Summer's snort lightened his spirits. "Let a bossy cop know my knees were shaking as I climbed down from the roof? Never." She stood, but she held his hand, as if she was as reluctant to walk away as he was to see her go. "Is this the chance you've been waiting for to tell him?"

TJ nodded slowly. "Yeah."

She squeezed his hand. "Let me know how it goes." Then she pressed a kiss to his lips, bent to ruffle Lucy's ears and walked back toward the street parking.

It was on the tip of TJ's tongue to ask her to go to dinner with him.

She would.

No matter how the conversation went, Summer would be on his side. She'd be prepared to step up and fight for him if it came to that. He'd seen how fierce she could be in her own defense, and there was no doubt in his mind that she applied that same effort on behalf of her people.

But he waited too long and she was gone.

"You ready to go, Lucy?" he asked as he rolled up off the bench. As expected, Lucy followed his motion, ready for whatever he asked.

As they jogged back to his apartment, TJ tried to script the conversation with his father, but he was having trouble imagining what the response might be.

Other than disappointment.

After he showered and changed clothes, TJ headed to his parents' house, the place he'd grown up. Leaving Lucy at home had been the right decision, because she was sensitive to tension in the air, but he wished for her backup as he walked through the door.

Bee and Lila were setting the table, while his mother banged pots and pans on the stove, dishing up what looked like an Italian feast of her homemade lasagna, fresh garlic bread and oven-roasted asparagus.

"Good. TJ, grab the lettuce out of the refrigerator. We need a salad." His mother bustled around him, pointing with her directions and pressing a quick kiss to his cheek as she went. Since that was her usual level of guidance when it came to her supporting chefs, TJ dug around in the vegetable crisper to find that she'd already chopped up carrots, onions, broccoli and bell peppers. All he had to do was the lettuce. One thing about his mother: she never failed to plan ahead.

"Your father's late. Something came up at the station," she said as she peered over TJ's shoulder. "He texted, so…"

Her eyes met his as they tried to guess what might have come up. TJ plopped the salad down on the table, the last bowl to hit it and the deadline for on-time arrivals, before he could come up with a good guess.

Then his father was walking in the door.

As always, the chief kissed his wife first and then hugged Bee and Lila. When he turned toward TJ, his eyes convinced TJ that whatever had happened, it had involved him.

Had Red Kelly contacted him? Explained TJ's plans?

His father hugged him tightly and then pointed at the table. "Let's sit. Can't let the food get cold. It's my favorite."

Since his father said some version of that same thing about every dinner, no one was really sure what his favorite meal was, only that Kay Shepard was the responsible chef.

TJ met Bee's stare across the table. She didn't have any better idea what was going on than he did, if he was reading her face correctly, but she knew he was at the center of it, too.

"What are we talking about?" Lila asked as she motioned around the table. "A whole lot of subtext and not many actual words for me to follow. You know I hate being left out."

Since no one had any answers, they all turned to the chief.

He finished piling asparagus on his plate and passed TJ the serving dish before propping his elbows on the table. "I had a meeting with Rainey. It ran long." Then he inhaled. "We were talking my retirement, but instead of ironing out the transition timeline, she was pretty set on arguing about my replacement."

His father pinned TJ with a stare. "She was as convinced that she needed to find a good candidate for the job as I was certain that I had already trained my replacement. She wasn't so sure that my candidate was interested in the job."

No one said anything.

"Why would she think that, TJ?" his father asked before picking up his fork to take a bite. "Did you tell Rainey you didn't want the job before you even told me?" Then he peered at TJ over the top of his glasses, and TJ could see Bee and

Lila exchange a glance before they dug into their own dinners.

The cold in the pit of TJ's stomach made it harder to find the right words, but he finally shook his head. "I've only admitted it to one person. She isn't at this table, but it's not Rainey."

Lila sighed. "As the only person who isn't a cop or cop-adjacent at this table, I might not be tracking all the clues here…" Lila said before patting their mother's hand. "Sorry, Mom, high school principals are definitely the cops of the academic world. Even I could see that TJ was miserable at being stuck in the station. He's never once said he wanted to be chief of police, has he?"

The way she peered at her father, only missing the glasses but otherwise nailing the expression, would have prompted a smile, but everything felt too precarious at the moment.

His father blinked but returned his stare to TJ. "Do you want to be chief?" He set his fork down and tangled his fingers together.

The urge to dance around the subject was strong.

He also wished he'd invited Summer. She would firmly prop him up, make this easier.

But there would never be a better time, so TJ said, "Not right now."

His father blinked before leaning back in his chair.

"What do you want to do, Thomas Junior? What

is your plan?" his mother asked. In her eyes, he could read encouragement to keep going, to get it all out.

"I want to keep my partner. Lucy is too important to me, and I love working with her. That's the best part of the job. Not too many chiefs are K9 handlers." TJ licked his lips as he wondered if his father would fill in the blank that they didn't know a single chief of police who was also on patrol with a police dog. "Because she's so important, I want to run for the regional director of the Eastern Division of the South Carolina Canine Officers Association. That way I can work on the policies that dictate the treatment of Lucy and other officers like her." He realized that it was easier to sit up straight and tall after he'd gotten all that out. "And I'd really like all the Shepards to help me win."

TJ braced himself and turned to his father.

The chief didn't react at first, but after a moment, he nodded once. "Okay."

"I'm sorry, Dad. I just…" TJ wished he'd come up with better words. "This is right for me."

TJ wanted him to say something. Even an argument would be better than silence, but his father folded his napkin and stood. "I understand, TJ. I'm going to step outside for a minute. It has been a long day and a long two weeks."

Before anyone could argue, the chief opened the sliding glass door that led to the expansive deck on the back of the house. TJ's mother and father had ended almost every day there, swinging together as the sun set.

TJ turned to his mother. "Should I follow him? I feel like there's more to say."

She rubbed her forehead as she did anytime she mediated between the chief and one of the kids. "No, not right now. Let's finish dinner and see if anything changes. He needs time to process."

Bee asked, "Should I take his plate out? He's missing his favorite dinner." She smiled at their mother as she squeezed her hand.

Their mother shook her head. "If he's hungry, I guess he'll sit back down at the table or raid the leftovers later. We aren't catering to him on the deck." Then she smiled at TJ. "When's this election?"

TJ met Bee's stare across the table. Her tiny shrug said she wasn't sure the best way to proceed, either, but she picked up her fork. "I'm going to pull up the COA membership list tomorrow and see who I know. You tell me when it's time to start making phone calls, Tommy."

She grinned at the way he narrowed his eyes at the hated nickname.

"If there are any people you'd like me to flirt with, give me a list. Not an excessive number or anything," Lila said. "Ten or fifteen, but no more."

"Lila Elaine Shepard. Flirting for votes?" their mother said in a scandalized voice. The twinkle in her eyes made it easier to laugh along.

Just as Lila had intended all along.

"Only a reasonable number," Bee added dryly.

They laughed and the conversation resumed, but no one had forgotten who was missing. By the time they cleared the table and washed up the dishes, TJ knew he couldn't leave without some kind of conversation. He waited for Bee and Lila to head home and hugged his mother tightly. "I'm going out to say goodbye."

She patted his shoulder. "Do that, Thomas Junior. Your father wants everything for you, so you remember that, but you don't let him change your mind."

When TJ stepped out on the deck, the night sounds of bugs and frogs and the occasional call of a mockingbird overlapped the peaceful flow of the creek that ran at the bottom of the hill in the backyard. The sun had set while they were eating, and it was impossible to miss how peaceful it was.

His father had his feet propped up on the rail, fingers laced together over his stomach, and his eyes were closed. It was a shame to disturb him, but TJ couldn't go without saying something.

"Dad, I'm leaving." He stepped up and touched his father's shoulder. "I hope we can talk about this tomorrow."

His father shook his head, and the knot in TJ's stomach tightened painfully.

"No," his father said. "Monday's soon enough. This is police business, so we'll handle it in the office." He met TJ's stare. "I should have never brought it to the dinner table in the first place. I promised your mother when you joined the department that here it would always be family first. I just..." He shook his head. "Rainey surprised me. That's all. Why didn't you talk to me before I heard it from her?"

Fighting the guilt that settled over his shoulders, TJ crossed his arms over his chest. "I thought I had time to figure out the right way to approach you. I really only told one person that I didn't want the job. I guess that was my mistake."

Trusting Summer with that information in the middle of the storm had been easy enough. He wished he hadn't now, but he should have immediately told his father...right after leaving his assignment and wrecking his police car and surviving a hurricane.

"Well, if it was Dr. Patel, when she came to see me today, she was ready to defend your honor and do whatever it took to set things right for your career." He shrugged. "And she never said a word about your choice to turn down a promotion."

TJ pursed his lips. "Knowing her like I do, the words were probably burning her inside."

His father grunted. "Now that you mention it, she did have the look of someone with something to say."

"Pretty much always," TJ agreed with a sigh.

His father's laugh made him feel better. Whatever rocky times were ahead, they'd be okay.

"Before I talk with Rainey about her replacement search," his father said slowly, "take some time to be sure this is really what you want." Before TJ could answer, he held up a hand. "I know you think you're sure, but..." He sighed. "The need to save Dr. Patel convinced you to leave your post, and she was ready to tell me you didn't want this job. I've made a lifetime with a strong-minded woman myself. I understand how attractive they are, but just be careful you aren't making a mistake here. I'll talk to the mayor next week."

TJ crossed his arms over his chest as he considered his father's advice. His first instinct was to squash the suggestion that Summer had been the one to make his decision for him, even if it was clear how much influence she had.

Enough to convince him to leave his assignment, to ride out a hurricane, to rescue a rooster.

Had she manipulated the circumstances to bring out this resolution, the one she believed was right? She'd had coffee with Bee, Lila and Rainey. It would have been simple enough to use Rainey to work all this out.

He hated the idea.

TJ hated the discouraged tone of his father's voice, too, but there wasn't much else to say, so he left. With some rest, they both might have an easier time talking.

But he had to find out if Summer was working behind the scenes.

As he was walking out to his truck, he pulled out his phone.

Summer answered on the first ring. "How did it go? Did you tell your father?"

TJ tilted his head down, exhausted suddenly. More than anything else, he wanted Summer to be the person who cared enough to be anxious for his big news like this.

But not if he couldn't trust her to keep it safe or to support the decisions he made on his own.

"I did, but someone else told him first." TJ paused. "Did you tell Rainey I wasn't going to take the job?"

Summer hesitated, and the plunging sensation in his chest took his breath.

"No," she said, but the uncertainty confirmed his suspicions. "Well, not directly."

"Not directly," he repeated slowly.

"No," Summer said, "but I really wanted to."

TJ waited for her to say more. He wasn't sure what he wanted her to say, but he needed her to add more words.

"Was it bad?" she finally asked.

"The one thing I needed most was to tell him myself. Whatever you did? I lost my chance." TJ knew he carried a big chunk of responsibility for that because he'd wavered for too long.

He'd given Summer this opening.

And he might not ever be able to see her the same way.

"It's late, Summer. I'll…" He didn't want to overreact and make his mistake bigger in the heat of the moment. "I'll talk to you next week. Good night."

TJ ended the call after he heard her soft "good night" in response.

As he drove back to his apartment, he wished clearing the air with his father felt better, but losing this new, sweet thing with Summer might be the worst thing to happen yet.

CHAPTER EIGHTEEN

AFTER A WEEK crammed full of work, Summer was running out of steam on Friday afternoon. Every day had been fully booked, sometimes double-booked, and they'd had an emergency surgery on Tuesday that had thrown even that plan into disarray. The tabby had swallowed a bright red ball, and getting it out was the only solution. She and Natalie had done good work, but the schedule had been wrecked ever since.

On top of that, preparations for the shelter's event were in full swing, and Jewel had taken the seed of the idea and built on it to include an actual adoption event for the shelter animals and a beagle rescue based in Savannah. She, Hank and Hattie had been scrambling to make sure the shelter showed well for this community event, and Summer was so thankful for their dedication even as she worried about the strain.

Then there was TJ and where they'd left things. She hadn't called because of how he'd ended the conversation. “I’ll talk to you next week.” To her, that indicated she should wait.

But waiting was not easy for her. At all. As soon as she had a spare minute and any energy, she was going to plop herself down across from town hall and wait for him.

“I should walk over to the shelter, just to see how things are going,” Summer said as she slumped in a chair next to the table in the clinic’s breakroom. As soon as she caught her breath, she would do that.

As long as she had time to do so before the next patient.

“I have two pieces of good news, Summer,” Kima said from the doorway.

Forcing herself to sit up straight took too much effort, so Summer only held the position for a second before smiling gratefully at Kima. “I need the boost.”

“Your next two appointments canceled.” Kima moved over to the refrigerator to take out one of the energy drinks she loved. She plopped it down on the table in front of Summer. “Looks like you could use this.”

Summer was tempted. “The few times I’ve tried these, I was pretty sure I was drinking straight gasoline.”

Kima pursed her lips. “I don’t understand. Are you complaining?” She laughed as she opened the can. “And did it work as promised? I thought so.”

Summer smiled as she rolled her head on her shoulders to ease some of the ache there. "Does that finish us up for the afternoon then?"

Kima nodded. "Natalie's cleaning up the exam room now."

That was a huge relief. "Let's not try to make up for a whole week ever again."

"I don't think you'll get any argument from us. Dr. Forsyth could never have managed this. The times we shut down, it took weeks to get all the canceled appointments covered." Kima sipped her drink.

When Dr. Forsyth had bragged about only evacuating twice, he'd never mentioned how often he'd closed the office down in advance of a storm. That would have been helpful information. "How often did he close for storms?"

Kima shrugged. "I don't know the total, but each time he moved into town to wait out the storm."

"More than twice?" Summer asked.

"Oh, yeah," Kima said with a frown. "Might just be for an overnight in Horizon because of high winds or expected flooding, but he would clear appointments before and after."

Summer wondered if there was some confusion over the word "evacuate" and that was how Dr. Forsyth counted only twice. It wasn't important now.

"I hope the next time we're facing one of these

storms, you and Natalie can discuss the right way to handle all of it." That reminded Summer that she needed to get back to finding or creating safety plans for the clinic. If things ever calmed down, she'd get right on that.

"We will, Summer. Before this storm, you were pretty..." Kima trailed off, and Summer imagined she was hunting for a friendly way to say "professional."

"You were very rigid. We're working as a team now. I like it."

"Rigid" was worse than "professional" any day, but Summer nodded as she absorbed that. They had made progress, so she was going to have to be happy with that.

If she had a spare minute, she would celebrate all the progress she'd made since the storm.

Because of the storm?

Hank, Hattie and Jewel were energized. They were also using her first name and actually welcoming her when she walked into the shelter.

Natalie and Kima had gone above and beyond to help her get the clinic's patients taken care of.

Her mother had been positive about this fund raiser in a way that made Summer believe she might stop telling Summer to sell and move back home soon.

And at some point over the last week, she'd set that idea completely aside herself.

She might still have some doubts about hurricanes and her ability to live with them, but it had receded in the face of the community that surrounded her and the clinic and shelter. They needed her here, and they were also prepared to support her when the time came.

The shift in her thinking from being certain she had only herself to rely on to understanding that it didn't have to be that way was a work in progress, but that progress felt right.

Being less rigid was nice.

She was going to keep it up.

"What's the second piece of good news?" Summer asked.

"Your parents are here." Kima held up a hand as Summer jerked upright. "You were with a patient when they arrived, so they decided to take a walk around outside. Catch your breath. Drink some gasoline if you'd like. Then, when you're ready, go see them."

Summer met her stare. "You sound as if you actually know my parents and how their visit can be…" A blessing and a curse? What was a nicer way to say that?

Kima didn't need her to fill in the blanks. "Summer. I know parents. I have parents. I am a parent. I also know the week you've had. Catching your breath makes perfect sense here."

Grateful for the encouragement, Summer nodded. "You and Natalie have both been amazing. I'm lucky to have you."

The way her office manager brightened at the words reminded Summer that she still had room for improvement, but she didn't have to fix everything today.

That was a lesson she would have to learn at some point.

The next item on her to-do list was welcoming her parents to Horizon. It was going to be her home. She wanted them to like it.

Summer stood slowly. "All right. I'm going to go find my parents and show off my clinic and shelter. Be right back."

As she stepped outside the side door, Russell Crow squawked from his usual spot under the outside stairs. This had become his greeting ever since they'd stopped trying to force him back into the pen near the shelter. Since it had replaced the aggressive crowing, Summer didn't complain. One quick survey of the driveway, yard and tree line didn't turn up her parents. Their luxury SUV was parked behind hers, so by process of elimination, Summer decided they'd gone to the shelter.

Since her mother had been in frequent video phone calls with Jewel, it made sense that she'd jump in with both feet for the last-minute preparation. As much as her mother loved schmoozing at fancy society events for her causes, she never hesitated to get her hands dirty.

"Yes, this is where your Hall of Fame needs to go," her mother said as Summer stepped inside the shelter's office. She also never hesitated to give her opinion.

Summer had no idea what was going into this Hall of Fame, but the way Jewel immediately clapped her hands told her it was a popular idea. She had a sneaking suspicion it would also cost more money, but it was impossible to argue with the results of Jewel's vision and Hank's hard work and budgeting prowess. The office had been transformed with a fresh coat of bright white paint, an area rug with a vaguely geometric design in pale grays and blues, and so much organization that Summer was beyond impressed. The whiteboard hung opposite the desk, and all the to-do items had been erased.

Her credit card was still hot to the touch, but the shelter was ready.

"What have I missed?" Summer asked to draw their attention from the TBD Hall of Fame.

"My baby!" As her mother squeezed Summer close, she could smell the mix of roses and vanilla her mother had always preferred. It was her signature scent, and every lady should have one, according to Lynn Patel.

"We're going to put up a bulletin board, a pretty one," Jewel said with a nod to Hank. Summer watched him make a note and hoped he might be able to find one in his magic secondhand store. "So we can take pictures of all the happy matches we make here. Inspiration for us and for anyone who walks through the door looking for a pet." She patted Summer's shoulder. "I see where you get your brains, Summer. Your mother is one smart cookie."

Summer grinned at the way her father's eyebrows shot up toward his hairline, but he had never been one to push her mother from center stage. She slipped out of her mother's arms to approach her father. "Your brains are also very good, Daddy."

He humphed before he raised an arm, so she could slip underneath like she had a hundred other times growing up. "Thank you for noticing me. The brainstorming has been fast and furious. I was backed into a corner before I knew it with no way out."

Summer pointed at the workroom off the office. "Want to see the rest of the place?"

He nodded. She would have explained where they were going, but absolutely no one was paying any attention to them. Jewel and her mother had bent over the laptop Hank had set up to discuss the shelter's website and whether or not a color change would be enough to update it.

If Summer guessed correctly, her mother would favor a fresh design.

Which would cost more fresh money.

"I sure hope this thank-you becomes the shelter's most successful fund raiser yet," she murmured as her father followed her into the quiet workroom.

"Your mother won't accept any less," he said as he clasped both hands behind his back and did a slow revolution to take in the room. "Spotless." He nodded.

It was. For her father, this was a rave review. She led him out into the play yard where two volunteers were cleaning up and playing with four of the smaller dogs. She waved at them and then went to the container that held treats to grab four. Her father waved off the offer, so Summer fed the dogs through the fence.

"Did you get to see the clinic at all?" she asked as they stopped in front of the shelter. If he had no questions or even additional comments, this was going to be the shortest tour ever.

He shook his head, and the nerves kicked up in Summer's abdomen.

She'd expected there to be a little hesitation, but what if he never thawed at all?

"You two trying to leave me behind?" her mother said as she trotted out of the office. "I swear I could brainstorm with Jewel until the sun comes up, but I'm not here to see her. I want to see every inch of your home, baby. Now that you've invited us here." She squeezed Summer tightly and then wrapped her arm through her husband's. "And if you don't get over your issues right now, Jay, I'll send you to sit in the car."

He frowned but didn't argue.

"Summer, your father's feelings were hurt when you left. Walk away from your husband, whatever, but not your parents." Her mother cut a glance toward her father, so Summer took that as a prompt.

"I'm sorry for hurting your feelings, Daddy, but I couldn't stay in Atlanta. The whole town was talking about me and Dixon." Summer rolled her eyes. "For that matter, my own parents couldn't stop telling me about how I was making a mistake, a hasty decision I would regret."

Her mother had the courtesy to show some remorse. "And then I kept it up when you were under the barrel of your first hurricane. I am sorry. I think we wanted the life we pictured for you and Dixon more than you did. We made a mistake."

Then she nudged her husband with an elbow forcefully enough to startle a grunt from him.

"I can't apologize for wanting to guide you, Summer," her father finally said. "You're our only daughter. Your happiness is my first job."

It wasn't an apology, but it was probably the closest she would get.

Suddenly, it was clear to Summer exactly why she had such a problem admitting she was wrong.

"The two of you..." Her mother threw her hands up in the air. "Carbon copies."

Summer laughed at the way her mother said aloud what she was thinking. "I won't apologize for making my own way here in Horizon. The ride has been bumpy, but every day it's clearer to me that I can be happy right here."

She held her breath as she realized TJ had been right about that.

He'd been right about everything. The sinking feeling in her stomach as she imagined admitting that to him was familiar. Learning to be independent without being so hardheaded would take some time, but she had to work on it.

This reconciliation with her father would be good practice.

She waited for her father to meet her stare.

When his shoulders relaxed, she was cautiously optimistic that the thaw had begun.

"I am sorry you were hurt when I moved to Horizon. I love having my own clinic. My team is good there and here at the shelter. With enough time and some money, they can both be successful." Summer covered her heart with a hand. "My definition of successful, which you know is nothing to sneeze at. I am so happy you're here to see it, Daddy. Thank you for coming."

Russell Crow decided to enter the conversation with a loud crow, which wasn't the punctuation she hoped for, but her father's interest was immediately captured. He hurried across the lawn to observe the rooster more closely. "You have a chicken?"

Summer sighed. "Honestly, I think the chicken has me at this point. If you hear of anyone hoping to adopt one, please send them my way. Otherwise, I believe Russell Crow is the clinic's new mascot."

Her mother snickered. "Russell Crow. I love it."

Summer shook her head. "He grows on you. This whole place does." She took her mother's hand. "Let me show you the rest." When her father made no move to follow, she said, "Dad? Are you coming?"

He glanced at her, but hesitated.

Almost as if he'd choose Russell Crow over the rest of the tour.

"He will be here when you come back out, Dad. I promise. I will send him home to Atlanta with you if you like." Summer grinned at how her mother narrowed her eyes in a clear threat.

Before they stepped inside, she pointed up at the dormer window overhead. "Dad, do you know what that piece is called?" She pointed at the fascia that had come loose before the storm.

He sniffed. "Window." Then he held up a finger. "Dormer window?"

Since he seemed less certain about that, Summer decided she'd been right not to call him when the "roof-thingy" was loose.

After a quick tour of the clinic's rooms, Summer led them up to her apartment and saw right through her mother's fake enthusiasm about how "snug" and "intimate" it was. She was relieved no one even tried to pretend that her parents would be staying with her. They had made reservations at the finest inn in Horizon, right off Battery Park. The sun was setting as they backed down the driveway to head into town to get some rest before the big day.

After she closed everything up and got ready for bed, she stared hard at her phone.

All it had taken to get back on track with her parents had been honesty.

Heartfelt honesty.

But for TJ…

Honesty might only open the door. He was going to need something bigger.

She owed him an apology…again.

Hey, remember when you promised you'd forgive me anything for a kiss? I messed us up again and I should never have let this go on so long because I can't admit when I'm wrong. Also, I thought of a really embarrassing story, but I can only tell it to you in person.

She bit her lip as she considered whether it was enough.

Then she added a postscript.

P.S. my parents are here. I really want them to meet you. Please come to the big community thank-you tomorrow.

She hit Send before she could second-guess herself. "Ugh. I hope this is not another story to add to my trove of embarrassing stories for the next guy." Since it was nearly impossible to imagine connecting with any other man the way she had with TJ, it was premature to be worried about what stories she could tell him.

That didn't keep her from staring up at the ceiling and worrying when she should have been sleeping.

When the sun rose, she wasn't well-rested, but she was excited anyway.

It was going to be a good day. She felt it in her bones.

CHAPTER NINETEEN

TJ GLANCED AT LUCY, who was seated next to him in the truck. She was focused on the large crowd milling around the lawn in front of Shoreline Shelter.

"Do you smell the food?" TJ asked. It was a silly question. Lucy's nose was a million times more sensitive than his, and the savory, spicy scent of Old Bay seasoning, shrimp and sausage cooking away was in the air.

"Looks like Charlene's running the food show, so you know it's good." TJ knew he was stalling, but he wasn't sure why. Everyone at the party was a neighbor or friend or family.

He was certain Bee and Lila were there.

There was almost no way his mother would have skipped the event, either. She never missed a party, and one where she wasn't cooking would be twice as exciting.

Whether or not his father made a conscious decision to attend, he would also be there because his mother's will was difficult to buck. That reminded him of his father's warning about strong-willed women and he smiled.

After five tense days on the job, walking carefully around the chief, it was nice to breathe freely.

"We're back on regular duty next week. That means less desk, Lucy." His patrol car had been cleared for service again on Friday, so they could get to what they were good at.

Red Kelly had reviewed the paperwork needed to declare he was running. Since it would be used to create a biography distributed to all the voting members, Red had made suggestions and forced TJ to edit it three different times over the week. Between that and the final report about the storm response to Hurricane Agnes, TJ had been hunched over a laptop for days.

"Awful experience," he muttered. He didn't want to repeat it anytime soon. "And none of this has anything to do with why you're sitting in the truck like a wallflower afraid to step on the dance floor."

Everything would be back on track.

Except for one major piece.

Stalling in the front seat of his truck could be laid squarely at Summer's feet.

He pulled out his phone to stare at her text.

"'Please come,'" he said and turned to stare at Lucy. "All of this mess between us and she's asking me to meet her parents anyway." It worried him a little that he hadn't hesitated to come when she asked. However his concerns about Summer and her influence were resolved, he didn't want to stay away.

"Let's go, Lucy," TJ said as he slid out of the truck. He searched for Summer without being too obvious, greeting people as he went and stopping twice for Lucy's fans. When he spoke at school events, he always told the kids that when Lucy was working, she would be wearing her vest, and it was important not to approach her without his okay.

When he and Lucy were off duty, they never went anywhere without fans lining up to say hello.

Eventually, he made it to the long row of tables where Charlene had dumped out the boil along the newspaper-covered surface. Rainey was filling two plates with the Sandlapper's always popular low-country boil, a mix of shrimp, sausage, corn and potatoes. He watched her hit both plates with melted butter and a dash of hot sauce as was only correct, but before she could turn to go, he said, "Mayor, do you have a minute?"

"Mayor?" Rainey glanced over her shoulder but turned back to him. "Just a minute. What's up, TJ?"

She crossed her arms over her chest, and he wondered what her hurry was. Then he realized he was standing in the way of her lunch. There was no sense in dancing around the issue anyway. "How did you know I was going to turn down the chief's position?" He wasn't sure why it mattered so much at this point, but he needed to know.

Rainey held up a finger. "First of all, you never had it to turn down. I'm the mayor. I hire the police chief." She exhaled. "You would be a good chief. You still may be someday, but the absolute misery on your face as you slumped over the laptop in the musty ol' conference room during the storm spoke volumes. Your father would have seen it if he hadn't been so certain he was right about everything." Her lips curled up. "He's a good man, but I wonder if he thinks he's ever been wrong."

She bumped his shoulder. "Not that I know anything about that, right, TJ? Takes one to know one, maybe."

"And that's all it took? No one told you to begin a search for your own candidate because the chief's was not interested?" Relief and dismay over doubting himself and Summer settled over his shoulders.

Rainey tipped her head back as she considered the question.

Then she shook her head. "No, that's it. I realized that, unless I actually had another candidate to put forth, I was going to need to sell you on taking the job. So, I went to Columbia this week, met with some colleagues and an old friend who is ready for this office, even if he doesn't know it quite yet."

TJ studied her face. She seemed pretty excited

about how that trip had turned out. Relief settled over his shoulders.

Rainey bent closer. "If you'll help me win your father's support, I will owe you a favor. A big favor."

He wasn't certain his influence would really help Rainey, but the prospect of having a favor to call in was tempting. "I'd be happy to meet your candidate. Maybe I can help there."

He offered his hand, and they shook on it before Rainey picked up her plates.

"Grab a plate and come join us. I'll introduce you."

TJ asked, "You brought him here?"

"It seemed like the perfect opportunity." She smiled. "You know I don't hesitate when I have a plan in motion."

Since the food was calling his name, TJ reached for a plate, but as he did, he saw Summer headed for the shelter. Was he ready to make his attempt at recovering their relationship or did he need a full stomach first? Then he saw his mother trailing behind her.

"I've got something I need to take care of first," TJ said, "but I'll head your way after."

Rainey pursed her lips. "Bring Summer with you. She can tell him how wonderful life in Horizon is as a newcomer."

TJ waved vaguely and waded into the crowd, Lucy at his side.

THE THIRD TIME her mother mentioned that she'd never attended a party where the food was served on soggy newspaper, let alone helped throw one, Summer decided that she needed a minute to herself.

To rest.

To enjoy the fact that so many of her new neighbors had shown up and appeared to appreciate the delicious food Charlene had served.

To keep from forcefully loading her parents into their SUV and pointing them back to Atlanta.

It had coincided with her father taking a phone call from Dr. Dixon Brooks, where they discussed their upcoming golf tournament and when Summer was moving back home. Her only comfort was that her father had sounded certain when he'd said, "Not anytime soon."

She slid into what she'd started calling "Hank's chair" with a sigh.

Their visit had gone better than she'd expected, even with these signs that any changes on their part would be slow to take hold.

"If you can't change them, change how you feel, Summer," she murmured as she closed her eyes. She'd always been able to do what she decided was most important, but not without some emotional strain. At some point, she had to let that part go.

"Oh, there is someone here! Good! I was hoping I could meet some of the cats you have available for adoption," a woman said from the doorway.

She pointed toward the hallway that led to the cat room. "Through here?"

Summer reached for her phone to text Hattie, but decided to wait and see how serious this visit got. Everyone was outside working the crowd, and Hattie had two of the shelter dogs on leashes as ambassadors. Her mother had been certain this was key to getting good responses to their donation requests.

"Yes, through here," Summer said as she led the petite woman down the hallway past the large indoor pens that were empty for now. "What kind of cat are you looking for? Kitten? Older cat?"

The woman sighed. "Good question. My husband says he is not a pet person, but he's getting ready to retire. I'm not ready to retire just yet, and even when I do, I'm going to need him to have another companion. Finding him a hobby has become my new hobby." She grinned.

As they entered the large open cat room, Summer really wished she'd called for Hattie's help because she knew adopting an animal out to someone who hadn't decided on their own to adopt was a bad idea. The shelter wouldn't do it, but there had to be a way to encourage this woman's interest.

"If this will be his cat, you should definitely bring him in. Is he here today? This is a great opportunity to test the waters." Summer was proud of that response.

"He is, Dr. Patel. He wouldn't have missed it, but he's caught up in a soap opera that involves the mayor, our son and a large audience of our friends and neighbors. Plus, he's on his second plate of Charlene's boil, and that is not the time to spring new ideas like pets on him."

As all the pieces fell into place for Summer, that this was TJ's mom, she heard, "I see you two have already met."

"Well, we haven't been formally introduced yet, which is sad because I thought I'd taught all my children to introduce their new friends to me," TJ's mom said with a sneaking glance at TJ. It was easy to imagine her doing the same with a rambunctious high school student to gently but firmly get them in line. "I'm Kay Shepard, Dr. Patel."

"If you had given me a chance, Mom, I would have gotten to it," TJ muttered.

Summer noticed the faintest hint of pink in his cheeks.

It was impossible not to commiserate, too.

Parents could be a handful.

"If you moved as quickly to introduce us as you did to tell your father you had no plans to follow in his footsteps just yet, I'm not sure I have enough time to wait for you, Thomas Junior," Kay Shepard said dryly.

It was tempting, but there was no way she needed to add a "Yeah, TJ" to the argument. Better smooth things over first. Then maybe she could have been right all along.

When Kay turned to Summer and said, "The whole town could see the writing on the wall, except for Tom Shepard." She patted her son's shoulder. "We've got all that straightened out now, Dr. Patel."

"Please, call me Summer, Ms. Shepard," Summer said.

"I will. And it's Kay," his mother answered as she picked up a sleek orange cat who came to investigate her. "Something tells me you and I are going to be seeing a lot of each other."

Where would she have gotten that idea? Was she referring to their kiss?

It was easy to picture Lila's delight when she'd heard about it, so Summer knew it wouldn't have stayed a secret for long.

Summer forced her lips into a straight line as she met TJ's stare. His expression was long-suffering patience, which confirmed that he'd already sat through an interrogation by his sisters.

She wanted to ask a million questions about what he'd been doing, how things were at work and with his father, and what his sisters had said about the two of them, but most of all, she needed to feel his arms around her.

That meant she had to get rid of his mother. Fast.

"It looks like Fox really likes you, Ms. Shepard,"

Summer said. "Maybe you should introduce him to the chief to see if they're a match. I'll be happy to wait here if you want to do that today."

And she'd insist that TJ stayed, if she could come up with a reasonable excuse.

"Actually," TJ said, "you might want to track Dad down for another reason. I just ran into Rainey, and she was carrying two plates of food."

His mother waved a hand. "Oh, that wasn't a plan to corner the chief. I saw her with a very handsome man before I followed Summer to force an introduction. If things don't work out with TJ, you should find out if he's single, Summer."

Then she pursed her lips and stared at TJ.

His slow inhale and exhale matched the one that her own parents provoked not too long ago perfectly.

"He's the man Rainey is planning to hire for chief of police. He's here. Today. Out there with the chief who has no idea." TJ tilted his head to the side as he waited for his mother to react.

"Oh," Kay Shepard said slowly. "That's probably...okay." She handed Fox back to Summer, who cuddled the cat close to her chest. Something about a cat's purr made it easy to believe everything would be okay.

The fact that Kay didn't sound fully convinced made it easy to understand why she brushed TJ out of the doorway. "Just in case, I'll go." She patted his shoulder. "You two kiss again and then come help."

When she was gone, Summer met TJ's stare. "The thing about us is that we don't have to learn how to argue. We've got that part down. We're also getting a lot of practice apologizing."

He nodded and moved close enough to touch. "Yeah. My turn to apologize this time. I'm sorry. I had this doubt, this idea that you had maneuvered me into making this decision. I honestly thought I had kept it all contained only to find out that there was only one person in Horizon who didn't know." He wrapped his arms around her arms. "You're dangerous. You could convince me to do things without too much effort, but you won't. You'll argue until we're both tearing our hair out, but you'd never manipulate." He cleared his throat. "I know it's hard to believe, but I made a mistake."

It hurt to think he would believe her capable of manipulating him, but they had needed so many resets because of her own stubbornness. Giving him one this time was the right answer. She also understood what he meant about how dangerous this thing between them could be. He'd already changed her, and the fact that she was desperate to settle this between them and move on meant she'd do almost anything for him, even if it hurt.

Summer closed her eyes and said dryly, "We'll have to commemorate this day for the rest of our lives. TJ made a mistake."

His lips were twitching. "I'm okay if we forget about this as long as you forgive me first." Then he groaned. "TJ made the same mistake he's been making, rushing in, making assumptions based on too little information. That was completely about me, not about you, and I understand if you want to run over my foot with your car to even the score."

Summer ran her hand over Fox's back as she considered that. "Maybe we're both a little bit messy, after all. I'm glad."

He brushed hair off her face before scratching Fox's ears. "I need you to promise that when I'm being unreasonable, you will be immovable. I hate that I've missed so much of you this week. I'd much rather hear all the words, even if they're loudly grumbled in my general vicinity."

Her laugh made Fox shake his head and leap out of her arms to curl up in his bed.

This was the key to why they worked. TJ saw her. Maybe he'd gotten confused for a minute, but he knew who she was. Asking her to lean into that person instead of fight her impulses was the key to her heart.

"That is an easy promise to keep," she said as his arms slipped around her waist.

"You never made any rash vows to forgive me anything for a kiss, but I'm hoping a kiss will be a powerful incentive," he murmured, his eyes locked on hers.

"I didn't, did I?" Summer pretended to consider it. "I don't see how it could hurt to try."

Their smiles melted as their lips touched.

But she wasn't foolish enough to make any rash promises that his kiss would get him out of trouble.

When he leaned back, TJ said, "I didn't see the shelter before, but this place looks great. I want to hear about all the work you've gotten done since the storm…" He wrinkled his nose. "But…"

Summer straightened her shoulders. "But somewhere out there in the middle of most of the population of Horizon, your father is about to meet the man who will be replacing him."

TJ rubbed the center of his chest. "When you put it like that…"

Summer brushed his hand down before tangling her fingers through his to lead him down the hallway. "First we find him. Then we'll run interference."

His laughter caused the silly, fluttery glow in her chest. "Am I being bossy, Officer Shepard?"

They were grinning at each other when they rejoined the crowd around the food tables.

TJ's mother immediately did the "get over here" jerk of her chin that all mothers knew, so Summer threaded through the crowd. When they stopped at the table where Chief Shepard, TJ's mother, the mayor and a very handsome man were seated,

Summer saw that Bee and Lila were on the fringes of the crowd watching the show.

"TJ, I was just introducing your dad to my friend, Trey Douglas. We worked together in Columbia," Rainey said as she raised her eyebrows at him.

Summer wasn't sure what she was silently communicating, but TJ got the message. He rounded the table with his hand held out. "Nice to meet you. Rainey's told me a lot about you."

Trey turned to face Rainey with one eyebrow raised. "Yeah? Okay, good. I haven't really decided whether to pursue this job yet, but I appreciate the warm welcome."

The way the chief's arms were crossed firmly over his chest made Summer think the welcome was lukewarm at best.

"I thought it was a great opportunity to show Trey how friendly Horizon is." Rainey stood taller and addressed the crowd. "We'd be lucky to have him step up when the chief retires. Trey's a military veteran and has served with the South Carolina Law Enforcement Division for more than ten years."

Summer thought the man in question appeared ill at ease.

And the chief's impassive expression made her wonder if this was just a bad idea or the worst, but Rainey pasted on a determined smile. "Please stop by and welcome him to town."

Kay patted Trey's shoulder. "We'll let you get back to your food, but Rainey left out a very important piece of information. Are you single, Trey?"

TJ did the long-suffering son eye close again before he draped an arm over Summer's shoulders. She wasn't sure if he was telling his mother to stand down, that he and Summer were together, but it was sweet to stand there next to him with the whole town watching.

Trey eventually nodded. "I am. Is this one of those small-town things I'll have to adjust to if I move here? I've never had a question like that on any other job interview."

Kay grinned happily. "Oh, it's not a job requirement, more like a strong incentive to support your hiring. If you want the job, that is. You've got big shoes to fill, so a little extra crowd support from people who enjoy romance couldn't hurt."

Trey surveyed the crowd before relaxing in his seat. "Yes, ma'am. I see your point."

Summer wasn't sure which part of his answer did it, but the chief thawed a degree or two when he heard it. "You won't find any better frogmore stew in South Carolina than Charlene's."

Rainey and TJ communicated silently, and Summer decided it was a positive conversation when Rainey pulled out her chair to sit. "Miss Kay, would you like to grab a plate and join us?"

"TJ, grab your mother a plate, then you and Dr.

Patel pull up a chair, too. I have some questions for you both," his father said before sprinkling hot sauce over his plate.

Summer followed behind TJ this time as he navigated the crowd and smiled at her mother at one of the tables near the back. She wasn't sure what kind of questions the chief might have, but the certainty that she had the answers she needed was growing.

CHAPTER TWENTY

AFTER SUMMER'S SUCCESSFUL community thank-you-slash-fund-raiser wound down, TJ decided it had been an excellent day. He was certain Rainey would agree because her candidate for chief of police had been evaluated by an informal panel of tough customers, and it seemed like there were only two people left to convince.

His father had maintained his stoic expression for most of the afternoon's conversation, but there had been a brief moment of connection when Trey had mentioned his captain. It sounded like Trey's mentor and the chief had some history. They had worked together on task forces throughout their careers, and the chief had ended that line of conversation by saying, "Remind that reprobate he still owes me a hundred dollars. He lost the bet, no doubt."

It was the kind of conversation that raised more questions than answers, but his father's almost-smile convinced TJ that it had opened up the door to getting his father's approval.

The other person who remained unconvinced was Trey Douglas. Columbia had been home for a long time. The kind of police work required would be different.

And then there was the fact that the population of Horizon appeared to be eavesdropping on the entire conversation. TJ and the chief accepted that, but Trey's uneasy scans of the attentive crowd suggested it would take some getting used to.

If Rainey could convince Trey, she might have pulled out a difficult victory. The chief had shaken Trey's hand and given Rainey a peaceful nod before he and TJ's mother pitched in to help clean up.

Then, before they'd left, his father had made a point to invite Summer to the next Shepard family dinner. His mother's smile was brighter than the afternoon sunshine, but Summer's was a close second.

"Are you sure you don't want to wait until morning to head back to Atlanta?" Summer asked as they trailed her parents down the driveway. "I can call the inn to make sure they still have a room available."

Summer's father shook his head. "Easy roads between here and Atlanta. Besides, Dixon and I have a tee time tomorrow. Can't miss that." He turned to TJ. "Next time, you and I will hit the golf course. Never met a golf swing I couldn't fix."

As they shook hands, TJ said, "I need all the help I can get, Jay."

He and Summer had both progressed to a first-name basis with all the parents over the course of the afternoon. She hadn't attempted to call his father Tom yet, but TJ totally understood the hesitation. Everyone else went with Chief. Until there was a new chief in town, there was no reason to change.

"Call me when you get home," Summer said.

"That's my line," her mother answered before hugging them both, "but I definitely will. I love seeing you so happy, Summer." She winked at TJ. "Even if it isn't at home. Next time, we'll plan something elegant. There's nothing like a string quartet and some dry banquet chicken to really open up the pocketbooks. Scout out some venues, m'kay?"

Summer stifled a sigh, but nodded until her mother was in the SUV.

TJ wondered if Summer and her father had ironed things out as Jay Patel stood in front of his daughter. "Speaking of pocketbooks," he said as he reached into his pocket, "add this to your fund-raising total." He offered Summer what looked like a folded check before pulling her close. "You are on the right track here."

Then he hurried to the SUV, slid into the driver's seat and backed down the driveway.

They waved until her parents were out of sight. Then Summer's shoulders slumped. There was a sheen in her eyes that made him think tears were right there, fighting to the surface.

TJ grabbed one of the blankets Hank and Hattie had piled up to be washed and returned to the shelter's shelves. "Could I interest you in a walk down to the beach? We could watch the sunset?"

Summer tilted her head to the side. "Sunset is still hours away."

He nodded. "I know." Then he held out his hand.

She slipped her hand in his. "If we can sit in silence for part of it, possibly with our eyes closed while I drool on your shoulder, I like this plan."

TJ smiled as he imagined the two of them snoozing on the beach, Summer with her face pressed into his shoulder. They were quiet for a bit as they navigated the very faint path through the trees and grasses.

"I should have warned you, though, that it's farther than I thought the first time I walked it. Now that Hurricane Agnes has come through, I believe it might be exactly the right distance," Summer said.

Was she nervous or just thinking out loud? TJ realized that things weren't quite as settled between them as he'd thought. What would be causing nerves at this point? He couldn't let that go on any longer.

When the trees cleared, TJ spread out the blanket in the rocky sand. Here, where the rest of the world was so far away, they could settle everything.

If he could just figure out how to start the conversation.

"I didn't know that you played golf," Summer

said as she lowered herself down to the blanket and kicked off her shoes. Her grateful sigh came from down deep inside.

TJ followed her lead and then immediately stretched out to stare up at the trees overhead and the blue sky beyond. Something in him relaxed when Summer stretched out next to him and pressed her forehead to his shoulder.

"I don't play golf yet. Your father can fix that." TJ closed his eyes.

Summer's head popped back up so she could stare at him. "You don't play?"

He shook his head. "There's only so much a man can listen to about Dr. Dixon Brooks and not make a rash decision to take on a new hobby, master it and then engineer a way to embarrass him at it." He hadn't even known about his jealous bone, but apparently it was in his spine somewhere because he'd made a snap decision to beat Summer's ex-fiancé at his own game. "I decided that becoming an orthopedic surgeon would take too much time away from you."

Watching her mouth drop open almost made the idea of wearing golf pants acceptable.

"My hero," she said before pressing a kiss to his lips.

Yeah, the pants would be worth it.

"You really don't have to do that. We'll continue to hear about Dixon, believe me, but he's in a whole different world from the two of us," she said as she returned to resting against him. "I think they're starting to understand now that they've seen Horizon. And us."

Us.

Whatever she was concerned about, Summer was thinking in terms of "us."

"Did your father make a donation to the shelter?" TJ asked as he studied her face.

She squeezed her eyes shut. "Yeah."

He waited to see if she'd expand her answer before prodding, "And how do we feel about that?"

"We?" she asked.

"You and me. Us." TJ watched her closely.

"I feel..." She inhaled slowly. "I know it shouldn't matter. I should be able to do this on my own. I *can* do this on my own...with some help from the friends and neighbors who showed up today." Hearing her say that convinced TJ she was already planted in Horizon. Her roots would only grow stronger every day.

Imagining what those days might look like was easy.

She pulled the check from her pocket and opened it before closing her eyes.

Then the first tear slipped out, followed by an inelegant sniffle. TJ would have teased her about it, but he was caught in that moment.

"I'm never going to get over wanting them to be proud of me, am I?" Summer asked.

TJ couldn't look away from her. She was beautiful all the time, but this vulnerable Summer was special. She didn't show this to anyone else.

The weight of that responsibility and the desire to keep her safe made it difficult to speak.

"And they are," he said softly. "How could they be anything but proud of you?"

She brushed a tear away. "They exasperate me, but they still showed up for me." Then she frowned. "And I am realizing…"

TJ raised an eyebrow.

"I lectured you about how you had to just… rip off the bandage." She shook her head. "I may have to come to terms with the fact that I give terrible advice."

Surprised, TJ laughed. "It wasn't terrible advice."

She brushed that away. "It really was. And that whole thing about doing the right thing even when it's hard…" She stuck her tongue out and blew a raspberry. "I've spent my whole life afraid I'd find the one time they wouldn't come around. It makes perfect sense to tread carefully to avoid risking your father's respect, TJ. I'm so glad you did this your way instead of mine."

He'd been so worried about her influence on his decision and how he was changing.

What he heard in that moment was that she was changing, too.

And he loved who she was, but imagining who they could become together was exciting.

"Do you think we have a chance at being happy together?" she asked, her eyes locked on his face. It was another vulnerable moment. He could read her fears, but the fact that she was talking to him about them was new and special.

They weren't who they had been a few weeks ago. The two of them were so much better together.

"Leo thinks we'll need to order two pizzas, one for each of us, so our budget may be a little out of whack, but that seems doable to me." TJ brushed his hand over the single frown line on her forehead. "What do you think?"

"It's more pizza. I see that as a win-win solution." Then she leaned up to press her lips against his. "I'll keep my promise to never stop talking and muttering at a loud volume. You'll keep your promise to wipe the slate clean with a kiss. When the next hurricane comes, I will follow all your directives."

TJ narrowed his eyes skeptically until she laughed.

"Okay, let's not think about future storms. I found Horizon. I found you," Summer said softly. "I've never felt more confident about what the future holds."

* * * * *